NEW WORLDS
FROM THE
LOWLANDS
FANTASY AND SCIENCE FICTION
OF DUTCH AND FLEMISH
WRITERS

NEW WORLDS FROM THE LOWLANDS

FANTASY AND SCIENCE FICTION OF DUTCH AND FLEMISH WRITERS

compiled and edited with an introduction by
MANUEL VAN LOGGEM

preface by
ISAAC ASIMOV

Cross-Cultural Communications
Merrick, New York
1982

Published by Cross-Cultural Communications, Stanley H. Barkan,
Publisher, 239 Wynsum Avenue, Merrick, N.Y. 11566/U.S.A. Telephone:
(516) 868-5635 in cooperation with the Foundation for the Promotion of
the Translation of Dutch Literary Works, 450 Singel, 1017 AV
Amsterdam. (The Netherlands)

First Edition
Library of Congress Catalog Card Number: 81-86630
ISBN 0-89304-054-1 Paperback

© Cover art by A. C. Willink

Cover design by Karel van Laar
Bookdesign by Paul Groenendaal
Printed and bound in the Netherlands by Tulp bv – Zwolle

Contents

6

Introduction

by Manuel van Loggem

People read in the hope of benefiting from it. Some types of reading material, like scientific handbooks, are written to convey knowledge, the usefulness of which cannot be disputed.

But there are people who spend a great deal of time and even money on literature: artfully constructed fancy in which characters, invented by a writer, participate in events that we intentionally take for granted. If this is skillfully done, if style and plot take us into their grip, a peculiar situation arises in which we are involved in a psychological process called identification. This enables us to merge our own feelings with those of the fictional characters and to share their experience. Occasionally this occurs with such an impact that we are apt to be profoundly moved by what, in essence, has nothing to do with our personal fate.

This is a strange thing, for we do not respond only to agreeable experiences of the heroic or the fortunate. It is remarkable that what thrills us most are those emotions we would try to avoid in the humdrum reality of everyday life.

The emotions that invented characters can arouse in us can be subsumed under three main categories: pleasure, sorrow, and anxiety—causing laughter, tears, or the jitters—though they usually manifest themselves in various combinations and transitional states—such as irony, gloom, or tension—with their corresponding inner and outer signs. It is still debatable whether or not love and hate can be classified under pleasure and sorrow or if they represent a category of their own. But that's beside the point. We are posed with the problem of how we can enjoy disagreeable states of mind that are engendered by the act of reading.

The reason is that in literature the "as-if" principle reigns supreme. When we start reading, we accept the primary precondition for the enjoyment of fiction in a mutual agreement with the author that any kind of imagination is feasible so long as the methods used can convince us, can produce what Coleridge called in his *Biographia Literaria* "a willing suspension of disbelief." It sometimes even happens that the events evoked in our imagination tend to overwhelm us. In its most manifest form, we can see this when people faint during a movie scene which arouses so much vicarious fear that they cannot bear to watch. Most people are susceptible to scenes on an operating table, even though they know that the blood on the sheets is nothing more than ketchup.

The delights of reading are primarily revealed in private, and that's why the effects of literature are less conspicuous than those experienced in a social surrounding like the theater or a movie house. It is also easier to stop reading for a while than it is to walk away from a public performance.

But everyone knows from experience that the act of reading can sometimes stimulate almost unbearable emotions.

We can only solve the riddle of how a rational human being can identify himself with as-if characters if we assume that—in the course of our development from lower organisms—our brain-system retained many qualities of our former state. Our brains leak. A cat is a well-organized system of reactions. Man is not. In our early infancy, when we are still little animals, we develop feelings—such as dependency, hate, and anxiety—that very soon become inexpedient. But they don't lose their power. Their influence remains very strong, even if our reasoning tells us that they have not only lost their usefulness but are even harmful in our adult life.

The layers in our brain that stir certain emotions generated by certain stimuli are not adequately isolated, which means that reaction patterns from different periods in our development can influence each other in a contradictory system of either harmful or useful feelings and behavior. That is the reason why a football fan, identifying himself with his favorite club, is able to hate his opponents with such a fierce enmity that he is inclined to hurt and even kill them, although his ability to reason might tell him that his countryman (his brother in a war on a broader scale) is a mere participant in a game that may be forgotten or valueless by next season.

This aficionado suffers from what one could call a partial loss of ego, a state of mind left over from his earliest infancy. A newborn baby is totally dependent for its survival on its parents', which in most cases means its mother's care. It is presumed that it cannot distinguish between its own body and the vast source of warmth and food from which it sucks its life-fluid. But after those first months in the peaceful dimness of amniotic ocean, the infant has to learn that its mother and itself are different entities. The child becomes an independent ego with a gradually strengthened "I-awareness."

But in states of deep emotional disturbance, such as can occur during a football game, the regression to the former situation, in which the distinction between inside and outside worlds becomes blurred, is so strong that rational thinking is overwhelmed by the remembrance of the egoless past.

It is this regressive state that, in turn, induces the rift in man's rational faculties which not only causes mob-excitement, belief in magic, or blind patriotism, but also the impact of literature.

In the act of reading, the as-if system is experienced as a state of reality. But the loss of "egoness," which enables us to relive the vicissitudes of the characters in the story, is never complete. There always remains (except in cases of insanity) a remnant of conscious thinking which teaches us that what we go through can never be as bad as would be the case if the fate of the fictional figures were to befall us in ordinary life. However fiercely we might experience the emotions evoked by reading, they are always more or less diluted by our sense of reality, and it is this very dilution which gives us the pleasure and profit we derive from literature. In vicarious participation we can, without real danger, experience the emotions we tend to suppress in normal life, according to the laws of the pleasure principle.

Reading is, therefore, a homeopathic phenomenon. Diluted poison serves as medicine. And literature is the most enchanting and profitable vehicle to make bliss out of the inherently miserable human condition.

Appearance and Reality

No one can create out of a void. Fiction must be based on experience, and every writer has his own way of dealing with reality, his own blend of fantasy and that specific kind of truth that has passed through the filter of imagination. Literary truth, of course, can never be literal truth. Even a purely autobiographical story, with the author speaking as an "I-witness," gives us no guarantee of being in tune with the truth and nothing but the truth, however earnestly the author might have done his best to tap his memory as faithfully as possible.

Unadulterated truth, however, is very rare in literature. A selection and twisting of the facts are always involved. Some writers use material that they consider to be remnants of a reliable memory, while others suppose that everything they produce derives from pure imagination.

In a study of the methods writers use to arrange their impressions, a number of experienced writers were asked to concoct a story on the basis of four intentionally blurred pictures. Many of them used events from their past, representing almost unchanged and recognizable problems that were occupying them at the time, while others hid themselves almost completely behind to products of their fantasy.

These are two opposing tendencies in the craft of writing, but neither fantasy nor the description of real events can ever be mutually exclusive. Even the most bizarre products of the imagination may contain experiences, dreams and nightmares, or wishes of the maker. No one can state with certainty which belongs to unalloyed invention or to creative reproduction.

Fantasy

This condition also applies to the most honest offer of untruth there is: the kind of literature called Fantasy, which, at first glance, seems to be constructed from mere flights of fancy.

Fantasy is made of material that, at any rate according to the rules of rational thinking, is completely out of tune with the laws of nature as we know them. In this light the adventures of Tom Thumb, Little Red Riding-Hood, Puss in Boots, or Snow White are pure nonsense.

Modern Fantasy is nothing more than the fairy tales of yore, in the garments of our own time. Children love fairy tales, for they still believe in miracles, and some grownups read them with relish because they want to believe in miracles or because they realize that there is more in heaven and on earth than is dreamt of in their philosophy.

In the Netherlands, there is no tradition in this field, whereas in the Anglo-American language area, Lewis Carroll is considered one of the great literary masters. Yet there are excellent representatives in the realm of fantastic writing in Dutch, the common language of Holland and Flanders (the greater part of Belgium). But the official handbooks of literature ignore them, with Belcampo as a striking exception. Most of the writers who occasionally stepped outside their bounds for a bout of fantasy have made their reputation in other fields. In this collection Simon Carmiggelt, Hugo Claus, Jan

Wolkers, and Harry Mulisch must be mentioned as outsiders who have made a successful trip into the unknown. It is only later that a tendency can be seen for specialists—most of them born after World War II—to emerge.

Still, we can observe in the history of Dutch and Flemish literature a steady stream of fanciful works, running beside the main river of acknowledged currents, always discernible, though seldom mentioned by scholars and teachers.

In the later Middle Ages, the Netherlands produced *Charles and Elegast* and that crafty fox of world renown, Reynard. One might even say that, in the field of early science fiction, the Netherlands has played a prominent role.

We then have the following chronology: in 1708, a certain Hendrik Smeets's *Description of the Mighty Kingdom Krinke Kesmes*, pure fantasy of the future; in 1777, Betje Wolff's *Holland in the Year 2940*; in 1788, John Schasz's *Voyage to the Country of the Apes*; in 1792, Arend Fokke Simonsz' *The Future Year 3000*; in 1794, published anonymously, *Historical Description of the Moon, Its Inhabitants, and Its Best Form of Government over a Period of 4500 Years*; and in 1813, the poet Willem Bilderdijk's (recently reprinted) *Short Tale of a Remarkable Air Voyage and the Discovery of a New Planet*.

After that, a long silence set in until, in 1916, the journalist Kees van Bruggen scored an astounding success with *The troubled Ant's Nest*, a typical novel of doom about the destruction of life on Earth by an interplanetary poisonous gas, with only one man and woman left to repopulate the planet.

From that time on, there has been bustling activity in the marketplace. Frederik van Eeden and F. Bordewijk published tales of fantasy, and before World War II, the first publications of Belcampo (pen name of Herman Schoenfeld Wichers, a physician who can be considered the doyen of Dutch Fantasy writers) began to appear. He is still active. In this anthology, in which the writers are chronologically presented, he occupies second place. The first is reserved for Rein Blijstra, who died in 1975, and who may be considered a pioneer in the field of pure SF with his collection of stories *The Planetarium of Otze Otzinga*. Louis Paul Boon, third in the order of age, died in 1979.

The intention was to compile an anthology of still-living Fantasy writers from the Netherlands, but since the collection would not truly represent the state of Fantasy and SF in Holland and Flanders without the contributions of the two dead masters—Blijstra and Boon—they were included.

Kinds of Fantasy

It is almost impossible to invent a theme that has not already been used. Most of the stories in this book can be subsumed under a particular heading, though there are some that escape strict categorizing.

The Modern Fairy Tale

In this kind of story, the events are of a purely imaginative nature. They cannot occur in a world governed by the laws of logic. Their style and plot owe much to the atmosphere of extreme cruelty and unhampered fancy with which our children are initiated into the world of the weird. A clear example of a modern fairy tale is Louis Paul Boon's contribution, a variation on the Bluebeard theme. The stories by Carmiggelt, Claus, and Hamelink can also be put into this category. People become animals, puppets come to life, old people shrink into nothingness. It is all reminiscent of the olden days, but the tone is different. And there's no happy ending.

The Second World

Even professional philosophers play with the problem if the world in which we live could be a reflection of an unknown reality. There is a school (solipsism) which avers that the world of phenomena can only exist in the mind of the beholder. Others consider the visible world as the manifestation of a hidden, higher reality. There are also philosophers who believe that the universe is nothing more than a dream of a godlike creature and that our own dreams are mere reflections of this universal mind.

The ordinary man, too, is often beset by a hunch that what *is* can't be what it *seems*, and in his fearful assumption of an all-pervading mystery, he peoples the world behind his visible surroundings with creatures of a higher, lower, or totally different order than nature has to offer him. Thus the ghosts, doppelgängers, dybbuks, devils, witches, werewolves, and vampires are born as reflections of mankind's fears and hopes. Anton Quintana's story is a fine variation on the theme of the double-crossing double.

From earliest times on, beings from the realm of death haunt our tales of fantasy, incorporating our ever-lurking collective fright, often suppressed, of the ultimate unknown. In Kees Simhoffer's contribution, a ghost from the recent past, a victim of the most atrocious crime in history (the Holocaust) penetrates into the present, unable to leave the world he was forced too soon to abandon.

Even while we are sleeping, when the mind is at unrest at night, the censor deep inside us takes his own nap, permitting the most horrible visions, our distorted fears and wishes rise from the depths as nightmares or dreams. Fantasy is replete with them, often disguised as the real stuff from which our world is made. Dreams come true, are shared with others, show prophetic tendencies, or materialize when we wake. Everyone knows from his own experience the close relationship between dream and fantasy. So it's little wonder that the literature of fantasy owes so much to the pregnant symbolism and meaningful distortions of our dreams. Olga Rodenko writes in a cool style, with a tinge of mock innocence, about the illusions of people who think they are living in a place which doesn't exist at all and in which they themselves can only be shadows of a dream.

Another prevalent theme is the slightly modified recurrence of events usually from the very remote past as an example of the recycling principle in the history of the cosmos. Biblical themes are often a favorite subject for this this-has-happened-before kind of story. In this collection, there are many such specimens. Belcampo describes how the Last Judgment, according to *Revelations*, takes place in his native village of Rijssen. Lampo and Hellinga allude to the birth of Jesus, and Paul van Herck foretells a second flood, announced by a certain Noah who wants to buy animals for his ark.

Horror

A specific kind of Fantasy is called Horror. Of course, Horror, as such, is not confined to horror stories. There are many traditional forms, and one man's terror might be another man's joke. Horror is meant to be horrifying. People who like the genre like it very much. The more shivers it evokes, the more pleasure it gives.

During fear, adrenaline makes the heart beat faster, provokes cold spells or hot sweat, and causes a disturbance in the normal rhythm of breathing. It is still a matter of contention between scientists whether adrenaline causes the symptoms or the other way around. Whichever, adrenaline was probably a very useful hormone in primeval times. It prepared the body of primitive man for immediate and efficient flight in moments of danger. Now its manifestations have become obsolete remnants of our past and are often harmful in our present state of civilization. The system of hormonal secretion has not caught up with the evolution of the mind, and we must painfully learn to live with this discrepancy. We can suffer from outbursts of anxiety or a permanent apprehension for which we don't even know the cause, and we often need the help of highly paid experts to tell us the root of our harmful feelings. Whether this helps is a matter of debate. All we know for sure is that all forms of anxiety derive, in essence, from the fear of death. The ultimate annihilation is perpetually present in our life.

As already mentioned, the arousal of diluted disagreeable sensations can be very useful and give us a lot of pleasure. That's why Horror occupies such a permanent place in the realm of Fantasy. Skillfully constructed nightmares are better digested on paper than when one is asleep and powerless.

For that matter, education has prepared us for the joy of invented apprehension. From the tenderest age, we are raised with blood-curdling adventures of sadists and innocent victims. The fairy tales of Mother Goose and the Brothers Grimm are literally dripping with blood, and whole armies of doting parents have threatened their brood with a menacing bogeyman or some other supernatural master over life and death. This seems terrible, but it is probably necessary. Without the regimen of fear, no human community can exist. The Devil is the keeper of morals. How can we sustain a well-organized society if our destructive impulses are not regulated by fear or punishment, either from conscience or the institutions of social justice?

Every man strives for immediate satisfaction of his desires, and this is most often contrary to the interests of his neighbors or society as a whole. The beast in us must be kept within bounds. One of the methods of teaching us this most difficult lesson our civilization imposes on us is through Horror in literature, and it is ancient. We all know the story of Cain and Abel, Lot's wife, and the terrors John revealed to us. Later on, readers took their fright with the help of lonely mansions, apparitions from the grave or clattering skeletons, preferably with rusty chains around their ankles. At the moment, that is child's play.

We now know the fear from inside better than our forebears. We all harbor a source of horror in our minds. That's not just the result of education or an inherent personal fear of death. From the recent past, we know that what John bequeathed us as the result of his apocalyptic visions may become horrendous reality with the ultimate nuclear bang. Since Hiroshima, the Day of the last Judgment —when the sun turns black, the moon falls from the sky, and the stars are wrenched from their course—no longer strikes us as an aberration in the brain of a religious fanatic.

Horror is amply represented in this anthology. Wim Burkunk was probably inspired while gorging on a fresh, young herring. Marty Olthuis, specialist in what she calls "quiet horror," announces in a way that makes the skin crawl the death of her cat. Ton van Reen describes a modern witch trial, Frank Herzen's contribution is about a meat-eating flower, and Patrick Conrad sticks to old, reliable craftmanship with a Poe-like story of blood, worm-infested corpses, putrefaction, and plain madness.

E.S.P.

Extra Sensory Perception is represented here as all phenomena investigated by parapsychologists, such as telepathy, clairvoyance, and telekinesis. Not so long ago, the study of these phenomena was considered a legitimate scientific occupation. Professor Rhine's laboratory at Duke University was world famous. The results with his Zener cards, designed for proving the existence of telepathic forces in gifted subjects, were astounding and utterly convincing. But, alas, those times are gone. There is growing doubt about the scientific reliability of many ESP experiments. Rumors about unskilled use of statistical data and downright cheating by some of Rhine's collaborators are getting stronger and stronger.

But in the field of Fantasy, the secrets of the mind are still frequently used as proven facts. Numerous are the tales of telepathists, often grouped around a Supreme Mindreader who collects and distributes the mind waves of his subjects. Hypnosis, too, is not a problem in fiction; neither are soul transference and second sight. That thoughts are able to materialize is an easy trick for fertile fantasists. Though very popular in Anglo-American fiction, it is remarkable that in this collection the ESP variety is represented only by Harry Mulisch. In his story, the Word becomes Flesh. The exchange of souls between man and animal, described by Marty Olthuis, also might—with a bit of good will—be included in the ESP category.

There is so much extensive research available on Science Fiction that only a brief excursion into this type of literature is possible. Dutchmen were early pioneers in the field of futuristic fiction. Despite this, in contemporary SF, they are rather poorly represented, though lately quite a number of competent SF authors from the Netherlands have been given the attention they deserve. Most of them belong to the category of explorers of man and society on our own planet in the future. Since the landings on the Moon suggest that no life is possible on the barren deserts of our satellite and pictures relayed from Mars and Venus have demonstrated that we cannot expect recognizable life forms on the nearest planets, the writers of futuristic fiction have necessarily confined their imagination to the exploration and extrapolation of the future on Earth and in our own minds.

Einstein proved that the velocity of light cannot be exceeded and that voyages to faraway stars are physically impossible for a single generation, though there might be a small chance for deep-frozen (cryogenic) individuals. That might also be a reason why modern and honest science fiction writers have left outer space for what it is: a perpetually unattainable goal for the human race, though nobody knows for certain what the future really has in store for us. Anyhow, no tendrilized life forms near the system of Betelgeuse for Dutch SF authors.

Time travel, however, is excluded from this dictum. Jaap Verduyn and Peter Cuijpers describe confrontations with our brothers from the past; Bob van Laerhoven prepares a surprising deception for those heading for the Middle Ages; and, yes, there is a short, satirical story about a tiny spaceship landing on Venus by Ef Leonard.

There is a special type of story, made famous by Eric von Däniken. In pseudo-scientific speculation, he tried to prove (and with remarkable success to many hankering for a new form of religion) that the astounding technical progress of mankind is the result of the intervention of extraterrestrial visitors. The tales of mystery from the Bible, only convincing with a supernatural explanation, then become SF stories.

Rein Blijstra provides an interesting variation on this theme: God as a hobbyist and his wife as the determiner of our ultimate fate.

Many of the current themes of modern SF are found in contemporary Dutch futuristic fiction. Carl Lans confronts us with an overpopulated world in which space and breathing material are strictly distributed. In my own contribution, man is depicted as an incorrigible animal, and Hugo Raes gives us an impression of a gloom future, a poetical evocation of the sun's impending blackness. In Ward Ruyslinck's story, the white doom we all fear manifests itself as a soft snowfall, and Bob van der Goen speculates about the tyranny of excessive sound, a not too improbable picture of a very near future. Eddy C. Bertin presents a surprising variation on the subject of the omnipotence of a universal mind, Julien C. Raasveld takes his cue from H.G. Well's spine-chilling forecast of the reign of insects as the dominant race on Earth, and Karel Sandor describes the tribulations of a religious group that expects blessings from on high.

A quick computation shows that 20% of the 32 stories in this anthology are of a more or less cheerful nature, 22% are neither cheerful nor gloomy, and about 60% are infused with the spirit of doom. People of a more optimistic turn of mind might arrive at a somewhat different classification, but the overall proportions can't be too far off.

I don't think that this dominance of doom is just a reflection of my taste preference. I have tried to compose a representative and readable anthology of contemporary Fantasy and SF in the Low Countries. I have chosen the stories for literary value, merits of style, clarity of language, an interesting theme, originality in the handling of the plot, and preferably an ending with a surprise twist which enhances the impact of the story by the agreeable shock of the unexpected.

That there are so many shiver-arousing stories to be enjoyed is not my fault. But it can't do you any harm. Vicarious fear is good for all of us.

Rein Blijstra (1901-1974)

was from early on a prose writer of distinction, and recognized as such by his contemporaries. By profession, he was the art editor for a daily paper, internationally recognized as an expert in the field of modern architectural construction, and one of the pioneers of Science Fiction in the Netherlands.

Behind Otze Otzinga, the handy Frisian, of course lies the famous carpenter Eise Eisinga from Franeker who built a beautiful planetarium (completed in 1780) which is still a fascinating sight.

However, Otze went a little further than Eise. Much further, one could say.

Otze Otzinga's Planetarium

Otze Otzinga was the amanuensis for the laboratory of astronomy at the University of Franeker. A stout man with a face that was perhaps a little too ruddy; on first impression, friendly to the point of submissiveness; jovial in his speech, but upon closer inspection not really the comfortable and contented man he made himself out to be. To be sure, there was a reason for this. Otze, from a poor family, had been discovered by his primary school teacher who saw in him a budding genius. This good man did not rest until he had seen to it that Otze had been admitted to secondary school, after which, no doubt, he would go to the university to continue his studies. He was not the only one to suppose this, for others who knew Otze and who were equally confident of his abilities were convinced of this. They were disappointed, however, because Otze was just a mediocre high school student, and despite years of diligence he did not graduate. He was already seventeen by then and had to learn a trade; the choice was not difficult, since it had gradually become evident that Otze's intelligence resided not in his head but in his hands. And so, he was taken on by an instrument maker at the engineering laboratory of the university and was still relatively young, not yet forty, when he was appointed as amanuensis at the astrophysics laboratory.

This, in itself, was not a bad—indeed it was quite a responsible—position. Nevertheless, it seemed that the initial hope and desire to reach the highest pinnacles of science and the subsequent letdowns had deeply affected the young Otze, and though he could not be called dispirited, he lacked the carefree zest for life of a happy person. He was always busy, busy with something, too intently busy.

Especially of late. Of late? The last few months, you could say, perhaps even—although less obviously—the last few years. This was impossible to detect accurately, for, ever since the beginning of his marriage, Otze had made use of the attic as a place to escape to; a study and a workshop where he passed a great deal of his spare time. Exactly what he was up to up there was not always clear to Boukje, his wife. She did suspect, in any case, that he took naps there after lunch, although it was clear that he did occasionally do something else, as he would at certain times come down with ingeniously made models of intricate machines. He also made old-fashioned things like ships, trains, and airplanes which he then proudly displayed somewhere. Such exhibits never lasted long, for, after a time, Otze would produce something else for which the earlier works had to make way—usually being given to neighbors and friends.

He had, however been busy for the last few months without anything tangible leaving his hands. Boukje was just starting to be worried when, one afternoon, Otze invited her to go up to the attic with him. He was looking pretty smug, and with reason, for, as she entered the workshop, a strange spectacle awaited her.

This time it was not the model of an obsolete machine or of a modern one that Otze had fashioned; it was at first sight not much more than a bunch of little spheres floating around the attic like tiny soap bubbles, seemingly without a particular purpose. Some of the little spheres radiated an unpleasant light, others were dark, still others were grouped together in little clusters, and in among it all, almost motionlessly, drifted dark and light mists of nondescript dust.

Otze looked at her as if he were expecting a compliment, or at least a comment from her, but she did not understand much of it and merely nodded wisely a few times, which evidently did not mislead him because he asked: "Don't you see what it is?"

"No," said Boukje. "I can't quite place it."

"It's our solar system with a portion of the Milky Way and the rest of the universe," Otze said proudly. "A model made to scale." He pointed to the little globes: "The sun, the earth, the planets, Alpha Centauri, Arcturus, Betelgeuse, Andromeda. Some of it I painted on a moving piece of cardboard, but they won't notice that anyway, it's too far away for them."

"For them?" Boukje asked in surprise. "For whom?"

"For the inhabited planets. I copied creation," said Otze proudly. "I had to alter the speed of light slightly, and therefore their time

23

reckoning has been altered as well. This world created by me is now eighty days old, but their Earth is now—according to their own calculations—about two million years old and the whole of creation, three million years. The earth revolves around the sun in more or less one three-thousandth of one of our seconds. I can check it exactly for you..."

"No, don't bother, it's too complicated for me anyway," said Boukje. "But what do you want to do with this?"

"It's truly amazing how quickly that little race on Earth has developed," Otze said, not heeding her question. "It's happening so fast, I had to make it all stop a couple of times in order not to miss too much of it. I can't do that now, though; they would notice. The beginning was rather dull: I took some stripped atoms from the lab which I let go among a number of neutralizing gravitational fields. For a few days I didn't pay much attention since it just kept on slowly expanding and there wasn't much to see. But then, suddenly I noticed that a couple of the atoms had released little bodies that began cooling off. I set them aside for observation under a magnifying glass, and what do you think comes into existence? Life! Plant growth! At least something that resembles it."

"Those little globes just started to get moldy," Boukje supposed.

"That's putting it very domestically," said Otze, somewhat insulted. "Life was generated. I created Life! Our molds are too big for those things. Discrete, microscopic life. And, afterwards, life you could easily observe with a magnifying glass. Ferns, enormous ferns, at least for the dimensions there. And trees—and after that there came very strange animals. I hadn't expected those at all. And you know what?' he said mysteriously. "Those things started making themselves from themselves. Animals that stood in swamps, and animals that lived in forests, and finally very tiny naked beings sprang up, and they look like us. They're still there now." He looked at his wife with a gaze full of anticipation.

"And what of it?" she asked gruffly. "What are you going to do about it?"

"I don't want to do anything about it, but they want to do something. They're going much too fast. At first I shut the whole thing down once or twice out of curiosity, but now I want to do it because I'm afraid they'll go off like an alarm." Otze laughed. "You know, the funny thing is there's a Franeker there as well and a university, too. But that one's already been shut down. Hilarious, really. The

24

learned types here should know about that. Then, no doubt, they'd be whistling a different tune. There's a fellow down there who also made a planetarium, a very primitive one. It's a tourist attraction now. The man's name was Eyse Eysinga. He's already been dead there for centuries."

"Otze Otzinga," Boukje cut in sharply, "you're playing with fire. You're a dabbler, not a researcher. You don't know what you're doing!"

"They don't know that there, either," Otze grinned. "And they know they don't know anything. They're all agnostics down there, just as I am. At first they even believed in me for a short time, but that's all over now."

"In you? Why you?"

"I can't help it," he said shyly. "For a little while they worshipped their creator. Well, that was me, wasn't it?"

"So, that was you, was it!" She took a step forward and clenched her fists. "That was you, was it? Boastful ranter! The great inventor who was too stupid to finish high school. Do you know what you are, Otze? You're presumptuous, an unbeliever, a blasphemer. You'll come to a bad end one of these days."

"Certainly, I'm allowed to create a world according to my own conception," declared Otze. "That isn't forbidden. I wasn't intending to copy the almighty Creator. It didn't even turn out the same," he ended haltingly and somewhat perplexed.

"So much the worse," interjected his wife. "That means you deviated from the divine plan. That means you've sold yourself to the devil."

"Oh, nonsense!" said Otze. "Those are just old wives' tales. The Creator set to work just the same as I did. And it got out of hand with Him, too; no devil entered into it. We became independent, just as they did, there. Except, it's funny, just the last few days they haven't been making any progress. You should see this." He gave Boukje his magnifying glass. "First they fired off little things in the direction of their moon and one has already gone all the way around, and then they moved on to a planet closer to their sun and then on to another farther away and that seems to have worked, but they don't seem able to get very much farther, somehow. Just the same as us, they can't get any farther. How can that be?"

"Because you can't see beyond your own nose," said Boukje decisively. "Those beings seem to be independent, but they aren't.

25

Those beings are dependent on you, just as you're dependent on..."

"Other beings," said Otze. "As if you stepped between two mirrors. You see yourself reflected again and again until the farther you get the smaller you become. What you don't see are the ones that keep getting larger." He wavered for a moment. "But who can tell whether the little ones aren't getting more powerful."

Boukje laid her hand on his shoulder. "Come on, Otze," she said. "Don't let it bother you. Nothing is going to happen there, as you yourself say. They aren't making any progress. They haven't surpassed us yet. They won't go any farther than your imagination, I'll bet." Her tone of voice sounded almost compassionate. "And if they tried..." She didn't finish her sentence and glanced at her watch. "It's time for you to go to the lab. You have to hurry. A short walk in the fresh air will do you good."

She climbed down the narrow, dark-red stairs with him and watched him until he disappeared around the corner of the street. With a worried look on her face, she went to sit down in the easy chair by the heater as soon as he was out of sight. She was not at all as certain of a happy ending as she had pretended to be in front of Otze. He had not been quite right of late: too distracted, steeped in thought too much, given to strange outbursts about his minor position in society, about the fact that he was not being recognized and how people like him—inventors, inventors of genius with no scientific background—were never recognized. He was terribly confused, that was plain to see, now; but she could not talk to anyone about it—not with the priest, not with a professor, not with the police. Being relieved of his position, scandal, and perhaps, being locked up in an asylum could result.

With a sigh she got up and went to the kitchen closet. "The poor fool," she muttered, as she climbed the stairs again, armed with a broom, a dust cloth and a dustpan and brush. "The poor fool. He sees them fly, even though of course they're only dangling from strings." And with a sturdy swipe of her broom, she dashed the sun, moon, stars, and nebulae to the dusty floor and then swept up the whole business without noticing that here and there the little globes were crackling ominously or dissipating in mushroom-shaped clouds. "I should have done a major clean-up in here a long time ago," she thought as she carried the dustpan laden with heavenly bodies down the stairs.

Belcampo (b. 1902)

is the pen name of Herman Pieter Schönfeld Wichers, a solicitor's son, who studied law and medicine and became a physician for students at Groningen University. But it was never a full-time job. Belcampo spent most of his time writing Fantasy stories, which brought him fame, moderate wealth, and his own undisputed place in Dutch literature. His first book The Wanderings of Belcampo *was an immediate hit. In his* Stories by Belcampo, *originally self-published in 1926, he already used most of the themes that still feed the imagination of contemporary SF authors.*

When Easter has elevated the minds of men and higher thoughts occupy ordinary people, it often occurs that the Devil, always good for a mean trick, lies in wait to pick his victims. What then happens is akin to a revelation—Belcampo's Revelation in Rijssen.

The Kruutntoone Plan

Every salesman knows where the small town of Rijssen lies, and any inhabitant of Rijssen will tell you: "It is a station on the Amsterdam-Berlin railroad"—but no one will ever mention what happened there on Easter Monday night. That has been hushed up totally by both press and public. There were enough people present— it isn't that; no, it is because everyone who was there regards that night as a rotten patch in the garland of his days. Let me, therefore, have the pleasure of relating here in detail those colorful events, too remarkable to be consigned to oblivion.

It all began with a meeting in the Crown Inn, convened for the purpose of devising ways and means of protecting Rijssen as much as possible against the consequences of the current world depression. In his opening address, the chairman mentioned the ruinous effect Japanese competition had on prices in our Eastern provinces, causing the large jute factory—mainstay of Rijssen's economy—to become unprofitable; the workforce was put on a three-day instead of a six-day week and Rijssen's income had been halved, and a return to the old farming ways was out of the question because agriculture was in a sadder state than ever before.

The chairman went on to point out that the factors influencing our economic life so unfavorably would in all probability be of long duration. "Changes are needed," he concluded his speech. "We are in an intolerable situation which will inevitably make beggars of us all. The question is: what can we do? We have no power over world events. All we can do is work in a limited sphere, but within these

27

limits it is our duty to do whatever we can for our own survival and that of our wives and children."

However, when it came to making actual proposals for improvement, it was the usual story: the spirit was willing, but the mind was weak.

Stupid proposals were put forward, a great many of them. Some were impracticable, others depended on the most fantastic profit calculations. Some were rapacious in the extreme, some offended against public morality—yes, there was even a suggestion that Rijssen should be turned into a center of sensual pleasure. Of all the proposals submitted, only one was finally selected for further consideration, and that was the one put forward by Kruutntoone, the old bronchitic cabinetmaker.

Kruutntoone said that if they wanted new ideas, they should not confine themselves to Rijssen alone, but look around elsewhere. He had done just that, and his eye had involuntarily fixed itself on the town of Ootmarsum.

Because of the ancient Easter traditions that are still observed there, an annual increasing stream of visitors pours into the town, with a stream of money in its wake. "Why," continued old Kruutntoone, "could not Rijssen have had its own ancient Easter customs, of which no knowledge has ever penetrated to the world outside? Rijssen is known to be a conservative town, so much so that it sometimes attracts ridicule. Well then, would it not be perfectly plausible if in such a town ancient customs were still being kept alive? A reputation we already have; the question is, now, how to turn it to profit."

A committee was appointed to examine the Kruutntoone proposal further and assess its feasibility. The world of scholarship was represented on the committee in the person of a young lawyer, the son of Rijssen's notary, widely renowned for his sharp intelligence and originality of mind.

After roaming the heath for a week, he brought out the following report:

For those of you who have never had the opportunity to attend the Ootmarsum Easter ceremonies, the so-called 'vlöggeln', I shall begin with a brief description of this custom.

In the afternoon of Easter Sunday, all the townspeople assemble in a field designated for the purpose. Four young men are in charge of the proceedings and go around distributing leaflets on which are printed two lengthy poems. The people then join hands and form a long line and, with the four young men at the head, set out along a prescribed route through the town, singing the songs on the leaflets which those who do not know them by heart have pinned on the backs of the people in front of them.

Some of the old farmhouses still have the traditional double barn doors leading to the threshing floor which has a pole in the middle. These doors stand open and everybody has to walk around the pole, which means that everybody sets foot on the threshing floor. Other houses, usually cafés, are entered by the back door and left by the front. On the counter, drinks have been poured for each of the four leaders, to be drunk in passing. The procession end in the main square where the column winds round and round until the whole square is packed with people. There the two songs are sung right through once more, and after the last verse, the young children—who have, meanwhile, joined their parents and have been sitting on their father's arms or shoulders for some while—are lifted up in the air three times, amid loud cheers. That is the end of the vlöggeln ceremony.

Attempts at discovering the origin of this custom have so far been unsuccessful. I am flattered to be able to lift the veil. We are here undoubtedly dealing with a religious custom, as is evident from the text of the two songs. If we study the meaning of Easter, our investigations will naturally lead us to Exodus 12 : 12 : "For I will pass through the land of Egypt that night, and I will smite all the first-born in the land of Egypt." To the intelligent interpreter, this means that there must have been a time when Easter was the feast of the sacrifice of the first-born. One step further and the significance of the vlöggeln ceremony will have become clear to us. The entire community gathers together and forms one body which visits the houses where the first-born of the past year lie ready to be killed by the priest, at the head of the procession, with the sacrifical knife. Everyone had to take part in the murder, hence the joining of hands, and everybody had to walk by the dead child and the blood which he himself had helped to shed. The singing fits in perfectly with a ritual act; a continuous hymn of praise to God leading the singers into a trance, making them deaf to the voice of their own hearts. Finally, they express their joy in those children which they have been allowed to keep. It is as if they wish to say: "We are no murderers.

29

Our children are dear to us, which shows, O Lord, how great has been the sacrifice we have made to thee."

When in the course of time customs softened, the human first-born were replaced by those of sheep and cattle, while, at the same time, it was precisely the first-born children that were lifted up at the end of the procession by parents in whose eyes could be read the joy at this fortunate modification. Later, the lambs and calves were left out altogether, and much later still, people lost the understanding of what they were doing, though they persisted in the custom, with a vague sense of something sacred, very remote. Nowadays, it is no more than a touristic sight for visitors, and the attraction is all the greater because anyone is free to join in.

So much for the vlöggeln tradition.

We should now turn our minds to the question of devising an Easter custom for Rijssen, also rooted in religion, and, if possible, with an even greater capacity to attract visitors. I think, gentlemen, that I have succeeded in finding one.

We all know that in the Christian religion Easter celebrates the resurrection of Jesus Christ on the third day after his burial, but few people know of a little legend connected with this event which, together with so many biblical legends, fell into the background at the time of the Reformation.

As the Gospels tell us, watchmen were placed by Christ's tomb, Roman soldiers who had taken part in the Crucifixion. When they saw—so says the legend—how an Angel of the Lord opened the tomb and how Jesus rose from the grave in all his glory, these rough warriors became, at a stroke, susceptible to the divine truth. But at the same moment, they also saw in consternation how black with sin their past life had been—yes, that they had helped nail their own God to the cross. In despair, they prostrated themselves and begged to be made pure, to be redeemed from the eternal damnation which would surely be awaiting them. Their prayer was heard. From the open grave there rose flames, hissing and crackling, which seemed to call out to the supplicants: "In us you can be purified, in us alone." Without further thought, the soldiers threw themselves into the fire, armor and all. Thus the tomb of Christ swallowed up its own guards.

Taking this legend as our starting point and making use of the common regional practice of lighting large bonfires at Easter, we could devise a kind of annual purification ceremony, the origin of which could be presented as follows:

To the early Christians, still partly tainted by pagan notions and moreover, inclined to profess their new faith with excessive fervor, this festival presented an opportunity to be cleansed of even the blackest sins through voluntary self-immolation and, thus, to enter upon the joys of heaven. These sacrificial acts were accompanied by solemn rites and demonstrations of rejoicing from the bystanders. As in Ootmarsum, the nature of the sacrifice gradually changed: instead of throwing themselves into the fire, people would offer their clothes and, after performing a purification dance naked around the fire, they would put on new clothing. Later still, the offerings became limited to certain easily replaced items of clothing, and, nowadays, we find market stalls erected in a wide circle around the fire, where one can buy anything from loose scraps of cloth to complete outfits for immediate sacrifice.

I should therefore like to make the following proposal: Firstly, we need a publicity campaign, of which I am willing to take charge. I suggest we concentrate chiefly on the three largest cities in the country, because that is where most of the people live who are interested in old folk customs.

Next, a large Easter bonfire will have to be built in the middle of the Schild Square. All around, close against the houses, we will erect stalls where food and drink must be available in large quantities. It must be impressed on all Rijsseners how much it is in their interest that our venture succeeds and how important it is that they offer their full cooperation in every respect. On Easter Sunday, a large number of extra trains and buses will be required to cope with the influx of tourists.

After midday, not a single Rijssener is to show himself out in the street. All the window shutters are to be closed, and where there are no shutters, the curtains must be drawn. The town must look deserted, for that is what tourists like. Only the cafés and restaurants remain open, of course.

At eight o'clock in the evening, the ceremony begins. All the people come out of their houses and go to the Schild. They gather around the unlit bonfire in silence and sit on the ground for a full twenty minutes—even the tourists are expected to do so; the tradition requires that everyone present takes part. Strangely attired men with halberds see to it that there is no disobedience; anyone unwilling to comply will be hit on the shin with the halberd. During these twenty minutes, the church bells will start ringing. When the fire is lit, all will join hands and walk slowly, in concentric circles around the pyre, chanting a somber song in seventeenth century Rijssen dialect. Visitors must be encouraged as much as possible to join in. When the fire is fully ablaze, the sacrificing begins. Long poles have to be ready to deposit the offerings onto the fire, for the heat will be so great that the people have to keep a respectful distance. The Rijsseners then take off their mourning clothes, and when all have brought their offerings, a great dance of joy commences, a chanting and a jigging in which everyone can take part. The fire department will have to be on the alert throughout the night.

This is the outline of my proposal, the details of which still have to be worked out further. I am convinced that this plan, if properly carried out, will arouse great interest all over the country and will offer our citizens ample opportunity to make money. It is therefore with the fullest confidence that I put my proposal before the committee.

Since none of the other committee members could have devised anything remotely similar, let alone anything better, the young lawyer's words were greeted as glad tidings, and a week before Easter a news item was launched in all the major papers in which, as many of you may still remember, visitors were for the first time ever invited to witness the secret Easter customs in Rijssen. The Telegraph published a leading article by Professor Casimir, discussing the origins, symbolic meaning, and ethical significance of the Rijssen Easter ceremonies. On Easter night, many a Rijssener lay tossing about restlessly in his cupboard bedstead.

The hordes of visitors, mostly from Amsterdam, that poured into Rijssen on Easter Monday, had an impression of having landed in some kind of Northern Pompeii, an impression further strengthened by the sight of large numbers of fellow tourists seen thumbing through booklets.

This was the Rijssen Easter guide, compiled by Mr. Wingerdhof, retired schoolteacher, a man who, like a horse, enjoyed his rest standing up, posted in the middle of the Schild, the main square which is the scene of all major events in the town. Today, his habitual place had been taken up by piles of osiers, beams, tar barrels, baskets, old rush mats, the seats and backs of chairs, two dilapidated settees, two sails from Paul's windmill on the Wierden Road (which had come off in one of the winter storms and would never need to be repaired, since Paul had been milling by steam for the last five years) the wooden parapet of a bridge, Toldiek's old rowboat which some youths had pulled up from the mud where it had been stuck for two years because the river Regge was so low. All these things could be seen at a first glance, but how much more was concealed in the funeral pile! Had not cartloads of juniper trees been brought back from the heath? Had there not been gangs of boys who, marauding at nightfall, had made off with anything combustible? Chicken coops, dog kennels, whole fences and summer houses even!

No, today there was no room for Mr. Wingerdhof. Anyway, he was not allowed to be out in the street; he had to be indoors like all the other Rijsseners—he had to play his part. He had to act the sinner, locking himself up at home and struggling with his remorse, a humble mortal, settling his yearly account with God. They acted their parts well, for the tourists believed it was genuine and looked, half curious, half embarrassed, at the closed shutters and the drawn curtains; there was no place for mockery, the deadness was too severe. The Easter guide explained it all so beautifully. Strange, how these people cling so tenaciously to their religion, there's something enviable about it, better than always chasing after money, as we do in the city, thought many a visitor. Their interest in the town had been awakened, and they looked at it far more attentively than they would have looked at any other town. They looked at the grass between the cobblestones, at the low roofs, the muck heaps in front of the houses, the barn doors, the chickens and the cattle that can be seen from the road, and then they sat down at Schutjen's or at the Crown on the Schild for a drink and a bite to eat, while in the center of the square the stack of firewood seemed to grow gradually more menacing as the sun went down and the six halberdiers, who had been standing like statues around the pile all afternoon, gaped at by hundreds, began to show up more sharply, in their bright red uniforms, as the dusk deepened. It was warm outside, there was no wind, but there was tension in the air.

At eight o'clock the houses openend to let out the dark, silent figures of the Rijsseners. From all directions they came shuffling along, their gaze fixed on the ground before them, as though they

33

were peering into an abyss, arms hanging straight by their sides as though they were being dragged along, the women with their skirts flung over their heads which looked as if they were tucked under their backs like tortoise heads, the men with their coats turned inside-out, expressing that which is not fit to be seen, as well as their seperation from worldly values. The children stayed at home.

On arrival at the Schild, all knelt down and stayed motionless, close to each other, the women like clods of earth. The visitors also went down on their knees, of their own accord; no one needed to be hit on the shins. There they lay, hundreds of them; no sound, no movement, as rigid as if they had been buried under lava, under red-hot, all-enclosing lava.

And then the bells began to ring; first those of the Old Church, very softly but slowly swelling; then the Roman Catholic Church, then the Old-Reformed, then the Dordrecht-Reformed, then the Town Hall, then the Fish Auction Hall—yes, it was clear that a question was being asked here, more and more urgently; these voices from above, almost commanding, sometimes descending uncontrollably into discords. Yes, it was clear, something had to happen; it was impossible to remain prostrated; a deafening desire was being voiced up there, a demand was being made. The ladies and gentlemen from the city, they felt it, too, these tremblings; was this still the mere attendance at an old custom, this anxious throbbing, this seething of emotions? Was this the gratification of curiosity, the indulging of an interest in folklore? This groaning and pealing of bells above the silent people, was it Christianity or did it smack of savagery, of the jungle? Was this not Rijssen, province of Over-ijssel?

Suddenly the bells fell silent, for something was about to happen. The halberdiers came forward, each carrying a flame, which they laid in different places at the foot of the colossus; they stepped back, slowly, each with his eyes fixed on his own growing flame. Calmly and surely, the light spread an the people knew: now there was no escape, the craving was now within. The Rijsseners rose and joined hands, the strangers let themselves be carried along, they had no will, there was a tingling in their hands, currents flowed through them, currents of a great awareness: that something was about to happen here, that with the breakthrough of the flames a great heaviness would be lifted, and so they moved and the Rijsseners sang, but it was no song—oh, no, it was a chant, a stirring chant setting alight all those that heard it, as the flames set alight the wood.

The circles were forced to retreat farther and farther from the increasing heat; but the strangers resisted, they tried to get closer to the fire, a recklessness had entered into them. The inner circles were pressing back, they were choking; the strangers surged forward, and for a time there was silent pressure against pressure—and then the fire began to crackle, the wood began to leap, there were flares and flights of sparks.

"The song is ended! The song is ended!" shouted the Rijsseners, letting go each other's hands, to prepare the sacrificial rites...

Then, suddenly, all were startled by a voice from above. Look, there on the Town Hall balcony, from where Rijssen's burgomaster is in the habit of surveying his domain—there stood a man, a gentleman in appearance, though not now: he had ripped off his jacket, one bare shoulder poked through the tatters of his shirt, his hair hung tousled about his head and his eyes, deep-socketed, seemingly scorched into his face with a branding iron, commanded all who looked at him. His body cast a monstrous shadow on the wall of the town hall; when he spoke, it was as if a mighty demon was conducting an orchestra behind him. And his voice was sharp and raw, his throat parched by the heat.

"Friends from Amsterdam, Rotterdam, The Hague! This day is for me the Day of Judgment; on this day I wish to pass judgment on the life I have led hitherto. Yes, I see it now, I have lived in a bleached sepulchre, a paved tomb! That was no life, for, my friends, what is a life without God? It is as a bird cage from which the bird has gone. Here, at the sight of these simple-hearted people, the scales have fallen from my eyes. let them go on living with God, but let us—even though our life has been unworthy—being a life without God, let us at least die with God, in God, in this yellow, seething God, in this smoking, crackling God, in this God of turmoil and terror, in this all-embracing, all-cleaving, upsurging God. Let us end our life, our worthless life, in a tremendous final chord; we failed to make something of our life, now we have the opportunity to at least make something of our death. Yes, I feel how life wants to take its revenge on me. 'Scorned hast thou me,' it cries out, 'me, thy precious, thy once-only life. I brought thee forth out of nothing; I gave thee eyes and ears, the sense of touch, a brain, and thou hast scorned me, as if I were worth nothing. Destroy me now, I have no wish to

35

go on.' Friends, my life is right to say so. For this once we want to live, really live, I can see it in your eyes, tonight we want to live! Let us celebrate the feast of our own perdition, let it be a feast of unbridled joy. Hurrah! We shall destroy ourselves, we shall purge the earth of ourselves. We took nothing from life, we cared nothing for life. Tonight we give our life for nothing. See how the flames curl in lustful desire to embrace our flesh; flames, we are coming, we are ready, we hear the call of your hot passion, the eager licking of your tongues. You are a huge hungry nestling that has opened its mouth wide and screams for food. Here we stand, great yellow God. We are your worms and your flies. There is no need for the beak of a parent to throw us into your gullet! I 'll come of my own accord!''

And with a leap such as no one would ever have believed possible, the unhappy man winged through the air and landed in the middle of the fire. Through a gap in the smoke, some could glimpse how his clothes were ablaze for one instant, making him stand up once more before he toppled backward into the flames. Six men, two halberdiers among them, tried to climb the pyre to rescue him, but before they could get close, their clothes caught fire in the heat. Like shrieking torches, they ran among the crowd. This was the signal for universal madness to break out.

Respectable ladies and gentlemen who had never in their lives uttered an improper word, were suddenly tearing off their own and other people's clothes, stampeding to the fire to offer themselves in sacrifice. Scarves, costumes, expensive hats, bodices, panties— men's clothing as well: jackets, waistcoats, pants, crimping shoe-leather; an orgy of garments flew into the fire, and all around there was a jigging of naked bodies; the bodies of professors, lawyers, teachers, teachers' wives; naked parsons, bobbing and stamping, their hands groping for the flesh of the naked wives of cabinet-ministers. There they went rolling about on the ground, in lewd embrace; over and over they rolled, so that the circular imprints of the cobblestones were pressed into their bare backs. Old hags with dangling breasts reeled about shrieking and thrashed the men into a frenzy of lust. The air was filled with the yelps of women lying on their backs and the roars of riding men interspersed by the high-pitched screams of the hysterical witches. An elderly woman who had ripped off one of her breasts and flung it into the fire was rushing here and there, yelling at the top of her voice as she pointed at the round bloody patch: "Ladies and gentlemen, time is up. Look at my clockface, time is up!"

Whoop, there went the first one; scratched and bitten, she still managed to squirm away from under her panting mate and, with a bold take-off run, plunge into the flames, head first; the fat of her buttocks melted at once and squirted high into the air, in two jets like a whale's: a human firework.

Time was up indeed. Several others took the plunge. One small group had got hold of a ladder and propped it up so that they could dive into the furnace from above. At the foot of the ladder, there was soon a jostle and there could be seen swan dives, running dives, demivolts, followed not by the splashing of water but by the splutter of fat and the snapping of bones. Flame-filled skeletons aped the sides of ham in a burning farmhouse: they rose from the fire and circled around the church tower, accompanied by screech-owls and bats. Naked entwined couples were tossed into the fire by others.

"Hi there!" screamed the lady with the clockface, "Look at our way of coïtus interruptus!"

Huddled under the overhanging eaves of their old-fashioned houses, a few bewildered Rijsseners watched the spectacle, but most had fled into their homes where they sat trembling together. Out in the square, the madness continued. Half-charred bodies, rolling down from the pyre, crawled on blackened limbs back toward the fire like candle-scorched insects.

Some, unable to attain their goal, held a match to themselves. Young, blossoming women were seen embracing and kissing burning beams until they themselves were black all over. And the lady with the clockface was still scuttering this way and that, calling out to the couples that lay locked in each other's arms: "No more now, another fire is calling you, a better fire!" And she flung burning bits of wood between the all too amorous bodies—yes, the last couple had to be literally driven apart with fiery wedges. The upper half of a geography teacher suddenly started lecturing until he drowned in the molten fat of his lower half. A jeering crowd, half on fire, had stuck a blazing gentleman on one of the offering poles and carried him in triumph around the square. Every now and again, when a joint was burnt through, the impaled man lost a limb, and then the lady with the clockface who came jogging along behind, shouted at the figure aloft on the spit: "Mind you, keep your head up!" And the burning head stood firm, until the whole procession vanished into the sea of fire as in a thick mist, stared at by countless dogs that had come to the scene from all directions, lured by the almost suffocating smell of roast meat.

It was this same smell that had driven the last Rijsseners away. They sat up at home all night, listening. For a long time the noise continued, like the unrelenting roar of a great, outraged wounded beast, until close to midnight, the hour at which the fire was due to begin to lose its force.

Then the noise weakened fairly suddenly into a groan, and persisted as a soft whimper until the Almelo constabulary arrived at three o'clock in the morning; the Deventer police had also been alerted and appeared half an hour later.

At five o'clock an ambulance train left Rijssen, carrying what was left of the city-dwellers, and arrived at Amsterdam Central at half past eight.

Louis Paul Boon (1912-1979)

was a candidate for the Nobel Prize for his socially engaged novels. In his earliest works, he displayed an interest for what he considered to be reality behind the visible world. His fairy tale The Sad Blackbird *was written in 1962.*

Fairy tales are seldom of a funny nature and almost always cruel. Boon's fairy tale is no exception. It is not only about birds and bees, but about Bluebeard's wives and the mysterious turret room in the castle. Boon knew that erotic lust lurks in the most unexpected places, and this is a central theme in much of his work.

The Sad Blackbird

The other day I met a blackbird in the silent forest. He was sitting there whistling a little tune to himself. As I paused, he began to tell me the story of his life.

The forest was quietly minding its business, said the blackbird. Lovers came here to hide and mate to their hearts' content. Little old ladies went gathering wool and wood. Shifty layabouts came to share hares, maybe the odd dwarf, never a fairy to sleep with. People knew that somewhere an artery led to the heart of the forest where the owner lived in a fairy tale castle. The villagers did not know him, but sitting by the hearth at night, they would speak of him as of the werewolf. Yet they had seen him many times. They did not know it, but he was the stranger that came among them, disguised as a passing traveler. He healed the sick, foretold the future, and exchanged strange coins belonging to no currency of this world. After each time he passed through the village, someone or other's budding young daughter would be missing, even though he had warned: "I just caught a glimpse of the werewolf!"

Every year, he called at the carpenter's cottage where there was little to be healed or exchanged but where three ripening girls frolicked about the house. And each time, the lord of the castle in his disguise as a passing traveler thought: I wonder if one of the three daughters will be ready for picking this year.

One Saturday morning, he passed by as the oldest was getting ready to wash herself in the tub under the awning. She had jet-black hair, eyes that glowed like burning coal, and folds of flesh that were painted dark brown.

Fiery birds began to scream in the traveler's blood when he saw her climbing into the tub. The lonely evenings in his castle, where his only amusement was watching the logs in the hearth crumble to ashes, struck his heart with more terror than ever before. He picked her out of the tub and—wet and naked as she was—put her into his big traveling bag. He returned to the heart of the forest by a round-about way, and only when darkness had fallen and the shutters were closed did he take her out.

"Dance like the flames in the hearth, scream like the birds in my blood, and stay naked as you were in the tub," he ordered.

She obeyed—she had expected worse.

For a long time she remained his playmate, and he feasted his eyes on the deep folds in her flesh that were such a beautiful shade of brown. It was the color of roast chicken done to a turn. He had to swallow his saliva when he saw her, in his mind's eye, lying on a platter. But she never gave him cause for anger so that he could rage: "I shall stick you on the roasting spit!"

He prowled around hatching his plan, and one day he gave her a silver key and the newly laid egg of a blackbird.

"Carry these always in your hands, but be careful not to put the key in the wrong lock or to break the egg," he warned.

Then he settled down by the hearth and pretended to be asleep. Holding the key in her hand, she nearly died with curiosity and could not wait to find out which lock it might fit. Quietly she stole away and tried it in all the doors. At last she came to the turret room which she had never entered before. And behold, the key fitted. As she went in, even the darkest fold of her flesh turned pale. A large tub was filled to the brim with blood and in it floated the girls who had vanished from the village. In her fright she dropped the egg and it broke.

When she returned, he knew at once that she had violated his commands. However much he had played with her, now was the moment to roast and eat her. She looked delicious lying on a dish, nicely browned and decorated with parsley. Ruefully he finished the last morsel—a little kidney it was—and then gathered the bones and carried them up to the turret room.

Once more his evenings became very lonely, and he began to long for the carpenter's second daughter, who must surely have been ripe by then. Evening was drawing near as he came to the cottage, and he hurried to watch her get ready for bed. His eyes hung upon the low window, and he saw her loosen the shift that clung to her body. Her head was a flaming torch of red hair, her eyes were cat-green, but her skin was pure cream.

He hastened to put her into his traveling bag, to taste the cream of her skin in his castle, and so warm his hands in the fiery flame that so playfully licked her belly.

But when the taste of cream began to pall and he knew the tongue of fire between her thighs to be too cold, he gnawed his fingernails as before. Again he fetched the silver key and the newly laid egg of a blackbird and put them into her hands. Then he secretly followed her as she climbed the stairs to the turret. He peered up at the swaying of her hips and thighs—in the deep folds there now lay an almost blue shadow, such as one sees on milk—and his regret grew hotter and fiercer.

The key turned in the lock, and the egg cracked. It thrilled him that he could now punish her with impunity: he hung her up by the red flame of her hair. The great nail in the wall rusted at once.

Then he hurried to the carpenter's house, driven by an insatiable longing for the youngest, the prettiest, whom he had kept until last. She was more mischievous than her sisters and loved nothing better than playing pranks. When she tired of pranks, she would sit looking at her reflection in the brook. Her blond hair hung about her, and in it her little breasts played blindman's bluff.

She laughed when she saw that the passing traveler was there again, eying her from behind the bushes. She asked him herself if she could go away with him and if he knew any games. But by the third night at the castle, she was already tired of his games.

"You're too sad and old a bird for me," she cooed, "and I'm already bored with your song. Don't you know any others?"

Then he gave her the silver key and the blackbird's egg and said: "Look, the game goes like this: you must open the right door without breaking the egg."

She searched longer than necessary just because she enjoyed the search so much. Each time she stuck the key in a wrong lock, she laughed till her little breasts quivered in the shrubbery of her blond hair. Once she laughed so hard the egg slipped out of her hand, but she managed to catch it halfway to the ground.

The next evening she discovered the turret room. Curiously she bent over the tub and its contents. She looked at the clean-eaten bones of her sister in one corner and then at her second sister on the nail in the other corner. And when she saw the lord of the castle standing like a sad bird in the doorway, she said. "This is a joke I can't laugh at."

He could not kill her. She had opened the turret room, but she had not broken the egg.

"I have no power over you," he said. "I'll give you the heart of the forest and the castle, my fortune, my silver key and my egg. Let us live here together for many long years and be as happy as we can."

In answer, she threw the blackbird's egg into his face. It broke and the yolk made a large yellow stain. And look: the lord of the castle shriveled up. He became shrunken and black, but the yellow stain stayed on him.

I changed into a sad blackbird. What happened to her, I don't know. Perhaps she still lives in the heart of the forest, in the castle. But I sit here alone and whistle in the rain.

Simon Carmiggelt (b. 1913)

is the most famous columnist in The Netherlands. Everyone knows him as the somewhat melancholy jester who turns his flashlight on the simple fate of ordinary people with the superior touch of pity and the irony of wonder. But once in a while, he turned his hand to the writing of pure Fantasy, like in Nothing but Nonsense, *the title of the collection from which* Ouija Board *has been taken.*

Ouija Board

"See you, Uncle Henry, I'm off now!" I announced, entering his den, overcoat already on, where, as usual, he was dozing over a book, with Doody, the almost hairless bitch, pressing herself against his legs.

"All right, my boy," he answered absently, looking at me with the pensive, unfathomable amiability of a very old man waiting for his death as he would wait for a train, surrounded by the saddening retinue of bric-a-brac and stand-up collars. It was this image I retained when some moments later I heard my footsteps on the moss-green drive and turned to look at the ugly, old house on the little river Vecht, where for the past month I had been interrupting his foggy monologues everytime I entered his room. We never got beyond the topic of the weather, and that was why I avidly accepted an invitation to pass the evening with some former friends in Amsterdam.

I was prepared for anything when I entered the apartment. I would even have welcomed a game of shuffleboard with enthusiasm. But there was more. On the round, oak table in a room lined with books, the bottles were standing ready beside the crystal glasses, so it was no surprise that the rather stiff introduction soon gave way to a convivial heartiness. In the beginning I had to get used to the stupid fact that I was forced to address an overweight, artistically inclined lawyer affectionately as "Hank", only because we had entertained a kind of friendship a quarter of a century earlier, when he and I were totally different people. But those bottles contain a twilight in which the years glide away with a soothing ease.

Oh, yes, Hank. Of course, Hank. And may I now drink the health of your wife Annie—a woman with a soul of stone and hair coarse as a horse's tail. Here's mud in your eye.

It was a cold-blooded, matter-of-fact little group but not as invincible as more conventional people. The conversation went well—sly, caustic, without scruples—as befits intelligent quitters with a capacity for self-ridicule. Hank told us about one of his cases: a very popular store owner, the gentle sandman of the neighborhood with a glued-on smile of helpfulness, turned out to be the perpetrator of an extremely perverted crime. Mention of the nameless, mysterious passer-by followed. I cited Poe's "Man in the Crowd" in an obstinate wish to be counted among the literates with this bunch of highbrows. They all noticed my intention, but I forged ahead bravely and broached the subject of my Uncle Henry.

"I've been living in the same house now for weeks on end, but to tell the truth I know next to nothing about him. I wouldn't be surprised if it turned out that at night he digs for corpses in his garden or that he's the leader of an infernal gang of water rats. He might've murdered my aunt, and maybe now she haunts his bedroom with a transparent body. In that case, his murmuring, which I can usually hear from my bed, wouldn't be as solitary as I've always thought. I mean, an old man like him is a mystery from the moment you start doubting the sincerity of his stereotypical gentility."

While talking about ghosts, we arrived at the topic of spiritualism. It was a favorite pastime in this group, not because they believed in it, but just for some good fun at parties.

"Shall we turn the glass on the Ouija board?" Hank suggested. Our hostess arranged some alphabet cards in a circle on the table, placing an upturned wineglass in the center.

"What now?" I asked sceptically.

"We put a finger very lightly on the foot of the glass," Hank said, looking suddenly remarkably tense as he took over. Once we had done so, the glass started to turn around, passing the letters. At first I thought Annie was pushing it, but I soon realized my suspicion was unfounded; it was genuine, no doubt about it.

"A real spirit!" Frits cried with a mocking irony, playing his usual role of the buffoon of the gang.

"Is there an intelligence present?" Hank asked the room.

The bottle moved to the Y, E and S.

"So what?" Frits retorted. Laughter broke out but was hushed down with angry hissing from Hank.

"For whom is the message?"

"F-O-R F-R-I-T-S," the glass spelled. Then, like a divine punishment, a painful announcement popped up about a certain Lisa, which made Frits's wife red with anger, whereas everyone else smiled with sarcastic understanding. My stupidity urged me to ask guilelessly: "Wouldn't that be a case of telepathy?" to which Frits, who showed signs of difficulty in keeping his usual expression of disdain, answered coolly: "It probably is, and I know very well who's been thinking it here."

The row flared up, the more violently because the booze had flowed freely. We had all become very susceptible and prone to irritation, our essential drives lying close under the skin... "No quarreling now," Hank at last shouted. "Let's go on." The glass again wobbled around, formulating unspoken thoughts, turning our party into a kind of spiritual striptease. At last my name, too, came up.

"Who sends the message?" Hank asked.

"Uncle Henry," the glass replied.

"Go ahead."

We were sitting tensely and saw the announcement develop slowly and hesitatingly. When the glass stopped, there was written on the paper: "I have fried the dog, and it's delicious."

"Is that all?" Hank asked with a voice full of suppressed joy.

"Yes," the glass spelled and stopped.

"Your uncle must be a real gourmet," Annie suggested and poured again. For more than half an hour, we discussed the case with the most unexpected comments and discharged our nervous tension with booming laughter. Till midnight we remained together—then the party suddenly burst like a punctured balloon.

"You'd better go home, otherwise your uncle might start tonight with the gardener," Frits said and even offered to drive me. One hour later I got out at the gate. The sound of the engine died away. With great effort I managed to walk up the drive and saw that the light in my uncle's study was still on. Don't laugh now when you see Uncle sitting with Doody at his feet, I thought.

He was sleeping in his armchair, but was startled awake when I stumbled into the room. Still on the brink of his dream, he looked at me with fear in his eyes.

"Hello, Uncle," I said jovially. "Still up?"

"No, my boy, no..." he said, staring absently. "As a matter of fact I thought you would be..."

The sentence trailed off in a yawn.

I sat down in front of him. The clock was ticking with tired monotony.

"Where's Doody?" I asked.

He looked embarrassed—or was it only my imagination? "I took Doody out for a walk tonight, but she ran away," he said with marked uneasiness. "She's never done that before. Very funny..."

"Yes, it is," I replied. Then I saw that the table was only partly covered by a cloth on which a dirty plate was placed, the napkin neatly folded beside the knife and the fork. Uncle followed my gaze.

"I've had a snack," he explained softly.

"What?" I asked fiercely.

"Some cold leftovers in the kitchen," he answered. Was there really such a shy look in his eyes? The silence became heavy.

"You want something to eat, too?" he asked in a naive tone.

"No, thank you," I hastily said.

We remained sitting for a while, he watching me with an arcane stare while I fought a fanatical desire to get to the truth.

"I'm going to bed," I suddenly announced. I shook hands with him and turned into the dark corridor leading directly to the kitchen, but when I got there and started to search the room the door creaked and Uncle Henry stood on the threshold.

"So you do want something to eat!" he said angrily.

I didn't know what to say. He evoked so much loathing and fear in me that I left the kitchen as quickly as possible and climbed the stairs to my room. Sitting on the edge of my old-fashioned guest-bed, ruminating over what had happened, I heard him go to his bedroom, soon followed by the sound of his mumbling soliloquy—a colorless rumble.

Terror sharpened my thoughts. I paced the room. "I have fried the dog, and it's delicious." Tomorrow all clues would be destroyed, but now I still had a chance to solve this Doody business.

Suddenly I was inspired by a ridiculous idea. I put out the light, sat down on the floor, and started to bay loudly with a hoarse and raucous sound—just like Doody used to do.

Now he'll react, I thought, and repeated: "Woof, woof, wruff!"

Meanwhile, continuing zealously with my imitation, I heard a clattering noise in the corridor. The door to my room opened and Uncle Henry appeared on the threshold, in a long, white sleeping gown, with a candle in his hand. His sallow face was drawn into an ecstatic grin, and the light shivered.

"How's that possible...?" he rasped in a whisper.

46

He moved towards me and just when I wanted to jump up and throw my accusation into his face, I made a gruesome discovery in the approaching light of the candle. My arms had changed into gray-haired dog's paws, and I sensed—with devastating clarity—that my head had deformed into Doody's shapeless mug.

"Uncle, Uncle," I wanted to scream, but I could manage nothing better than a desperate "Wraff, wraff, wruff..." Groaning and whining I saw how Uncle Henry laid his hand on my head, and I heard his voice, shaking with passion: "Tomorrow, Doody... To-morrow night we'll do it again..."

Carl Lans (b. 1913)

studied violin but became a teacher, and after that spent most of his life as an official in the Department of Social Affairs with the Dutch Ministry of Defense. He became known as an SF author with more than 70 radio and TV plays. He collected his stories in Worlds Beyond the Horizon (1970.)

Most good writers of SF take only a small step into the future, describing events that are not too far removed from the present. Overpopulation is a well-known menace of our age. It is possible to pack people away in living cells of computer-regulated pyramid-cities. A man gets used to his surroundings. But there will always remain those who try to escape from what is considered good for them. They are called rebels.

The Aegean Sea

The old man looked at me.

Of course I didn't see his real face—merely his psycho-image. But it doesn't end there. Some time ago I had already started seeing *facial expressions* in personographs.

The man on the graph looked at me like a beast of prey.

That beast-of-prey expression was native to all the population levels of Thague. A constant population of 12 million people, born beneath the energy dome with which the Builders had protected the pyramid city eons ago from the soupy bacterial atmosphere outside, have live there ever since, caged up in their residence cells. Beasts of prey.

I was a Froit.

Every personograph circulates decennially through the Selector, is analyzed and—if rejected—is thrown out. My duty as a Froit consisted of directing individuals to lower-city levels. Or to the Exterminator, depending on the extent of their degeneration.

I had nothing to do, however, with the unknown individual from the lowest level whose graph I was holding in my hand, at least not functionally. His psychoround-factor was still far below the fateful point of consignment. Indeed, the Selector had not selected the graph.

I had stolen it!

That was a criminal offense.

For a long time I had understood that my psychoround-factor was rising, imperceptibly yet persistently. I knew I was approaching the end of my mental health and possibly had reached it. I would at last,

like all Froits before me, have to be exiled (regrouped, as it was called) to one of the lower levels. Or, if there weren't any residence cells
free, I would be finished off.

Shortly, the automatic trap-floor would open up beneath me, and
I would be removed.

At the age of four, at the command of the Automat, I was deposited in the transport chute by the female individual who took care of
me. In this way I slid along many dark channels to one of the thousands of youth-cells.

The Builders of Thague, in a time lost to memory, had—despite
the acute shortage of space—taken precautions so that at least children would not be entirely deprived of badly needed calm and space.

The youth-cell—a space or Ruhcell—that served as an exercise
compartment surrounded by six sleeping cells, was a realm I remember as a paradise: besides space, it had thick, sound-proof
walls. Fed into this inviolable Ruhcell along with five playmates, I
got the chance to develop my greatest stability.

But all too quickly, drilled by the Automat that taught me during
sleep, I understood what I was to expect upon entering my four-
teenth year: Examination Day. The Automat of the legendary
Builders imprinted in me the attacking strategies as well as the defense strategies. Yet, above all, on Examination Day my stability
would decide my placement in society, be it high or low. Even so,
Examination Day was more than a test: it was a matter of life and
death. Presumably, the Builders hadn't looked far enough into the
future, and none of us had the knowledge to fathom our indestructi-
ble Automat, let alone improve it.

Later, as a Froit, I understood more. On Examination Day, the
personograpghs were imprinted for the first time with the char-
acteristics of every individual who survived that day.

Besides his stability, which determined his future level, the psy-
choround- or decay-factor was measured as well. His resistance.

Nobody's nervous system is—in the course of time—impervious
to idleness, lack of space and the noise of a sea of people, whatever
the level. Some degenerate slowly, others quickly. Many so quickly
that their placement on any level is senseless.

Therefore, the all-vital psychoround-factor was not only electro-
nically measured but also practically put to the test. On Examination Day!

I remember this day quite clearly. Automatically, the trap-floors of our peaceful paradise, the Ruhcell, and the ringcells began to give way. We had to go out.

Two got scared; they hesitated too long and tumbled into the removal tube to the Exterminator. The ones who remained, including myself, overcame our fear of the Examination and without so much as an inkling were tossed in among the perverts, the psychopaths, and other sorts of lunatics.

I won't go into details about the unspeakable things to which they subjected us. Should even half of the numerous brood-members, bleeding, sometimes castrated, finally reach the safe Ruhcell again, that would be a lot. Yes, the psychoround-factor was thoroughly tested.

By means of balance and cunning, I was the only one of the six who escaped annihilation. Somewhere in the uppermost level, a Froit was studying my freshly imprinted graph. I was a good specimen, and my tendency to disorder would only become discernible at a more mature age. I could even endure some schooling!

That's how I became a Froit. A Froit enjoys esteem. He lives on the Upper Level. He gets the sun, and now and then helps the Automat in distributing residence cells.

As a Froit, however, I knew where I would end up. In the end, even I was not a match for my environment.

No match for the Tridios in adjacent rooms, nor for being packed inside a crowd no matter where I stood or went. No match for my constricting, eternally humming night cell.

Nor for my colleagues' blinking, their mannerisms, their screaming, their psychoses, their phobias. That gets contagious.

In the end I would have to reach the point when I would break down or become a zombie.

From this fate, I would have to flee.

That is when my investigation of the twelve million nameless people of Thague living in their string of little residence cells began. Investigation of their graphs continually circulating in the Selector. Forbidden investigation.

What I was looking for was otherwise modest enough: one elderly individual who still had a low psychoround-factor. I was looking for one stable individual.

What I was doing was not merely forbidden, it was senseless.

And here, suddenly, I had found it!

From out of the graph, the psycho-image of the old man stared at me. Of course I didn't see his real face, only a combination of curves.

A 0.3! And the bearer of this factor even lived on the *bottommost* level.

That anomaly proved that he was staying there of his own free will or, more likely, was hiding there. His technique for repressing the dreaded factor, consequently, had to be based on a secret he did not wish to share with anyone.

The problem of finding from among the millions of residence cells a particular one kept me busy the entire afternoon. It is possible that because of this I delayed a little too long once or twice in replacing processed graphs, whereby the trap-floor for Finishing Off opened up under two or three individuals, instead of their being conveyed to lower residence cells previously made vacant.

But, then, wherever work is being done, mistakes are made.

What Thague was like in prehistory, nobody knows. It is said it was situated by water, water that was undrinkable. But water doesn't stay on the ground; it flows through pipes.

So that's just a story.

The real Thague starts with the Builders. They found a Force that —how isn't known—created idleness for the masses. And later, when the supposedly poisonous bacterial atmosphere was formed, the Builders of that Force created transparent energy domes above Rodam, Tricht, or whatever the names of those old cities might have been.

They created the inviolable residence cells as well as the inde-structible chute-network that fed the cells. Even our food. By means, it is believed, of altering certain substances.

However this may have been, the Automat has been regulating us for so many centuries that nobody knows where it is located. The legendary Builders created everything. There was, nevertheless, one thing they could not create.

More space...

Thus, when that was finally impossible, the occupation of the modern Froit came into being: continual regrouping of individuals according to levels. As soon as they were no longer able to be main-tained, the Selector tossed out their graphs. I regrouped the graphs on the appropriate level and placed them in the corresponding section of the Selector.

If this graph were accepted, then a cell was free somewhere on the level in question. If not, the graph would just lie there, and after a short time the trap-floor opened by itself beneath the unsuspecting individual.

This system of little residence cells, known only to the Automat, concealed a puzzle; how to discover a mature individual with an impossibly low psychoround-factor. I had to wring out his secret before it was too late. Before the Selector threw out my own graph.

How could I find the cell that housed this individual? I had to think it out.

That night.

On the other side of the web-thin wall, I heard the Techno Derek hiccup and snore. Derek's snoring cut like a saw through my brain. Under such circumstances I had to reflect, find the stranger before it was too late.

It was the beast-of-prey expression of his psycho-image that led me to the explanation at last: the man must have made himself master of a Ruhcell down there on the Alpha-level. The space cell of a youth-group. An overwhelming space of eight cubic meters, where, between sound-proof walls, he could move freely, could run, shout, carouse, copulate with his surrogate. Live life to the full.

I pushed my ears shut but the Techno's snores came through my nostrils. Oh, his turn would come. Now I had to think. All of a sudden, I had the answer: the Ruhcell Board on the Alpha-level; on which every cell light discretely matured from dull red to bright white; *on which their numbers were also given.*

Carefully I slid open the lid of my residence cell and stole outside. The shimmering nightly stream of individuals carried me along, around the entire circuit, until after two fruitless rounds I managed to make an exit.

I arrived at the Selexcenter inconspicuously. I looked only in passing at the little lights on the master Ruhboard. An unoccupied cell is not recorded there. Many white lights flickered brightly: tomorrow it was Examination Day for the brood raised there.

Squeezing my way past machinery, I reached the Metab-section where the running consumption curve of every Ruh-system is projected. To this record my hopes were now turned.

After all, immature individuals my receive a blank personograph, but their consumption is still registered. Ergo, the Consumption Curve of that particular Ruhcell could lead to a trail. An old man does, after all, consume different kinds of things than a youthful brood.

I pulled the dusty handle, and the entire curve appeared on the screen.

As I stared at the dimly constructed image, something slowly sank within me. There was no aberration anywhere. Nowhere.

The stranger had thoroughly fortified himself against being traced...

But not entirely.

Before my time, no one had even known that there was yet a third checkpoint: the Control Curve!

The two complete images of Supply and Removal could be brought together on a third screen (what it was for, nobody had previously known). With this, their mutually fixed relation at each point of their young growth could be graphically plotted.

Not only had I discovered the existence of that unusual curve at the time, I had even been able to deduce what it was for!

It turned out to be no less than a fine tuning of the controls on both previous curves! This was the greatest discovery of my time.

Undoubtedly.

But no one questioned me.

What did those low lifes—the Metabs, Technos or the Inspec—care about the fine tuning of controls, controls in which these lazy bums didn't show the least bit of interest?

I engaged the combi-regulator. Made contact.

And heard a voice that uttered a terrifying scream. Panic pulsed through my intestines, alarm bells jangled through my nerves. I quickly turned away, with clawing hands.

But no one was standing behind me: I myself had produced that scream.

For, in front of me on the screen, there was one curve, strongly deviant among thousands. One curve, made up of *false* ratio figures: in one of the ring-cell systems lived a 12-year-old ghost brood with a metabolism of barely 10. It turned out to be Ruhcell

S.M.3471, Alpha-level, near Carrier Chute 8.

It was 4 o'clock in the evening. I had prepared myself completely. Among other things, I had taken my personograph out of the Secret Selector and destroyed it. Since no individual can exist without a personograph, the floor of my cell would automatically open up. It would appear to be suicide, so no one would inquire about me. I shut Carrier Chute 8 behind me and put it into operation. I laughed, supposing the impossible, supposing my hypothesis had missed the mark; then I would soon be in a tight spot there on the lowest level of Thague. Among the milling pile of degenerates and lunatics where the straggler is tortured and maimed in ways even the Metabs and Technos above hardly dared to whisper about:

Slowly, inch by inch, Carrier Chute 8 went down. At last it came to a halt and pushed me outside.

It was stuffy and dark. Economical discharge-electrodes, hidden in niches, provided a dim, diffuse light. I crept along in the tunnel walkway. To the left and right, at arm's length, rose smooth gray, impervious walls.

Shallow niches with closed lids betrayed cells, meter after meter, where individuals were penned. At certain times the Automat drove them out, all at different times. In this way, the millions still had some walking space. This was their only means of keeping their psychoround-factor above the extermination point.

That it was at present quiet, suggested danger. I smelled it in the stale air. And suddenly I could hear it.

From a side-tunnel, shrieks and screams accosted me. Clutching my paralyzor firmly, I threw a glance in the direction of the little group. Perhaps Sculers, belonging to one of the many hazy sects. They were in the process of flaying a young victim in a way no sexotape would wish to record. They were not in any hurry...

A small group of individuals was already closing in around me, so I knocked imperatively on the lid of one of the adjoining cells. After eternal seconds, a spy-window in the cell lid was opened. A wrinkled mouth squeaked out a word, to which I sharply responded. The miracle happened. Seconds later, I was inside—safe.

The silence of soundproof walls fell coolly over my shoulders. The human surf of whole Thague, responsible for my crippled state,

54

slowly faded from my eardrums. I was back in my youth—in the calm of my ring-cell, leading into the Ruhcell.

"Even my residence-cell here is sound-proof," said the old man.

His breathing came difficult and squeaking. Wrinkles like his I had never seen before.

"I am eighty," said the old-timer. "When I came here I was for-ty-eight, just like you."

Thirty-two years ago, the miscreant had nestled himself here and had extended his residence into the adjacent Ruh-system?

"No, it was like this when I arrived," said the old man. "I only had to make sure that the consumption in the ring-cells continued."

A vague threat was coming from him. Was it in the atmosphere? Or in his statement?

Thirty-two years! Since his arrival, three youthful broods had been deposited here via the introchute and straightway pushed through the chute to the Exterminator by the Elder.

"You'll get used to it, as well," he said.

Of course I would get used to it, to that infanticide. I merely had to ensure that their consumption curve continued. And after ten years, on Examination Day, their blank graphs would also automatically be thrown out by the Selector above.

On that day, there were so many broods that didn't make it, it wouldn't come to anyone's attention.

Once again a thought of warning wanted to loose itself from my subconscious—in vain, for envy had the upperhand. All those years during which the worry about my worsening factor had been haunting me, the old fox had enjoyed everything life had to offer—space, calm.

I saw something move in his eyes. No, he had found more than this. After all, a man like him, descended from the uppermost level of Thague had known daylight, sun, moon—even plants.

What had he found in a big, empty, 24 by 24 - feet Ruhcell to replace all that...?

"On the other side of this passageway," said the old man, "lies something other than what you imagine." His eyes flamed: "There lies the Aegean Sea," he whispered in a squeak, "the Aegean Sea."

A sea? What *was* a sea? The old-timer winked and began to crawl through the hole.

I squeezed past the combifurniture and along the wall from which a tridiscreen and the accompanying tinny hubbub were missing. Cautiously, pointing my paralyzor ahead of me, I crawled after the old fellow. Until I entered a darkened, pleasantly warm space. Full of wonder, I straightened up; beneath my feet crunched gritty, unknown things, but I was listening to something else: *to space*. Because space can be heard. Without calculating, I knew that the old man's residence cell measured less than fifteen cubic feet: my main work cell measured 18. My luxury residence cell, 24. But this space, which certainly took up 500, didn't produce any echoes. Was it infinite?

A scornful remark came out of the darkness: "The first time you feel your innards turn. But what did you want? You have to get used to the Aegean Sea. The moon has gone down. If you wait a moment you can see the stars."

I had heard of stars. Their light didn't penetrate the murky, bacterial atmosphere; only the bright brown sun and the ash-coppery moon. Here, gradually, I saw the stars. But there was more. Around me something was in motion, as if—very slowly—the air was displacing itself; a fragrance was drifting through the atmosphere, a soft breath I didn't recognize, salt—and also other smells. Of plants?...

"Roses, if you know what roses are. Wait until the sun comes up."

His footsteps crunched away. Somewhere, metal was scraping metal.

The sun came up.

We were sitting on a terrace, in the middle of an "island," sticking up out of the Aegean Sea; water—blue and bottomless. Yes, *water!* The terrace was enclosed by a white picket fence. Growing up on it, "roses."

We sat at a tottery little table with a translucent orange screen above it that kept out the brightest rays of the brilliant sun. A sun shining warmly out of a sky as I had never before beheld it, bright azure.

All around, as far as the eye could see, there was a backdrop of snow-capped mountains. Close at hand: a low-lying coast, a desolate and peaceful Sunland, that gradually sloped to yellow shores.

Between the shore and our island-terrace flowed the Aegean, blue, in between many shoals and distant islands. On a few of them stood columns of ruined temples; elsewhere lay weathered blocks of stone—the rubble of pillars, several feet thick. The old man filled in the words I didn't know.

The expanse flowed around me, my gaze did not find a fixed point. Slowly the Aegean flowed along the shoreline... slowly...

"I could have killed you, intruder," spoke the old man when I opened my eyes with a start. "Later on you will ask yourself why I didn't. You'll come around to the answer some day."

The old eyes stared at me warily; within them lay a hidden excitement. Did the sly devil hope to win me over?

But why should I share his Aegean with him, if I could have it all to myself? His company was already getting to be too much for me. The old man's breathing rasped. At night I would have to listen to it for hours. And in the daytime I would stare into his knowing eyes that would follow me, as they were doing now, without telling me why.

I killed him on the first night. Opened the trap-chute. Exit old-timer. He had enjoyed his Aegean Sea long enough...

I went to the terrace and sat in the moonlight or at least in something that resembled it closely, staring into the peaceful distance of a sound-absorbing material. How had the old fellow created this masterpiece of illusion? It was strange—even more than strange; impossible.

The broken voice of the gray-haired miscreant spoke in memory. "It was here already."

The peaceful moonlit expanse breathed fragrance. Through the fragrance a thought crept up on me. A warning that had taken form. It was unpleasant, so I tried to escape it. But it kept coming closer and closer.

It was here already. Something started knocking at my temples. Fear. How many broods had already disappeared into this Ruhcell! For how long had it not supplied anybody on Examination Day!

For how long had this Ruh-system distinguished itself from all the others!

So—there was yet *another* way to find this cell. And camouflage against this was impossible.

You'll come around to the answer some day, the old fellow had said.

All around me there was emptiness. The same that had hung around the old man. And around all his predecessors.

In the emptiness I heard it: the soft knocking, far away, of a knuckle on a cell lid. The same knocking the old man had kept on hearing, getting louder with the years.

Of course, I was imagining it.

But, sometime, someone just as distressed and resourceful as I would have to hit upon the simple, statistical discovery. And knock. Urgently.

Perhaps in 40 years. Perhaps tomorrow.

On the horizon, far away over the Aegean, hung rain clouds. Motionless.

Naturally, they had always been there.

Manuel van Loggem (b. 1916)

the editor of this collection, has written plays, essays about the theater, novels and numerous stories, most of them SF or Fantasy. He was editor of a magazine called Morgen (Tomorrow) *in which many of the prominent young SF-writers in the Low Countries were given their first opportunity to publish. He now divides his time between writing and practicing psychotherapy.*

People being what they are, it is no wonder that they will still be what they are in the near or remote future. Man is an animal with an overweight brain, and this discrepancy is the cause of all evil. The hope for a better species of humans is in vain. To quote the old sage of the Bible: There is nothing new under the sun.

Fancyfuck

The twin elevations slightly lifting her unity dress of blue linen identified the passenger in the third seat of the city train as a woman. Most females hid the signs of their sex to a deceiving degree so that they couldn't be distinguished from men, but occasionally citizens appeared in the streets who were not able to conceal completely their personal traits of gender.

Breeroo felt uncomfortable. The sight of the hidden breasts excited him, though he could not define his feelings. He knew that he had already been watching her midriff too long and he averted his gaze. When he looked again in her direction, he saw that she was still staring at him.

The train stopped with a menacing hiss. Breero did not like the sound but the reason for his aversion escaped him. He managed to move in the direction of the woman. She smiled almost imperceptibly. In the rush he was pressed against her. Her body showed no resistance. As if by accident, Breeroo furtively stroked her breasts. Again he did not understand the motive for this movement.

The woman held his hand for a moment. It might have been by chance, but when Breeroc looked at her face he saw that she must have done it on purpose. Together they got out of the train. Again, as if by accident, they walked together.

"Are you going to the match, too?" Breeroo asked.

"Yes."

While walking in the direction of the stadium, he could not refrain from looking at the delicate movement of her nipples, now clearly delineated in their confines of thick cotton.

"I'm Breeroo, pedigree number W-3293," he said.

She smiled but did not answer. This was very unusual. The custom required that one mentioned pedigree number and serial letter after introducing oneself.

Together they went through one of the gigantic gates of the stadium, punched their tickets in the identifying-machines, and joined the hundreds of thousands who had gathered for the match.

Occasionally they were pressed against each other, and every time it was as if the woman took advantage of the opportunity to let him feel the litheness of her body under her coarse garment.

On the field, some couples were already rehearsing. The audience watched them indifferently. Breero sat down and focused the enlarging apparatus on a young couple which had attracted him with their graceful movements. He now saw that they were very young, the girl showing delicate breasts which shook lightly during the simple act of mating.

Again Breeroo felt the agreeable unrest in his belly. It made him anxious and angry. He looked at the woman in the adjoining seat. It was as if she shared his thoughts. She smiled and nodded.

A man in the front row leaned over to someone who was sitting at his side, probably a woman, to judge from the smooth face with the slightly Mongolian traits and the small, athletically built body. Breeroo did not know the kind. It might be a recently developed type. They were still raised by the pedigree-fathers who had not yet fully succeeded in mendeling out all unwanted properties of the newly created races.

"I envy you," the fat man said. "I'm getting much too heavy, so damned fat I can hardly get up without help. It's a pity you can't choose your own stock before birth. It's always a matter of luck which kind of body you get. Or of bad luck, as in my case. I wish I'd been born from better semen."

The other shrugged her shoulders.

"Every race has its advantages."

"You may be right. But why don't they raise only prime-stock?"

"They have their reasons."

The fat man was visibly shocked, realizing he had gone too far. He looked anxiously around but the other onlookers were staring off in the distance. Nobody showed the slightest willingness to have anything to do with the ill-placed and unexpected remarks of the overweight man. They all knew that the methods of breeding were not yet perfect. Weird and unpredictable properties could manifest themselves at any age. It was widely known that the pedigree-fathers occasionally raised deviant individuals for motives the masses could not fathom. They might have been created for the sake of scientific research in genetics. But it was generally assumed that one did better not to discuss these topics.

The fat man, reassured by the obvious indifference of the others, opened a can of beer and gulped down the drink, belching with voluptuous abandon. The sight of this unrestrained relish revolted Breeroo and he turned again to the arena where only one couple was still performing. The man stroked the woman's breasts with a swift, rotating gesture and simultaneously put his other hand between his partner's thighs. His member slowly swelled.

Breero panicked. He closed his eyes. He remembered the repression exercises when he was about five or six years old. The boys were standing in a line, the lower part of their bodies uncovered. Pictures of naked women and copulating couples were projected and after that a holograph of a large, erected member appeared. The boys had a pill in their mouths.

"Now," they heard a voice say from the speakers.

Only then were they allowed to swallow.

When their pitifully small members began to swell they felt a piercing pain that did not stop before the strange, disquieting erection withdrew. There must have been more exercises that were called behavior correction, but Breero dit not succeed in letting them enter his memory, hidden as he felt they were in remote recesses of his mind, barred by orders of a high authority deeply ingrained in him.

More couples had entered the field, well-known sports figures, though no top-performers. The sprint in which they excelled offered little opportunity for variety and was not very popular with the masses. The couple who reached orgasm simultaneously first had won. The large orgasm meters, put at regular intervals on the playing field, indicated the exact moment of ultimate frenzy with which the match ended.

There were some grudging cries of praise from the audience for the winning couple and then the field remained empty for some time.

"Why did I come?" Breeroo asked himself.

He seldom went to a match. He even disliked competitive games.

The crowds of avid buffs for the mating competition frightened him. Those passive masses, which in their humdrum life as industrious workers were united by a common spirit of obsequiousness to the rules laid down by the pedigree-fathers, often developed an incisive cruelty when watching the performance of mediocre contestants.

In the big factories, lots were drawn for tickets. Breeroo had won this time and he had come. It had not occurred to him to stay home——it was as though he had obeyed an order never put into words. He switched on the enlarging device for the game of fancy-fuck, which had started now. He looked sideways at his companion. She smiled and put her hand on his arm, withdrawing it quickly, as if she had touched him by accident.

The mating ballet, elegantly executed fancy groupings in swiftly changing compositions, was judged for speed, adequate penetration, richness of movement, and originality of bodily cooperation.

After that, the field was empty again. The audience remained remarkably silent, intensely anticipating the big match of the day: marathon copulation. The unity-human with the Mongolian traits, who might have been bred as a genderless creature, again addressed the man at her side. She spoke with such obvious emphasis that it was clear her words were meant for everybody within hearing distance.

"The pedigree-fathers know what they're doing. How was it in the past? Men reproduced by mating."

"It's a fine sport," the fat man said eagerly. "A very fine sport."

"Yes, a fine sport, I grant you that," the Mongolian creature answered, "but nothing more and only to be practiced by carefully selected and highly trained professionals. In former times, mating was the only means for the propagation of our kind. Everybody knows the consequences: chaos, the near-annihilation of mankind. The most inferior representatives of the human race, the morons and the brutes, were the most prolific. Hate and homicide, egotism and jealousy ruled the world and brought it to the brink of the all-terminating war. Who saved mankind?"

"The pedigree-fathers."

The crowd murmured the answer, full of pious respect, heads bowed. The fear Breeroo had felt the whole day and which he had tried to keep down with conscious effort now broke loose in him. He shivered and gasped. He clenched his fists and gradually the burning fright was subdued. The horrible suspicion could not be warded off anymore. Of late it had caused him sleepless nights.

He knew he was different in several ways from his friends, his fellow-workers, and the people he met casually.

The woman again laid her hand on his arm, almost imperceptibly longer than before. It helped him to regain his outward composure.

He had received his education as a pedigree-child in one of the communal foster homes and had been selected to become a factory worker. But he knew he was not fit for this work. He worried too much. He sometimes felt lonely or restless. He did not like the atmosphere in the factory, and he abhorred the strong bond with the other workers, propagated as the most desirable way of living.

"The community of your fellows is your real home," was the slogan. Breeroo knew it to be true, but he, nevertheless, remained an outsider.

Again he heard the Mongolian creature's voice:

"We have been bred from the purest mendeled-out stock. In this way the best servants, managers, white-collar workers, officials, or engineers have been created each according to the standards set up for him. There's no more hate among us, no envy, no need for a better life or more possessions. Everybody is happy with his task and place because he is born to become what will suit him most. And if, by accident, traces remain of our animal heritage, we can purge them in the contests. The pedigree-fathers, in their wisdom, have foreseen this need. The best semen for the best breeding-mothers ensures the best of all societies."

"The best semen for the best breeding-mother," the crowd murmured, and Breeroo joined in the chantlike recitation. The deeply rooted sequence of words was ready for release at the slightest incitement. But now he did not bow his head, like the others, when he heard the sacred slogan. He looked at the woman who had accompanied him to the playing fields and noticed her lips were not moving.

The penetrating sound of a gong boomed over the field, and the voice of the match leader announced the start of the most important event of the day.

A hush of expectation floated over the audience, and every spectator switched on his enlarging-screen.

The first male performer entered his mating partner with a carefully measured rhythm. An indignant roar rose up.

"Far too careful!" the fat man cried. "That way it's easy to keep it

63

up for hours! But that's no sport!"

More couples entered the field. Referees moved among them to inspect whether the rules were being honored. On the scoreboards the spectators could read the grade of excitement, the orgasm handicap, and the movement velocity of each participant. Occasionally a couple, one of whose partners could no longer muster the physical competence with which to continue, was removed from the field. The public hooted them away with the lusty wrath of a collective one-track mind. Again Breeroo's fear rose within him. For the moment he managed to suppress the pangs of an unknown desire, but he realized it provided only temporary relief and that the dangerous urge could not be cut off. It was lying in wait, ready to overwhelm him at the slightest stimulation.

He averted his eyes from the action on the field, immersing himself in the floating thoughts and vague images which drifted to the surface of his mind. The cries of the mob shook him out of his waking dreams, announcing that the game was over. He hastily made his way to the exit and was one of the first to reach the gate. Only then did he muster the pluck to lift his eyes. His companion was still near him.

There was not much traffic in the streets as yet, but Breeroo noticed litle groups of men standing guard at every corner, clearly identifiable as plain-clothes police. Their ill-fitting civilian dress rendered them more terrifying than their uniforms could make them.

The woman quickened her pace as if she sensed some kind of danger Breeroo was not yet aware of. His steps automatically fell into the same pace as hers.

"What's your name?" he asked.

"Jeanne."

Her answer made him uneasy.

"What is your pedigree-number?"

"I have no pedigree-number."

His fear was confirmed. She must be one of those natureborns about whom vague rumors were spread, miserable creatures who still seemed able to eke out a sordid existence in remote areas of sparsely populated country. Most of them had been tracked down and put out of the way. A few appeared to have survived, living an animal-like life, driven by passions that had died out long ago through the continuous breeding efforts of the pedigree-fathers. A

64

natureborn was aggressive and dangerous, posing a constant threat to the well-organized society of mendeled humanity.

It was not the fact that he felt drawn to a natureborn which intensified Breeroo's lurking terror to an almost unbearable sharpness, but the inevitable insight that he himself must belong to that detestable class of deviants.

During the past year, he had often doubted his origin. The hints, not only from his recent behavior and feelings, but also of what trickled through of his earliest experiences in dreams and flashes of memory, had become too obvious to be discarded or pushed back.

The woman began to talk. Breeroo now realized it was the first time she addressed him directly.

"Do you know your breeding-mother?"

"No."

"Hasn't it ever struck you as strange?"

"Until lately I seldom was bothered about it, though most of my friends in the pedigree-home knew their breeding-mother. Some of them were proud of her. My best friend came from one who had hatched forty children from a well-known strain of high-quality semen. We all envied him. But still, there were some who didn't know from whom they came. It wasn't that unusual."

"Haven't you ever longed to meet the mother you were raised in?"

Before Breeroo could answer, she had seized his hand and drawn him swiftly into the doorway of a house. A few moments later a patrol car passed. Breeroo wondered how Jeanne could have spotted it so quickly. She must have developed a special sense for hidden danger, sharpened by experience. He presumed she must be one of those natureborns who lived among the pedigree-people and had, till now, been able to remain under cover, awaiting their opportunity to vent their inborn aggression and hate against their betters.

The painful realization that he must be one of her kind made it almost impossible for him to continue his walk.

2

He knew what was expected of him, having seen numerous competitions on television, teaching him the right touching-process and the most gratifying sequence of movements for both parties.

In a blinding flash his thoughts and feelings were swept away, inundating his whole body with an all-encompassing whiteness, followed by a deep and dark comfort, saturating him with a bliss he had never known.

He saw Jeanne lying beside him, panting and smiling.

"Was it the first time?" she asked tenderly.

He nodded.

"Are you now sure of what you are?"

"Yes, a natureborn."

"When did you get your first inkling?"

"After I dreamt I was sucking the breasts of my breeding-mother."

"You said you never knew who she was."

"That's true, but I still dreamt of her. When I awoke I was scared. I had been taught that free animals, like mice and rabbits, monkeys and apes, suckle their young, but not people... except the natureborns, of course. From that time on I was constantly plagued by fear. But how did I arrive in this pedigree-world?"

Her voice was soft and soothing, as if she wanted to caress him with words: "When the small group of oppressors, who called themselves pedigree-fathers, seized power, the technique of raising new stock with deep-frozen semen and living breeding-mothers had already been invented. Large quantities of high-quality sperm had been stored. When it appeared that, with these methods of reproduction, the birth rate could be kept at a stable level and that all kinds of desirable species could be created, those left over from the great war and still clinging to the old customs were ruthlessly persecuted and liquidated, whenever the flunkies of that gang of rulers could lay their hands on them."

The bitterness in her words belied the caressing softness of her voice. The almost tangible hatred suffocated Breeroo. He still could hear the vibrating lure in the recorded voices of the pedigree-fathers —the propaganda with which his brains had been programmed from his early youth on.

"What you've got is enough for what you want and what you are. Enough is more than too much. Excessive is less than moderate."

And then again: "The pedigree-people are peaceful. They know neither hatred nor envy. The pedigree-world is paradise found."

But at the very moment the soft, slurring voice stirred the depths of his memory, he knew it had lost its magical power. The soulless, repetitive rhythm, which intensified the prearranged slogans, was nothing more than an echo from the past.

He slowly spoke the well-known sentences, amazed at being able to hear his own voice with impartial curiosity.

"That's what they taught me," he said, smiling. "I used to believe it. Funny, isn't it?"

"They're lifeless, cowardly mock creatures, without a soul of their own," Jeanne said sharply. "Out-mendelized yes-and-amen-nodders. They don't know love. All they have are their disgusting games because their masters have not yet been able to create them without any trace of lust and competitive drive. The rulers intended to stop the matches after they had served their purpose, but people appeared to be infected by the habit. They even became addicted, and that's why the pedigree-fathers, who are no fools, allowed the games to continue, as a fight against the remnants of what they call vice. It reinforces the puppetlike behavior of their subjects, created to keep the small group of pedigree-lords in power. That's why they fear us. We natureborns can't be manipulated to react as they want us. We always manage to conquer their methods of brain-invasion."

She then told him the story of his own origin:

"When the pedigree-fathers took over the government and installed the reign of the breeding-mother society, they did not succeed in killing all those couples who continued reproducing as their nature urged them. Many of them went underground in the community of pedigrees. In the beginning of the big breeding experiments, they could hardly be distinguished from the rest of the population. They could leave their homes, walk in the streets. Provided with forged identity papers, they could even work in factories. They got all the help they needed from members of their own kind who sometimes had attained high positions in the pedigree world. Some of their children, born in secret places, could be placed in the homes of sympathizing breeding-mothers who registered them with the authorities as their own semen-offspring. You must've been one of them."

She stroked his hand and kissed him long and passionately.

"This is what they call vice," she said tenderly.

"Vice and hatred," Breeroo answered.

"What do you mean?"

The ferocity in her voice shocked him.

"It's part of a lesson. Vice and hatred caused the decline of our former society, ruled by the natureborns. Those two items are intertwined. That's what they taught us. Vice and hatred brought the world to the brink of destruction. When you mentioned vice I felt compelled to fill in what you had left open. That's the power of education. I still have to unlearn a lot."

She now lay very still beside him. When she spoke again, her voice was flat as if teaching him a lesson she knew by heart.

"A great number of our people managed to escape the murderous attacks of the pedigree-henchmen. They founded a new society in the mountains where none of our enemies has any chance of entering without impunity. After all those years we natureborns have become a powerful community with a trained army, prepared to sacrifice our lives unconditionally for our people, supplied with the best weapons."

"Why?"

"To take over the government."

"Impossible. The pedigree-fathers are too strong."

"We are stronger."

The unshakable confidence in her voice convinced him.

"How do you know all these things?" he asked.

"I've visited the camps of our kind. There I've been told the truth. They've sent me back to locate people like you, who will be able to help us when the time comes for our armies to march."

"Have you also been sent to initiate people like me?"

She did not answer, but she embraced him with such vigor and tenderness that Breeroo was not able to fathom the sadness that briefly rose within him.

3

In the street a strong desire seized him to take her hand and only with a strong effort could he refrain from this dangerous gesture.

Jeanne, in her stiff unity-clothes, again looked like a pedigree-woman. She had hidden her long hair under a cap, and her breasts were better contained within the boundaries of her starched bodice than when Breeroo had met her for the first time. He now suspected her of having then shown the outer signs of her sex on purpose.

68

They were walking with extreme caution. There were still many policemen patrolling. People passed with obvious nervousness. Suddenly Breeroo saw a group running. Patrol cars shot noiselessly by. Jeanne seized Breeroo's hand and dragged him towards the protection of a porch, but the shock of the stiffening fear that engulfed him slowed his movements down so that he was not able to keep up with her. He lost his balance and fell. For one moment he saw her hesitate, but when a couple of policemen approached she ran away and disappeared into the doorway of a living-tower where it would be very difficult to locate her in the maze of cell-like rooms and passageways.

Breeroo was pushed into one of the wagons. It was dark inside. He could tell by hearing more than seeing that there were other prisoners. After a short ride the car stopped. The captives were blindfolded. When Breeroo could see again he was in a small room, a kind of mini-laboratory. On the wall there were instruments and gauges. A low, unbroken hum filled the air, soft but so deeply penetrating that it affected the heartbeat. The tension grew so strongly in Breeroo that he felt he had to let down his resistance. He wanted to shout, beat the walls and the shining implements, but when he started to groan and pant the door opened and a short man entered with an easy, almost gliding gait. His face was strikingly smooth, and though he could readily be identified as a man, he showed hardly any beard growth. It struck Breeroo that he had seen more of these kinds of people lately. He now remembered the Mongolian between-creature who had so fiercely defended the wisdom of the pedigree-fathers on the benches of the stadium.

"Perhaps they are the human race of the future; outmendelized till there are no more distinctions between the sexes. I wonder what the rest of their bodies look like."

He started. Suddenly a laser-image appeared in the room; a picture of a mating couple: man and woman.

Breeroo noticed that the measuring devices on the wall had been put into action. He immediately understood the meaning of this. His degree of lust was being measured after the sudden appearance of a picture that could only contain erotic excitement for natureborns. He knew also that the visible sign of his natural inclination could cost him his life.

His heart beat faster. He felt a strong tension of lascivious danger in his underbelly and he saw the needles on some of the screens deflecting in obvious agitation.

Now the memory of the repression exercises in his youth surged back in him. He remembered clearly the punishment associated with certain pictures, the bitter taste of sickness pills, the unrelenting drone of the soft voice, penetrating into the deepest layers of his brain, reinforcing the engrams, which now, after so many years, enabled Breeroo to repress the dangerous impulses which threatened to invade him. The tension subsided, his heartbeat slowed. He saw the needles in the instruments fall back.

Soon after that he was set free.

He still felt dazed. Then a deep depression set in. Jeanne's disappearance was so painful that his unexpected freedom gave him no relief. For hours he roamed the vicinity where she had been forced to flee, hoping that she, too, would be looking for him there. Only when darkness fell did he allow himself to realize that she would not come. He was so desperate, he took the risk of being picked up again.

Patrol vans shrieked along, sirens screamed, laser weapons flashed and in the street hung the sweet and nauseating smell of burnt flesh.

Breeroo felt his misery so strongly that he considered the upheaval around him a fitting background for his despair. It only fully dawned on him that the world he had known was on the brink of exploding when he found his way to the sprawling building where the factory, for which he worked, had built living-cells for its laborers.

He loved Jeanne. He knew the word from old books, but now he understood what it meant. His own being had been extended with her, and he missed her as a part of himself.

"Love means giving yourself away," he thought. "There's nothing to be compared with it. It makes people lose their selfishness. It is the essence and justification of life."

He knew that through the power of love he would be prepared to sacrifice his life for Jeanne. It made him reckless. He now took the direct route to his living quarters. It was remarkably quiet in the long corridors on which hundreds of doors gave access to the living-cells. When Breeroo entered the compartment and switched on the light, he saw Jeanne sitting in a corner. She remained motionless when he entered. The news apparatus was alive with swiftly changing images. Breeroo kissed Jeanne's hair and remained standing.

The news announcer was a smooth pedigree-being, a midway-creature, with carefully modelled, rather flat, impersonal features. He had a high, whining voice.

"Most of the natureborns, who have penetrated our cities, have been rounded up and are being annihilated. The situation is under control and there is not the least cause for alarm."

Breeroo knelt down and kissed Jeanne on the mouth. She pressed her breasts against him. He did not ask her how she could have known where he lived and why she had risked her life waiting for him here, but she answered his unspoken question.

"I suddenly realized I loved you."

"Did you know that I would return?"

She thought it over.

"No," she said.

"Why did you come?"

"I had a slight hope they would release you. But if it had turned out they had you killed by their underlings then..."

Her voice trailed off.

"Then what?"

"I would have avenged you in a terrible way."

The sudden hatred in her voice shook him less than when it had struck him the first time. It was a sign of love now.

The news announcer again appeared. He sounded more excited.

"In the capital a few buildings have been occupied by the natureborns. There is no immediate danger. The police control all strategic points."

Jeanne got to her feet.

"That was the appointed signal. The great rising is imminent. We must go to help our kind. The pedigree-people are powerless against our combined efforts. They're not bred for fighting."

When they left the building, the streets were full of disorderly groups, fleeing in all directions. The patrolling policemen had disappeared. In the distance a heavy rumbling could be heard, and occasionally big flames shot up against the horizon. A red glow quickly spread in the evening sky.

Jeanne took Breeroo by the hand. With firm purpose she cut her way through the crowds. After some time the streets became more quiet. Jeanne was still holding Breeroo's hand. Now she would not leave him in danger. Love was stronger than the fear of death. Love lifted the natureborns out of their animal past to the highest realms of humanity.

71

"Love," Breeroo thought, "makes gods of us."

They arrived at an immense assembly hall. There were all sorts of natureborns. It amazed Breeroo that the members of his own race showed so much variety in size, color, and shape. He was used to the soothing uniformity within the different species of pedigree-people.

Crowds of armed soldiers entered.

A swarthy, earnest man jumped upon the platform. His voice resounded through the vast hall.

"We will destroy the enemy! There will be nobody left! The disgusting products of a perverted breeding system must be annihilated! And as for the perpetrators of the crimes against us, we will take a horrible revenge for what we've suffered at their hands!"

The crowd shouted: "Revenge! Revenge!"

Breeroo saw that Jeanne was swept away by the general frenzy. He laid his arm around her shoulders. He now felt in every fibre of his body that he was a natureborn. He too, now, roared for revenge. An almost unbearable lust accompanied the visions of blood and death which the induced hate created in him.

Then he saw a group of newly found fellow-men approach.

They had taken Jeanne and him for the enemy because of their clothing.

He saw the hatred in their eyes.

He saw how they seized Jeanne.

"We belong to you!" he cried. "We are natureborns ourselves."

He only stopped shouting when they had kicked out his brains with their heavy boots.

Hubert Lampo (b. 1920)

is one of the best-known and best-selling Fantasy writers in Flanders. He calls him-
self a "magical realist". In his many theoretical expositions on his kind of writing
he heavily supports the mystical and murky thoughts of C.G. Jung about the collec-
tive unconscious. But that does not prevent him from writing Fantasy of a very
high quality.

The Bible is full of historical accounts of mystery and horror that more often
than not can be applied to contemporary situations. The birth of a Jewish prophet,
crucified as a rebel under the Roman procurator Pontius Pilate, is considered by
vast multitudes to be the most important event in the history of mankind. Writers
of SF and Fantasy have often tried to imitate the enigmatic magic of the Bible's
stories. Or they recast them into molds which SF writers call parallel worlds, which
is what Lampo does here.

Mr. Davidson's Son

A year ago I wound up here in the harbor as a chaplain. From the
first day on, I was struck by that modest little business. Its looks
weren't unsuitable at all, absolutely not, safely tucked away between a Chinese eating house and the Fierlafijn pharmacy, well
known of old. Yet I had the feeling from the start that there was
something not quite right about it. Presumably, as I think about it
now, because it rather belonged in one of the characterless streets
behind the Central Station, where the shabby children of the Dia-
spora who had come down here from the East preferred to settle, as
if it made them feel relatively safe to hear the trains race by, day and
night, and at ease, now they weren't stuck any longer in one ghetto
or another.

In the showcase where in the evening two weak bulbs burned
stood three seven-armed candlesticks. There were scrolls, and next
to other objects I connected with synagogues or other domestic de-
votions lay some records of religious songs. The books that weren't
in Hebrew, were a mishmash of every other Western language.
Among them I discovered, however, a Gustave Doré Bible. To me it
was something nicely familiar among the mass of religious, mystical, and perhaps even occult Jewish writings. Hadn't I seen a volu-
minous book about the Kabala lying there, or did I imagine it afterwards? Over the whole business hung a dusty smell of dying paper.
I presumed that the whole cellar was full of books, too, unavoidably
consumed by moisture and mold.

On the window was the name of the owner, Joseph Davidson. In the afternoon of the third day of my installation, I saw him standing in the doorway. He was a kind-looking man in his seventies with a neat square beard. Not without a certain elegance, he wore a yarmulke on his head. The fourth day we greeted one another. The next day he was not, as usual, in the doorway. Beyond the window, however, in the deep twilight of the store, I saw his yarmulke floating around. Before I knew what I meant to do, I pushed open the door, which moved a small chime.

"Good morning, Mr. Chaplain," he said helpfully. "How can the old Davidson be of service to you?"

Still baffled about my unexpected initiative I stammered something about the Doré Bible.

"A beautiful piece, Mr. Chaplain... A first printing, for years practically unfindable and not even that expensive..." Without pushing, he mentioned an amount which sounded absolutely astronomical to a beggarly fellow like myself. I hadn't a thought, by the way, of buying.

"Good Lord, even if you asked a tenth of that, I wouldn't be able to afford such an acquisition..."

"No problem at all, Mr. Chaplain. You may take the book home with you for a while. But do sit down, yes, go ahead and leaf through it quietly."

I was glad not to have postponed meeting my neighbor any longer by shy dawdling. It helped overcome the vague, unmotivated guilt feeling Jewish people have filled me with since the war, as if I'd been a party to the death of their millions of martyrs. Nevertheless, it wasn't my need for a surrounding other than the usual which made me spend so many hours with Mr. Davidson after that. Each time the shop door closed behind me and the little chime sounded, deepening the silence even more, although the gluepot simmered audibly on the black stove, the feeling overwhelmed me that I belonged here. Was it the silence that attracted me? We could sit quietly together for an hour or more, without the silence becoming oppressive. In the meantime, I would watch while Mr. Davidson deftly repaired the cover of some book or, as it often happened, tried to get an old watch going with endless patience.

Miriam made coffee in the meantime. There was actually no confidentiality between us. She was too shy to talk with others, even with someone who visited daily, as I did. Something keeps me from

74

calling her Mrs. Davidson. I don't know if they were married. I have never heard Mr. Davidson say that Miriam was his wife. Why should he have done that anyway? I have never heard my father say my mother was his wife, either. I guessed Miriam to be in her early forties, she could easily have been his daughter, but I am sure that Mr. Davidson would not have kept that from me. Nor would he have kept it a secret, either, if Miriam's son had been his son. The boy was about twenty-five. Now that I see that past year of my life go by in my mind's eye again, I am still certain that I never heard his name. Davidson kindly called him "boy", and as far as Miriam is concerned, how often did I hear her voice at all? He looked, however, as I had imagined David must have looked, with a beautiful blond head and the same sad eyes as his mother's. I used to call him Joshua to myself sometimes. Despite possessing the cool looks of an apprentice-prophet, or even a Greek Apollo, he had remained a child. Of course I could just characterize him as simple-minded, but then it would seem as though I'd taken him to be insane.

I had wondered about that. How could I have done otherwise?

It happened one evening around Easter. There was no sign of spring yet. The wind made the shop window tremble softly and hurled half-melted snow against it, which slid down the glass helplessly sad and turned to water halfway down.

"No," Mr. Davidson said all of a sudden as if answering something I'd asked. "No...". I had said nothing for at least a quarter of an hour, engrossed in a beautiful edition of the Jewish historian Flavius Josephus.

Miriam had not yet lit the lamps in the window, and I saw the old man stand by the glowing stove only vaguely, where he was refilling the water bowl of the glue pot. "Naturally I can understand that you can't help taking the boy for an idiot..."

"Not at all," I protested. "Where did you get that...?" and it bothered me that I sounded so weak.

"I don't hold it against you," he mumbled softly. "Could I deny that he is retarded?"

"Not really retarded," I consoled, "but simple as a child. What else could a deaf-mute seem but simple as a child?"

I did not feel at ease. From the silence of Mr. Davidson I realized that he understood how I lacked the one exact and tactful word for the boy's mixture of childishness and strange dreaminess. A word that did not exist by the way, I was pretty sure of that. At the same moment, I heard Miriam blow her nose softly.

"It's already totally dark. I'll put on the light..." she mumbled apologetically. Have I ever heard her mumble anything but apologies?

"We were talking about the boy..." said Mr. Davidson.

"He's a good, sweet boy," I added.

She looked at me gratefully, her Biblical eyes red with tears, but did not say anything anymore.

Everyone in the neighborhood knew the boy Joshua, as I will call him from now on. To live and let live is the motto here. Everybody was very nice to him. It was only because of being a deaf-mute that he had no intimacies with people. At the grocery store or the bakery, they would give him a sweet every now and then, and even the humorless pharmacist Fierlafijn let himself be moved to reach into his jars full of peppermints and licorice. What Joshua got, he usually gave away to kids, of whom there were always a few sitting on the steps of the church entrance. He couldn't be blamed for being so nonchalant about things that had been given him with a good heart. Instinctively, people seemed to cherish a vague respect for the retarded young prophet, and no one treated him with condescending cheerfulness as the neighborhood's idiot. Even the street boys left him alone and would sometimes walk quietly with him for a while.

At the end of September I got a visit from the district policeman, a big teddybear of a man, who was clearly confused about his task.

"It is not an investigation, Father," he said immediately in the hall. "The superintendant advised us to look around a bit first and to inquire among a few serious people."

"Out with it, officer."

"It's about that boy, that blond Jewish Davidson boy..."

"Is something the matter with him?" I asked, suddenly worried, as if I felt personally responsible for Joshua.

"Ah, nothing too bad, Father... Unlawful practice of medicine, the superintendent says. But if I'm right, he doesn't believe it himself, either..."

Relieved, I stood there grinning. "The poor thing is a deaf-mute and on top of it he doesn't have much brains."

"There you say it yourself, Father... It seems to have something to do with the laying on of hands. You have a pain somewhere, and the doctor doesn't know the answer, either. Then, at last, someone

76

else is called, someone who just puts his hands on the place that hurts, and presto, the pain is gone. That's what they say, at least!"

"Is it forbidden?"

"As long as they ask no money for it, everything's O.K. If they do, it's quackery, you understand? And quackery is forbidden by law..."

It was not difficult to convince the policeman that I knew nothing of the affair and that the whole story could only be slander. It seemed to me superfluous to bother Mr. Davidson with it. Nevertheless I began to study the deaf-mute more attentively than before, although I reproached myself every time I caught myself at it. There is no help for it. Today, early in the Christmas evening, I was witness to an odd occurrence which I've been putting off describing.

The whole afternoon I had been working in church. With the older boyscouts, I had been putting the finishing touches on the Nativity scene, a life-sized one even, because we had to make do with unmanageable manikins a man from a bankrupt clothing store had given us. It bothered me that Mary looked like a film diva from the Thirties, but I think my fellow parishioners rather liked that and found it appropriate. Presumably they saw in the shabby look of the doll a warrant of old-fashioned female decency. The bare fake-sandstone wall of the choir, which served as a background, worried me; it looked so poor.

Despondently, I was eying the whole affair once more. We had given the Messiah's birthplace much more the look of an old Flemish farmer's kitchen than of a true stable from Bethlehem. Well, that is one of our respectable traditions, after all. Suddenly I thought of the copper wall clock which hung at Mr. Davidson's. It wouldn't add much to the mystical atmosphere, but in the candlelight it would at least provide a nicely gleaming spot on that bare miserable wall. My old friend would be glad to lend it to me until Mary Candlemas, I didn't doubt that.

There was no one in the shop. I decided to wait a little and look around. Miriam must be shopping, the afternoon nap of Mr. Davidson was a little longer than usual, while the deaf-mute young man was probably feeding the gulls in the square.

The clock from Auvergne beat five o'clock. Slowly growing impatient, I sat down at the Empire desk at the back of the store where Mr. Davidson often sat writing in a thick cash-register book. I kept feeling like an intruder, in spite of the open shop door, and wondered if I hadn't better light the lamps. From that moment on everything went extremely fast, so fast that I could hardly suppress the thought that it happened beyond any measure of time. A car stopped in front of the door. Suddenly the shop stood full of anxiously silent people. Afterwards, I didn't understand how they could all have fit into that one car. It was a colorful group. Some were neatly dressed ladies and gentlemen who wouldn't stick out in the city crowd here or anywhere. Yet they were also unmistakably Jewish mothers, with colorful head scarves or spiky wigs, real Talmudic grandfathers, supplied with Moses-like beards and little curls around the ears, as well as pale younger men in long caftans, broad-rimmed hats and black boots. Without any doubt, I should have left my hiding place to warn the visitors that it could be a while before anybody came home.

I did not. Possibly I felt somewhat inhibited as a Catholic priest. I felt, by the way, that something was about to happen with which I should not involve myself. I was deeply touched by the appearance of a young woman who carried a child of about a year in her arms and formed the center of the silent group. I stood there breathless. I had only estimated the child's age. It was wrapped in a blanket from which the little feet were hanging powerlessly and white to my dismay. Suddenly I was sure the child was dead.

No one had yet uttered a word, but I heard the women sob in a soft moaning tone, deathly grieved, but filled with a patience which defied eternity. Suddenly, however, the complete motionlessness came to an end. Hurriedly the tall shadow of a sturdy man slid past the shop window against the light of the street lanterns. The door was opened, the chimes sounded thinly, and in the twilight a hand turned on the electrical bulbs. What I watched from my hiding place was like an authentic Rembrandt, dominated by the recently entered Joshua, however timidly he was standing there, dressed in his tight, washed-out jeans which made his tall Apollo's figure yet more impressive and his short sheepskin-lined jacket left in pawn by a sailor, but who'd never come back to reclaim it. With his back anxiously pressed against the door, he looked around bewildered, as if he made up his mind to take to his heels at the first sign of disaster. Then he stared in panic at the woman with the dead child, who came up to him smiling pathetically, while the tears were streaming down her face. I saw him turning as pale as death, his eyes filled with an unspeakable fear. "Rabbi," she pleaded, "Rabbi," after which something followed that I did not understand. Shyly the boy looked around him. I thought it was almost sure that he would run away now. But then I saw an immense, unprecedented light in his gray-blue child's eyes, now freed of fear, something like an eternal wisdom awakening from its deep lethargy. Then I saw how—still shy, but watched by everyone with adoration and in a silence that almost could be touched by one's fingers—he put his beautiful white hands around the little head hidden in the blanket. I got dizzy when I suddenly heard the baby crow with pleasure. The whole crowd broke out into such an explosion of cheer and gratitude, that I was able to leave the shop without being bothered. I realized, however, that the boy had seen me. He had looked at me for a moment from his forced silence, while the women were crowding around him like clucking hens and stroking the grimy sheepskin of his coat cuffs and grabbing at his beautiful hands.

Like Jacob with the Angel, I struggled uninterruptedly through the whole length of Christmas mass with a horrible inhuman feeling of panic at the thought that I would never understand it. That I would have to wait for another half of a life time without knowing the answer to a question that could not be asked. Whenever I exerted myself to close off my mind from that question, I could think of nothing else. It irritated me immensely. Let such things happen in the Scriptures. Not in the life of a poor chaplain who has finished college and seminary on a grant, I thought. If need be, I would try, even though I wouldn't succeed, to convert the whores in the neighborhood one by one to a better life, without getting into temptation. But no wonders, I thought, no miracles, no hocus-pocus that undermines belief instead of supporting it. As a climax, the sexton warned me after mass that he had let three gentlemen into the sacristy who wanted to talk to me.

With military correctness they rose as one, their caps in their hands. They were three sailors. I'd noticed them already during the service in the unsure twilight shed by the candles. But I was mistaken. They were not sailors, but airline pilots in uniform, as became apparent from the Pan American Airways badge on their sleeves.

"Excuse us for disturbing you, especially on Christmas Eve," said the oldest American, a mulatto with silvergray hair, who reminded me of Paul Robeson. "It seemed reasonable to us to wait until after mass."

"You don't have to excuse yourself," I stammered.

"All three of us fly for the same company," said the second, an Oriental. "Usually it takes years before we meet up again in the bar of some airport or other..."

"It takes an eternity sometimes," affirmed the third one, a blond Scandinavian. "We did not understand a lot of the mass, however. None of us is a Catholic."

"It's of no importance," I mumbled.

"We thought that in church we would find someone who knows where the Davidsons live these days... Could you tell us perhaps?"

"Indeed I can," I answered with such stress that it must have seemed that I had to convince them of something. "It's close by, but hard to explain. You know: left, then right, and right again... I'll change and then I'll walk over with you."

The cars in front of the bars seemed covered with dew, but later I noticed that they were covered with a thin layer of ice that sometimes gleamed in different colors in the light of the lanterns. On the square, where I'd often seen Joshua feed the pigeons with rice he had gotten from the grocer's, the three dawdled a little, to look at the sky trembling with stars. For people who spend their lives between heaven and earth, I found that pretty absurd, but possibly they were just homesick for the infinity which starts beyond the glass of their cockpit.

"A sky just like that night..." the Oriental said.

"Well, it was Christmas then after all, too, at the end of the war. For some minutes a magnesium torch had been hanging over the camp. Just like a star. Do you remember how the prisoners kept asking whether bombs would be dropped?"

"As if we knew anything about it..." the blond Scandinavian grinned. "We had even been shot down the day before and had been brought by a run-down truck."

"Fortunately we were just in time..."

"For what were you just in time?" I asked timidly.

"To help the Jewish girl deliver her child. Pilots were supposed to be able to do everything. To let the milk from our emergency rations drip through her and the child's lips with difficulty..."

"And to beat that swine of a guard to a pulp, who wanted to stop us," the mulatto said.

"So you're talking about Miriam. And her boy?"

"Yes, that was the poor child's name. She was still so extremely young. Lucky Davidson took pity on her and the baby. It hasn't been easy to find out where the three of them wound up later."

We walked on. Behind the rose-red light of the bar and café windows, people were busy celebrating. It hardly touched the feeling of solemnity which suddenly filled the icy cold night. I wished for it to start snowing.

"One more corner, and we'll be there," I called out.

The Chinese eating house was there. It even seemed to be pretty crowded. Although there were no more lights burning, I clearly saw that Fierlafijn's old pharmacy was there, too. But Mr. Davidson's bookshop, which should have been in between those two, was missing. Everyone would have sworn, by the way, that it could never have been there. With a staggering sharpness I was struck by the fact that the worn advertisement for some cough syrup or other began halfway on the restaurant and continued across the total breadth of the pharmacy. I knew at the same time that it had always been like this.

"It's not possible..." I shouted with a weary voice, and presumably it sounded to the others like no more than a hoarse whisper.

"Don't let it worry you, Father..." I heard one of the Americans say from afar, yet strangely close as if he hoped to console me with such a commonplace. "We, too, have in all these years only once succeeded in finding them again..."

I suppose they must have said goodbye, but I don't remember. Paralyzed, I realized that their martial steps were dying out for good in the quiet street. My head was completely empty. How long did it take before my hollow mind was able to ask itself a question again? The question, I mean, of what had begun, or what had ended?

Ef Leonard (b. 1924)

is a journalist by profession. He has written two collections of SF that were very well received, both by the critics and the readers.

There is no absolute truth. The laws of relativity reign throughout the universe. One man's grain of sand might be another man's whole planet. Everybody knows the infuriating buzzing of mosquitoes. There is nothing you can do about it. Once in a while you might defeat the enemy with an unexpected swipe of the hand. A stain of blood is the proof of success. But who can know what really happened?

Landing

Eagle XIII dove into the dense cloud layer that covered almost the entire surface of the planet Venus.

After a time the surface became vaguely visible, not entirely flat, but lacking the innumerable craters they had encountered on other planets. The crust did exhibit myriads of splits and cracks, small cracks and splits reminding one of the craquelure in the layers of old paintings. "Take a look on the left," said Dick Hainsfeather. "We have to make sure at all costs to stay as far away from that as possible."

Ginger, who exhibited the color combination of a red-spotted cow—red hair and milky white skin—looked in the direction indicated and nodded when she saw the vertical wall losing itself in the fog. She maneuvered the Eagle XIII slowly in the other direction, where the landscape was relatively flat.

Two low hills came into view, making her recall the undulating Sahara where they had been in training with about ten others for several months. The colors of the hills were also desertlike, a light ochre-pink, as if the sand-colored ground were lit up by early morning sun. "I don't think we have to look any farther," she said. "This spot looks fine to me. Who knows what we might come across if we fly over those hills, maybe even a city of Venusian monsters."

Dick Hainsfeather glanced to check the controls. Everything looked reassuring. He smiled. "The Planet of Mosquitoes," he said, "I must have read that book at least six times when I was young. Took place on Venus. Cities full of terrifying mosquito -like beings at least six-feet tall. It made a big impression on me then." He regulated something on the fuel supply.

Slowly, aggravatingly slowly, the surface of Venus came closer.

It was as if they were looking through binoculars steadily being focused a little sharper by giant hands. The cracks and splits became clefts, and fine hairline rifts became cracks, altogether forming an extremely intricate pattern, a kind of infinite spider's web.

Not for a moment did they panic, knowing that the now still extremely tiny, flat places would steadily grow larger and would, perhaps, extend to an area of a few square miles.

The vertical wall and the hills had now disappeared out of sight, retreating into the distant, misty horizon.

"Luckily, Houston isn't bothering us for a bit," said Dick. "I think it's a real pain when they start gabbing while you're busy with a landing."

"To the right of that little reddish hill," said Ginger tensely, correcting the steering. "It looks like an enormous mosquito bite. That little spot next to it looks really flat to me. Give it a try?"

After a few minutes they were hovering right over it. Another fifty feet, another forty, thirty, ten, five...

Once again a soft humming vaguely registered in her head. She wasn't wide awake, but her hand was incredibly fast this time. Almost before she had even felt the poisonous prick, her hand was already coming down with force on the right spot, right in between her beautifully shaped breasts, protruding like two low hills from the glowing landscape of her body.

On the ochre-pink of her skin trickled a tiny red drop of blood to which something silvery was sticking—little fragments that looked a little like insect wings from a distance, on tiny bent insect legs that were still twitching.

Venus rolled over resentfully on her side. "Blasted mosquitoes," she mumbled. Then she fell asleep again.

Olga Rodenko (b. 1924)

is not a prolific writer, but the few stories she has published show a sensitivity, a frightening sense of humor, and a deep insight into universal fears that turn every one of her contributions to the literature of the unconscious into pure gems.

Maurits Dekker, a famous Dutch playwright, once said that the world has no waiting room. Evidently he was wrong. We are all confined to a waiting room and we know well enough what we're waiting for, though we try to ignore this sad inevitability. And it never ends. Never. And nobody will ever know the real reason.

Kept Waiting

I had an appointment. This was really the chance of a lifetime, and I'd put on my double-breasted suit for the occasion. When it's the chance of a lifetime, you do that.

The doorman treated me like a mechanical part on a conveyor belt, but that's just their way of doing things, and I convinced myself that I could avenge myself a hundred times over once I got the job, and I told myself I shouldn't let such a doorman bother me.

And yet, the doorman was still bothering me when I was in the waiting room; I felt a bit shaken up. To be honest, I felt so shaken up that I didn't mind the little man who sat huddled in a corner one bit.

And I hardly noticed the painter, who came in a little while later with a ladder and a can of paint.

When the painter had gone, the little man started speaking.

"Are you also applying for a job, sir?" he asked politely.

He was a very old little man.

"Yes," I said, "will it still be long?"

"Oh," he said, "so you must be here for the first time, then?"

"Of course," I said, a little bit louder. "I've come to apply for a job. For private secretary," I added.

He nodded, the way little old men do, and I asked myself what job he could be applying for. He looked just like a toy monkey. I asked him.

"For private secretary," he said.

"Ah," I said with a smile, and slid the palm of my hand over the buttons of my double-breasted suit.

"Yes," he said, "that may surprise you, but when I first came here I was as young as you."

"What?" I said. "When you first came here? I must say, sir, you are persistent."

"That isn't the word for it," he said.

"It would seem that way to me," I said, "once you've been turned down."

"I wasn't turned down," he said. "I'm still applying."

"I don't understand," I said.

"It isn't a question of understanding," he said. There was a silence. Little old men tend to make mysterious pronouncements like that. It's best if you don't take any notice of them.

Then he said: "Did you see that painter?"

"Vaguely," I responded.

"As you get older," he said with a smile, "you'll see him better."

"Oh," I said, also smiling, "but I don't intend to wait here that long."

Again there was a silence. Little old men have that sort of smile, they always know better. The best thing is to pay no attention to them and to smile back.

"It's certainly taking a long time," I said after it had been quiet for a time.

"You are still impatient," he said paternally. "That's why it's taking so long. But he could come in any minute now."

"Who?" I asked.

"The man in black," he said, "with his right arm bandaged up."

"Oh," I said, "and who is that?"

"There are a lot of them," he said, "it's always a different one."

"All in black?" I asked with a smile, "and with their right arms bandaged up?"

"No," he said, "sometimes they just have an empty right sleeve tucked in their pocket, or a deformed right hand, or a hand made of metal or wood."

"I don't understand you, sir," I said. "Who are those people?"

"They take you from one antechamber into the next," he said.

"The longer I listen to you the less I understand," I said. "How many antechambers are there, then?"

"Oh," he said, "they're countable, but they run in a circle, and you always end up returning to the same one."

"How long have you been here, anyway?" I asked.

"Sixty years," he said, "or more."

"You are persistent," I said with a smile.

"That isn't the word for it," he said. There was a silence. I didn't

85

understand it at all. He was just like a toy monkey lying in the bottom of a toy chest.

The best thing to do was to smile.

"And why do all those people in black have something wrong with their right arms?"

"Well," he said, "it's hard to say. But you'll soon find out for yourself when the door opens. Then one of those official gentlemen in black will be standing there, and you'll jump up with a broad smile, extending your hand, because, of course, you'll be thinking it's the director himself, and then you'll see that he's looking past you, and too late you'll realize that his right hand is bandaged up. You understand, don't you? It has something to do with your double-breasted suit and your diplomas."

"No," I said. "I don't understand any of this. What's wrong with my suit?"

"Nothing," he said, "but it doesn't come down to understanding."

And again it was quiet. I was beginning to get impatient; to me it seemed a bad omen having to wait so long. On top of this, the little old man was bothering me.

"It's taking so long," I said.

"You're still impatient," he said with a paternal smile.

"Still," I said. "Why, still? I don't understand it, I don't understand any of this."

"It's not a question of understanding," he said. "Young people always think it's a question of understanding. When I first came here..."

"Sixty years ago," I said.

"Sixty years ago," he said, "I also thought it was a matter of understanding. And I was as least as sure of myself as you are. But in the corner sat a little old man. At first I didn't pay much attention to him, or to the painter, and when the man in black appeared, I walked toward him with outstretched hand, as you will soon be doing, and turned red and fiddled with my sleeves because he didn't have a right hand. But in the meantime I had been shown into the next waiting room, and I thought I was, in any case, definitely a step closer, because I still didn't know that there were many more antechambers, and that they run in a circle. Then I saw the little old man sitting in a corner, and wondered how he had gotten there so fast, since only a moment before he had been in the previous antechamber. And that's where I went wrong, you see, when I started wondering. The little old man sat in each of the following ante-chambers, in the same corner. But it doesn't come down to understanding."

"For how long did this little man keep you company?" I asked with an obviously malicious smile.

"About fifty years," he said.

"And then?" I asked, unsmiling.

"Then he wasn't there any more."

"Well, what happened to him?" I asked.

"He disappeared," he said, "and in the corner where he had sat I myself was sitting."

"I don't understand it," I said, "and what was that little old man doing here... applying for a job?"

"Yes," he said, "for private secretary."

"Then that little man was very persistent," I said.

"That isn't the right word," he said. And at that, we both fell silent.

"It's taking a long time," I said from time to time.

Finally the door opened and a man in black was standing in the doorway, and with a broad smile and an outstretched hand I walked toward him. Because this was the chance of a lifetime.

However, the man in black looked past me, and I noticed his right hand was bandaged.

"Excuse me," I said, "I mean—"

"Just a moment," he said, and motioned with his left hand into the room behind him.

"I mean—" I said.

But he had already shut the door behind me.

"Oh well," I thought as soon as I could think straight again, "a step closer, anyway."

"A step closer, anyway," said the little old man.

I turned around. Believe it or not, there he was. Huddled in a corner like a forlorn and forgotten toy monkey.

"I don't get it," I said, "Sir, how did you get here so quickly?"

"It doesn't come down to understanding," the little man said.

I sat down again and said nothing. The painter came in, the same one as before, with a ladder and a can of paint, and painted the edges of the ceiling and walls.

When he was gone, the little old man said: "A strange one, that painter."

87

"Why," I asked, "is his right leg bandaged up or something?"

"No," said the little man, "but he's got a very long index finger, and that's what he paints with."

I shrugged my shoulders. "That's his business."

"But the funny thing is," said the old man, "he only paints where the ceiling meets the walls. Just as if he were pointing out the limits. When I was as young as you, I sometimes thought that painter would drive me crazy. Young people are so quick to think they'll go crazy," he said, "and everything's really quite normal."

"Why," I said, "did you think that that painter was going to drive you crazy?"

"He just keeps on pointing," said the little man, "with his index finger. He only points so far and no farther. Young people always want to go farther, and that's why they think they'll go crazy as soon as they see the limits. That's just how young people are. And everything's really quite normal."

"Yes," I said, "if you're as patient as you are, sir."

"Patient," he said, "isn't the right word."

And both of us fell silent.

I had gotten a splitting headache. I felt as if my skull would burst at any moment.

"I have a headache," I said.

"That will go away," he said with a paternal smile.

"I don't get it," I said "I don't understand any of this. What happened to that door I came in just now? I only see one, and that's on the other side."

"You're already beginning to notice things," he said.

"What!" I said. "What's wrong with that door?"

He shook his head. Little old men have such an irritating way of shaking their heads.

"There is only one door," he said, "the door to the next antechamber. You've come for a job, haven't you?"

"Yes," I said.

"For private secretary," he said.

"Yes," I said, "what does that have to do with that door? I don't understand."

"It has nothing to do with it," he said, "nothing at all."

Then something dawned on me. "But the director," I said, "I can just ask for the director, can't I? Who else would have placed that ad?"

"Hm," he said, "the director."

"That's right," I said, "the director."

"The director," he said and shook his head.

I stared at him. I had a headache.

"I have a headache," I said.

"And your double-breasted suit is wrinkled," he said with a smile.

Just at that moment the door opened, and in the entrance stood a man in black. With a sigh of relief, I got up and walked toward him with an outstretched hand.

Too late I saw that his right hand was deformed, and before I knew it I was standing in the room behind him.

"Just a moment," I could still hear him saying. The door was already closing.

"Another step closer," said the little man.

I turned around. There he sat.

"I don't understand," I stammered. "I don't understand it at all."

"No," he said comfortingly, "it really doesn't come down to that, to understanding."

And a long silence fell.

Jan Wolkers (b. 1925)

is a sculptor and a novelist of international fame. All of his books have become bestsellers and some of the films made from them have enjoyed great popularity. Love and hate are closely related. There is a fair chance that Cain, the famous fratricide, loved Abel. The world as we know it will one day come to an end. And then, once again, a father will have to give his firstborn a name. "There is nothing new under the sun," says the melancholy sage Ecclesiastes in the Bible. This leaves little hope for mankind.

Last Quarter

Do I have everlasting life? I must be thousands of years old at least, perhaps even older, perhaps not. Does it matter? What do I still remember of that rotting fruit that hangs in a hairy mold in the purple sky? Yet there were six of us that came from there. Six of us! And we ate each other up like sewer rats. Why was I the strongest and the only one to survive? Was a worse punishment imaginable? Why did I not suffocate, why did there have to be enough oxygen to crawl about gasping, and eat bitter moss like a reindeer? And those years of waiting for other rockets that never came, how did I live through them? Why were no further attempts made, ever? Oh, yes, I see them passing over all right, like golden hoverflies. Sometimes I think they are coming closer, that they will land, but then they shoot past, high above, to more distant destinations. Later, rockets did land, small human-shaped Egyptian coffins with revolting contents. Before the sun reaches them and turns their bodies paper-dry, I crawl up to them feverishly, break them open and drag the corpses in to the eternal shade of the crater bowls. I eat them, I suck them dry, as a spider sucks its prey. Among the contents of their stomachs I look for pips and seeds. Here, in the gray shadows, I cultivate gardens that seem to have sprouted from nightmares. Melon plants grow tablehigh, their fruits burst open when they are ripe and melt away in a pool of red liquid. Bunches of grapes lie on the brown soil like poisonous jellyfish stuck together. I am very grateful to the Earth-dwellers for these gifts packed in stiff dead flesh. If Southerners arrive, who are used to eating dates and olives, stones and all, I lay them out in rows. In due course, a small oasis grows out of their loins. The trees burst into leaf, the flesh disappears. The skin remains, withered and brown, like the empty outer membrane of a puffball.

But now, since yesterday, last year... hours days months years fly... they are sending not only corpses in cocoons, but also living beings. What has come over them on Earth? Is there such a desperate lack of space? Are these doomed, convicted people? But there are children among them and mothers with babies. If I leave them, if I do not drag them into the shade, I hear them in the heat of the first sunrays beating wildly against the casing. Only for a moment, though. Then the plain is littered with burnt newspapers fluttering in the glow, drifting away like lazy crows on a warm summer's day.

I cannot resist the temptation to open some of them. But the beings that come out are alien to me, I have been unaccustomed for too long to the company of people. I kick them over the rocks, to my garden of horrors. There I throw them flat on the ground and put heavy stones on their arms and legs so that they are robbed of their freedom. I cut a shallow notch in their bellies into which I carefully slip seeds and pips. The plants shoot up alarmingly fast. The pale roots soon poke out of the flesh on all sides. Those who are strong enough and do not die at once in terror and torment, scream unceasingly with pain. I like listening to them, except when someone screams in a language I used to speak. Then I ram a stone into his mouth. Terrible, that Portuguese among these chilly rocks.

I sit at the edge of the shade. A few feet away, the sun parches the rock which pulverizes in the heat. But here it is cool. On the ground between my legs lies a thin strip of paper, a last memory of my origin. CALVINATOR it says on it. I tear off small bits, making sure there is one letter on each piece. Much has changed lately. I no longer torture Earth creatures and my garden of horrors is gone, the ground there is as arid as before. And the moss is still as bitter as ever. She has also taught me to lie down on my knees twice a day and perform a strange action which I do not understand. Sometimes I feel regret, and long for my garden of melons so tall I was unable to see over the tops. Why could I not cut open her belly? How did I know she would bear fruit in a different way? And yesterday it happened, a son. I now have ten bits of paper, with a letter on each one, and turn them over one after another. I must think of a name for him, but how should I still know any names? I pick out four pieces, the others I gather and crumple up. Then I turn over the remaining ones and place them in a row. CAIN it says. A strange word: CAIN. But why should it not be a name?

Wim Burkunk (b. 1925)

is an actor, director, and playwright. For a time, he had his own company, the Pocket Theater. Later, he tried his hand at writing stories which regularly won prizes in competitions.

"New Herring" is a delicacy to the Dutch, but the sea is being emptied and we must learn to be careful with what is left of the animal kingdom. Animals, too, must be careful with us, otherwise humans will soon become as expensive as new herrings.

New Herring

When the first herring surfaced in Zandvoort, stepped onto the beach, put on a bowler hat, opened up his umbrella, and walked away over the sand, it didn't seem odd, since the rain was so bad that day.

When it happened again, later on, it was at night. The man who saw it was rather drunk, immediately checked in with A.A., and since then hasn't touched a drop. The third time, however, it happened in beautiful, sunny, going-to-the-beach weather and caused a big stir.

"How do they do it?"

"Isn't it something?" said somebody else, and everybody roared with laughter when the herring was having problems with his tie. But a boy not more than eight years old audibly sniffed, saying: "It's just got a little motor in it. With remote control," and continued building his castle. His father reflected on this for a moment. He hadn't seen a key sticking out of it anywhere, but forgot about that straightaway when a lady, who had much larger dimensions than her bikini, walked by.

The strange thing was that nobody at that time paid any attention to where the fish were going.

In a couple of days, everybody was used to seeing herring pop out of the sea, then swim around in the lukewarm puddles along the beach for a while, and finally walk away, struggling through the loose sand in the direction of the boardwalk. By now, the majority of the bathers probably shared the spoiled eight-year-old's opinion of mechanical toys, although there was also a minority who wanted to regard it as an advertising gimmick. At this point, it didn't much matter to anybody any more. The novelty had worn off. The sun was shining. People were lazy and on vacation, and as a bricklayer from Amsterdam summed it up: "For all I care, let 'em send whales. Lying here's fine with me."

It was only several weeks later, after hundreds and hundreds of herring had already disappeared inland, that a contractor for excavation and demolition projects brought his troubles down to the police station. When his confusing story was written up as an orderly, official report, it turned out that he was working on a row of condemned houses, old fishermen's cottages, that had to be torn down to make way for the construction of new apartments and a beach hotel. During the past few days, his bulldozers had been put out of action by little objects that had been placed on the site—"doll houses," the man had said—of a tough substance that wouldn't budge even in the face of the mechanical force of a demolition company. When he wanted to drive right over them to level the site, it had cost him his caterpillar treads which were ripped to shreds as soon as they came into contact with the elastic substance of the doll houses.

A bashing with an enormous forklift resulted in nothing but a bent-up piece of scrap metal, while the houses were still standing exactly as before.

At the station there were more than a few snickers to be heard, and it was assumed the man had been drunk when giving his account. Because it was so busy, a low-ranking officer was instructed to make an on-the-spot appraisal of the situation—sometime when he was going that way anyway—and to write out a report at his convenience and deliver it to his superior officer. The contractor was advised to take a rest, as the construction workers' vacations were starting just then.

So it was at least a week later when the low-ranking officer delivered his report. Not only were there little houses, hundreds and hundreds of little houses, he said, but now there were also little hotels, apartments, and other little constructions that looked like schools or churches. And the strangest of all: beside every row of houses, there was a small vat; a kind of herring vat, said the officer, complete with a red, white, and blue flag. He had brought one with him.

When the little vat was pried open, it contained a bather who had been missing for some days. A naked bather. Properly pickled and cleaned.

Marty Olthuis (b. 1925)

has published only one book of stories about what she calls "quiet horror". When Close Your Eyes, Please appeared in 1966, the connoisseurs sat up and took notice. Here they heard a new voice in the choir of fear-evoking storytellers.

Since man has begun to wonder about natural phenomena he cannot account for, he has sought explanations for them. Two hundred years ago, Mesmer proved the existence of animal magnetism. But the results of his experiments are no longer accepted. There are still many among us, however, who wonder whether there might have been some truth to Mesmer's wild surmises. If so, the death of a cat can become a supernatural event.

"Hold my Hand," said the Cat

Antoinette is half convinced that her cat is a human being. Indeed, the cat looks intelligent and her eyes have a close resemblance to those of Antoinette's daughter. They are light green and incredible —you've never seen anything like it. Those eyes suck you towards them and inside, you're gone, nothing to be done about it... Just like Antoinette's daughter the cat sways her behind gracefully and when she rubs her head against you, she stands high up on her hindlegs and turns around like a ballet dancer, bending her forelegs elegantly, just like a circus horse. Antoinette's daughter also rubs up against you, but without all that to-do. She doesn't run screaming into the street as if she's in heat to attract men, far from it. The cat, too, amuses herself splendidly with weakly protesting little mice which try to get away in vain...

When they put on their look of melancholy or fear, you would like to enclose cat and daughter in your arms, they can get you to do everything for them, then. They sleep intensely, rolled up tidily, their noses tucked away in their limbs. Sometimes they purr with pleasure and throw themselves at you with such force that you go to your knees: they love with a violent straightforwardness. That is, if they don't look right through you, at something that's none of your business. Both have triangular faces and triangular pink mouths. They're both called Rosamunde. There are differences: Cat Rosamunde always and ever wears long white fur underpants.

The cat's boyfriend brings her animal presents. Once it was a bloody rabbit, its head dangling morbidly; Antoinette screamed with disgust. She forgot that in her refrigerator one such thing was lying in wait, too, brought by Rosamunde's latest lover, apparently

95

a materialist. He had disguised the present with ribbons and red roses.

Two days in succession puss and tomcat dined uninterruptedly, after which only an empty skin was left of the plump rabbit. His little feet stood upright on the terrace, strangely deserted without any further pieces of rabbit attached.

When the cat is petted, she enjoys a fine hand: the little fingers spread and flex themselves. Antoinette's daughter does that with her toes. I enjoy watching that so much...

Both Rosamundes have gone through a similar drama. The cat had just littered, every one of them an intriguing character. One had a bright red carnival nose and square eyes. Another walked rapidly backwards all the time. A third was called Windekind because he broke wind like a big creature, which didn't improve the atmosphere in the room. And the last could float slantwise on wooden legs with a high back, in a fairly spooky way. When all four of them showed their strongest side, it made quite a hubbub around the basket. Sometimes the cluster of cats, huddling together, would be looking at Antoinette, softly swaying, in mature wisdom. The harder she would laugh, the more neutral would become the reflective stares of the eight little eyes.

At the time of this litter, the mother cat caught her husband in adultery. Not decently hidden, but carried on openly under her own window. She looked at it with a shiver of fear and threw Antoinette a dark look. She swore off the tomcat who had provided her offspring for years, and the color of the next litter underwent a change.

Exactly the same thing happened to Rosamunde. She, too, changed men and the color of her babies. I can talk about it, because I am the second choice and my skin is dark. She went with me to a faraway country and Antoinette often cried. Cat Rosamunde stayed and offered whatever she could in the way of consolation: a lot.

And, unavoidably, the time came when the cat's laden belly was swinging to and fro. She continued to rub her head against you, tiresomely up on her hindlegs. A top heavy, strangely proportioned circus horse.

In the middle of the night she came to get Antoinette. She jumped up onto the bed and tapped her cheek, the penetrating eyes luminous as jewels: red, danger! Antoinette put the birth basket next to the bed, and Rosamunde lay down in it hastily and nervous. She spread herself as wide as possible, put her belly next to her as a thing apart, fear shot through her eyes with fiery arrows. Then she stuck out her paw to Antoinette—help... help!—who grabbed and stroked it. A contraction went through the little body, the light green eyes begged. The body trembled, shook, contracted; the little mouth opened, screamed without a sound. "Nothing to be done about it, it's in there and it has to come out," Antoinette said aloud. And suddenly she remembered what it had been like, giving birth. Involved in the birthprocess... taking over a piece of God's task... oh, can't you think of anything else? All the devils she'd sworn out of hell! "Nurse," she had called furiously, "this is a shame! How can you think of it! God is a sadist. I think it's a dirty trick. Couldn't he have done it a little differently? Don't ever get married. Don't ever have any children, nurse, don't do it—promise me!"

It had seemed of great importance that this woman would never go through it. She promised and put a wet washcloth on Antoinette's forehead. The doctor came and said, just not softly enough: "It's not going well; the nose is getting so pointed." There I go, boys, she had thought, resigned, almost cheerful. But it went differently, and with one big push all of a sudden the child was there. The feeling of liberation had been so enormous that she'd almost lost consciousness.

Everybody was busy, a soft reassuring murmur that went over her while she thought: Gosh, I've created a person, I managed that at least. Put together a complete person with life in it, that's the craziest of all. That something like that exists should astound you...

Her smile became so wide that her face didn't have room enough for it; everywhere little lights went on, a whole future of lights. She wanted to say something, but the sounds stayed behind her teeth. Good gracious, my teeth cemented together. Who did that?... Nice going. It had to be fixed quickly, for she wanted to talk to her child...

The mother cat gave a scream, a human scream. It was absurd, but the tears were streaming down Antoinette's cheeks.

Then a black, ratlike creature flapped into the basket. She looked at the clock as she always did during drastic events: 3:14. The mother cat bit and licked and ate up the rubbish. The little black cat was already looking for a nipple... I have to survive... It was so unsparing that it was almost embarrassing in its intensity.

A little time to catch breath. Then, again, that whole horrible business. Antoinette closed her eyes, she was so tired of it; she had enough of it. The cat said hold my hand and she did that, but for the rest she was of no practical use. Another scream, another little cat born. A red one this time, a sticky bundle of guts turned independent. She felt Rosamunde's belly; there was nothing left inside, it was over; the gentlemen are thanked.

The red cat child didn't do too well, it was panting and gasping for air. The mother didn't help; she turned away and ignored the child. Antoinette couldn't stand it: "Rosamunde, come on, you have to help the little red one!" The cat threw the little animal out of the basket and lay down with her back towards it. Oh, stupid idiot, hurry up! Lick the life into it, come on! Antoinette put the moribund animal carefully back into the basket. It was panting, grimacing scarily, gave a sob, turned still and stiff, was dead.

She rolled the tiny little body in a soft cloth, put it on the nightstand next to her and looked at it from time to time. She hoped it would come back to life one good moment, you never know after all...

The next day she buried the little red cat in the garden, the garbage can being unthinkable.

In a letter her daughter wrote:
At 3:14 European time our son was born, pitch black, very lively. He is half of a twin, but, Mummy—it's so terrible, Mummy. The other one died. He had bright red hair.

Harry Mulisch (b. 1927)

*is one of the most famous of Dutch authors. With his first novel, Archibald Stro-
halm (1952), he won the most prestigious prize for young writers in Holland. His
work has been widely translated.*

*In the adventures of Mr. Tiennoppen, the principal character in the collection
The Miracle (1955), themes are reflected that since time immemorial, have occupied the minds of fanciful storytellers. In the Bible the Word becomes Flesh. This is
also the case in Harry's story. Tiennoppen thinks and it happens. A subject worthy
of his maker.*

The Crown Prince

Mr. Tiennoppen rocked on his heels and whistled away to his
heart's content. Late summer was in full swing. The sap in the trees
was getting ready to run out, but everything was still green. The
sun was shining, no longer in a ravaging way, but already with the
gentleness of old age. It was better, a thousand times better than in
spring! Dressed in a white summersuit and a yellow straw hat, Mr.
Tiennoppen stood at the edge of the park whistling and rocking
away. This was the day of days. He had not been so happy for
months. There was a bustle and a gaiety in the air. Never had the
streetcars seemed so elated.

Mr. Tiennoppen had raised the day to his lips and drained it dry.
On this day he was not going to grow a day older, but a year younger. He loved humanity. Full of benevolence he looked at the things
around him, the cars, the cyclists, the city hall. Floris V had once
lived in it, but today it had discarded its look of mellow old age and
joined in the dance: a passacaglia in the late summer sunshine. The
doors were very low. People used to be small in those days. Mr.
Tiennoppen had often noticed this in suits of armour. The human
race is getting taller and taller, he reflected, biologically a definite
sign of the approaching end. Brontosaurians died out, and baccilli
possess life eternal. He who gets tall is at death's door. Mr. Tiennoppen reflected. He smiled and rocked. What did it matter? He
pursed his lips and whistled a loud note, far too loud so that the
sound collapsed into a tuneless blowing.

"Excuse me, sir," a voice beside him suddenly asked. "Pardon
me... is there anything worth looking at?"

Mr. Tiennoppen looked round, and saw a little old man pointing
at the city hall with his pipe.

"What do you mean? Yes, of course, there's the town hall."
The man, probably and old-age pensioner, looked inquiringly at
the windows and the steps. He was shabbily but neatly dressed.
"Do you think there might be a foreign Head of State in there?"
he asked.

"Not that I know of," said Mr. Tiennoppen, shrugging his shoulders. "I don't think so, and I've been standing here for quite a
while."

"Then what are you standing here for?"

"Why do you want to know?"

"Ah, you are from the police, aren't you?"

Mr. Tiennoppen laughed.

"I am standing here because the sun is shining," he said.

The pensioner looked at him in surprise and then uttered a whin-
nying laugh.

"Tell that to the marines," he exclaimed. "You are standing here
because something is going on over there in the city hall." Again he
pointed. "The City Council is probably receiving a foreign Head of
State. Why do you want to keep it to yourself?"

Mr. Tiennoppen shrugged his shoulders.

"You are quite welcome to believe that there is a foreign Head of
State. I don't care what you think, only stop bothering me."

"From which country?" the man asked eagerly.

"It is the Crown Prince of Bessarabia, for all I know," Mr. Tiennoppen suggested. He nodded with a smile and moved off to one
side, whistling away to his heart's content.

This is a wonderful world, he reflected. Leading a pensioner up
the garden path on a fine late summer day. What more could a man
wish for? Look, the streetcars and buildings were laughing too.
Even a few chimneys giggled stealthily. Mr. Tiennoppen stopped
whistling, and became completely absorbed in the day.

A little later, as people brushed against him, he was startled from
his daydreaming. A considerable group had gathered around the
pensioner: several other pensioners, a good many housewives, and
quite a troop of schoolchildren. They were all talking at once and
continually casting excited glances at the city hall. A few cyclists got
off their bikes. A moment later a man with a pedal-cart also stopped,
and more pedestrians joined the crowd. Now and again the pensioner pointed out Mr. Tiennoppen with his pipe, after which everybody would look in his direction and then turn back quickly to the

city hall so as not to miss anything.

Mr. Tiennoppen was inclined to point to his forehead, but he refrained. Even when one of the cyclists asked him at what time the Crown Prince would appear, he did not answer, but stepped further off to the side. The crowd was growing quickly. There were at least fifty people now. He decided not to worry about anything and to pretend he was having a nosebleed. He pressed his handkerchief to his nose and enjoyed the view. The weather was not getting any worse, and the city hall was a splendid building, Floris V had once lived in it.

Still he was bothered by queries. There were even people standing on his other side now. Mr. Tiennoppen firmly made up his mind not to budge another inch. A few minutes later, he was completely shut in by the spectators. He was seized by a momentary panic, when he noticed the proportions the crowd was assuming. But he regained control of himself. Here and there a policeman saw to it that everything went smoothly. From all directions the curious hastened to the scene, excitedly asking for information, and again and again the pensioner pointed at Mr. Tiennoppen with his little pipe.

But he remained silent and obstinate. He was pushed to the left and right, and all round him people were chattering. Children cried or sat on their fathers' shoulders, blowing paper whistles. People also leaned out of the windows of the adjoining houses. Some of them were wearing hats and coats; it was probably possible to rent standing places. A flag was raised somewhere, and soon the national tricolor was flying from every building. Herring vendors slowly pushed their fishcarts through the crowd, doing a roaring trade. From several windows streamers were thrown over the people. The police also had moved into action on a grand scale. Motorcycles with sidecars thundered back and forth, and a high-ranking officer (probably the Chief Constable) arrived in a navy-blue police jeep. Cars were no longer to be seen. The traffic had very likely been rerouted. Streetcars, too, had vanished.

Mr. Tiennoppen began to feel warm and ill. Behind him people pushed impatiently, and as the police had formed a cordon, it was impossible for him to escape. For that matter, he wasn't even thinking of leaving. He would show them. Yes, sir, he was going to stay here and enjoy the summer if it killed him. He raised himself on his toes and looked around. The whole square was one sea of heads. It would be easy to walk quickly across the heads from one side to the other without faltering and with little danger of sinking. Mr. Tiennoppen closed his eyes for a moment and then looked again, as if the situation were only now brought home to him, and then he began to tremble with fear. At the same time, the crowd started singing the national anthem. Shaking like a leaf, Mr. Tiennoppen uncovered his head while breaking out into a cold sweat. The singing was very uneven. A little distance away, they had already come to the seventh line of the national anthem, while here they were still lingering over the fourth. In desperation, Mr. Tiennoppen shredded his straw hat apart. What was he to do? People were singing and anticipating. Ought he to leave them under this delusion? He felt as though the responsibility were weighing on his shoulders like a planet. Everything was his fault, wasn't it? Wasn't it? His fault!

"Hip-hip-hip...!" shouted the pensioner, and the whole world cried "Hurrah."

And again:

"Hip-hip-hip...!"

"Hurrah!"

"Hip-hip-hip...!"

"Hurrah!"

"There is no Crown Prince!" roared Mr. Tiennoppen, and there was no one who did not hear him.

Silence descended upon the crowd like a shroud.

Pale as death, Mr. Tiennoppen stared into the myriads of eyes and moved his lips once more, but not a sound came out. He had emptied himself with the first shout. A gesture he wanted to make did not come off either. He started to quake with misery.

Then, in two groups, the answer from the people came. One half started to scream with laughter and howled because of the absurdity of his remark; the others flew into a terrible rage. Many people forced their way over to him, ranting and raving. Somebody gave him a push, which sent him staggering, and from behind he received a violent blow.

"I am speaking the truth," he groaned as a police officer dragged him outside the cordon. He turned around and stood face to face with the furious and laughing crowd.

When he wanted to say something further, the policeman ordered: "Clear out!" and gave him a push. "That way, the Koningstraat has been kept open."

Pursued by shouts and laughter, still clutching the shreds of his straw hat, Mr. Tiennoppen stumbled weeping across the roped-off part to the Koningstraat, down which a brass band now came marching. When he had reached the corner, the noise suddenly assumed alarming and bellowing proportions. He looked back, just in time to see, smiling gracefully in his white burnose, the Crown Prince of Bessarabia appearing on the steps.

Hugo Raes (b. 1929)

is a full-time English teacher. He might be called a pure SF writer, one of the founders of the SF-Fantasy movement in Belgium.
The BEMs or Bug-Eyed Monsters are well-known creatures in SF. They populate the remote planets on which bold explorers of space land. In a sensitive, poetic style, Raes describes erotic experiences on a satellite of Saturn: strange and remote and yet, somehow, very near to us.

A Sunrise

Then the sun set and it became evening. It was no longer so warm now. So he seized her tits and raised them lightly. She cooed, a laugh, and the thought, now her light will go on.

I am unscrupulous, conscienceless, corrupt, he thought, but it is her business if she likes it. He pulled her toot. She blinked, and he felt her trembling in irregular spasms. She was tensed like a spring about to be released. He felt the tingling in his joins himself. He felt carefully between her folds for her joins, which were firmly set together. It was a big one. Shall we play stretcher? And he grabbed her, not relaxing his sharp gaze, and stretched. Gurgling in a somewhat provocative way, she laughed. "You like this game, don't you," she said. He stretched and suddenly let go, then grasped again and went on repeating this.

After half an hour he heard her sighing, then rustling like a soft breeze at high speed. He deftly titillated her tapper (oh, mine is not so deep), making it disappear more and more, and a large pink patch became visible, expanded, and grew brighter in color. A glassy sheen came over it and the brightness became watery. He played gently with her breast-paws and waved all his projections rhythmically, which affected and delighted her greatly. "How you stir me up inside, Krisnamari; I never felt my inside so moved, so much in action as now," she sighed, and the hair on her back lay flat on her carapace. He went on like this for almost an hour.

Deliberately he touched the unpetrified external vertebra and received the shock. The first one hurt, but the second was less charged, and gradually decreasing in power to a constant level they effected him more and more pleasantly. Perhaps her charge was not decreasing, but he was getting more used to it. After forty minutes the closed circuit was accomplished, he noticed, looking at his chronometer. She is definitely quick, he reflected. The symmetrical waves streamed through him, and his organism sent them back to her. Normally this would go on for three hours, but she was quicker than the others and he knew her tower would certainly rise considerably sooner; so he must prepare for more hurried capsuling. He pressed nickle against the shining pink patch and waited in readiness. Again he looked at his timing instruments. They would have about thirty minutes before entering the next phase.

It was now completely dark. The sound of the planets had about reached night strength. Perhaps we had better have our night packet now, he suggested. She smiled and nodded, and they took it, accurately in the required places, so as not to forget any. In the meantime she made jokes and teased him and pressed her schoulder-fingers against his temples and said: "Here were your prehistoric ears, and that was your blob of a nose, but... what do I see? Yes, you've got a little lump, perhaps you will get one back again." He grinned and grabbed her by the repples and folded them over so that she complained and cried out; "Ow, you're hurting me." She pushed him straight in the middle opening, but he closed it smartly round her pale-orange stickle and squeezed. "Now I'm not going to let you," he said, and thought: I'll hold on to her till her tower comes up and while I am working on it. She was sensitive to it, he felt, and so he slackened his hold a little, squeezed less hard and saw that it gave her more satisfaction. I must not relax any more or perhaps she will pull it out when the tower comes up. His thoughts flashed quickly through the attention he was giving to the other parts. He pushed more firmly through her upper segments, so that she kept still and noiseless and seemed to be waiting, to have stopped breathing. The suspended tension lasted more than a quarter of an hour, and when she began to get more lively he saw his trembler vibrating more violently than ever. Then he clamped himself fast with his side hooks to her white and mauve scales, one by one, so that she felt the process for a long time.

The night was now sultry and Saturn was clear and neater to the world than ever before.

How long had they not discussed the night of love... prepared, described it? With some anxiety. It could so easily be a failure, it could easily be cruel. But as he felt her more securely and inflexibly joined to him, his hooks as though crystallized behind her scales;

but one with her joined as if grown together, his certainty became great.

Some time later he began to push her breast-paws down till they would go no further, entirely pushed in. In the meantime he stuck the thorn-shaped appendage for the first time against the curving, soft surface of her belly. She cried a little and water came out of her dark eyes, which were now less fiery. So he stopped and, instead, pushed still deeper between her segments and joins and rubbed violently between a few of her rings.

Now the parallel vibrations of her closed circuit were gentle enough for him to stroke her lubber. The discharges pulsed constantly through him and her as if they were one. He worked on her lubber and stroked and stroked. She licked the shining skin of his skull and teased him by withdrawing her lubber for a time and making it disappear altogether.

He gave a short, rather nervous laugh and knew that this time it would not be a failure. Otherwise he would hardly be allowed to again. They die so soon if it is not a success, and your identity is made public every time one dies. He had to laugh inwardly. But this one must not die. She did not know the ones before and arranged the night of love and waited for it so long, and after seeing her last week he had impressed on her that she must rest the whole time, so that she was as strong and powerful as possible, and that she must bathe a lot in the light of Saturn, so as to be charged. You do not get a sufficient charge in one night. "Have you done it often, as you seem to know so much," she had asked. He did not go into that, so she could not ask how many successes and failures there had been.

When her dark eyes, now burning more fiercely, saw his green belly with its irregularities, she felt violently stimulated. She suddenly realized that he was experienced. The uncertainty about the number of successes and failures made her rather anxious, so that the heat under her scales and her skin increased. Krisnamari felt it, gripped her firmly and more roughly between the rings. And he saw that snogs were coming through the upper nipples and that they were moving up and down and getting whiter. And he blew on them.

The sky grew lighter. Saturn was less sharply outlined. Dawn would soon break. It would happen in the next ten minutes, he calculated, after a glance at his timing instrument. Her folds were already becoming softer, her white lips wider and harder, and the smallest, transparent scales were sliding over each other. He could hear their strange sound. Then he made her big tummel go up and down, as it should, while he made little snips with the pincers, more and more, quicker and quicker, so that is seemed that she was being snipped on all sides, snipped into a thousand pieces, so quickly, more quickly, at last almost invisibly.

And then, just as the first ray of the sun probed the horizon, all her breast-paws stiffened. He clung closer to her scales, cutting involuntarily into her flesh, penetrated with the point of his hooks farther into her inside, and then softly and slowly, her tower began to rise, wet and shiny, higher and higher, inch by inch, red changing to pink, and whiter and whiter and the air stimulated it immensely, vulnerable, and the sun shone on it with more and more rays till it emitted a golden tinge. It rose higher and higher. He pushed away a little with his main grabbers and carefully watched the tower growing and approaching his own extremity. It went on and on. It seemed to take a quarter of an hour instead of the usual twelve minutes. It was shining unusually and it was whiter than he had ever seen one, and it went on rising, higher and higher, inch by inch, and he could feel her tits bouncing and her nipples snogging and saw her eyes staring at Saturn. Gently, but at a great rate, her toot tapped his thorn-shaped appendage, her tits wobbled in the motionless, hard-breast scales, and the radiating waves in the closed circuit tore through all his joins and hers. Her tower was now an almost perfect one, and just before he began the decisive phase he turned on the electric metal poker that poked her in the place left free by nature for which no corresponding male organ was provided. And just as the sun came right above the horizon he began capsuling. A shining, moist haze-like mist spouted out of him, over her tower, billowing and forming a bright cloche, shutting it off and protecting it from the air. And while he was finishing it, he noticed how quickly everything of his and hers was moving and making sound, and how brightly and gloriously the morning irradiated them.

Ward Ruyslinck (b. 1929)

is a librarian in an Antwerp museum. His SF novel Golden Ophelia *has met with remarkable success, both in the Netherlands and in English-speaking countries.*

The profoundest horror for a modern reader is not always evoked by moaning ghosts in isolated mansions but can sometimes be aroused by a description of minor discrepancies in everyday reality, in which depths are revealed which no one wants to know about. A snowfall in winter can enhance the landscape with the beauty of white innocence. But what the snow hides is unfit for human eyes.

The Snow Shower

One morning in May it suddenly began to snow, not just a few harmlessly drifting flakes, but a heavy shower that made it hard to see anything. There was no wind and the snow fell vertically, piling up like foam from a fire extinguisher.

People thought they were dreaming: such a heavy snowfall in May was extraordinary. Among the senior citizens occupying the benches in the city park, there were several who did not think it so exceptional. They could recall a Whitsun week shortly before World War II when it wouldn't stop snowing. Great mounds of it, they said, wedging their crutch or walking stick between their knees to free both hands to indicate how high the snow had been. The others, whose memories weren't as good and who did think it exceptional, silenty stared with burnt-out old man's eyes at the thick woolly shreds coming down past the chestnut trees to rest on the lawns. It was a peculiar sight, like a trick of the eye. If you stared long enough, it looked as if the chestnuts were shedding blossoms. "The funny thing is," said the fraternity, "it's not at all cold." Indeed, although they were wearing only light summer jackets, they did not feel cold. "A remarkable natural phenomenon," they observed, and so had a topic for conversation.

That day most of the children were late for school, but the teachers were not angry. They said nothing about it, because they also found so much snow in the midst of spring most unusual. But they accepted it; it was an exceptional event and may well have inspired a new saying to be added to their stock of pedagogical lore: *Snow in May, its gets in the way, but the children cry hurray!* The teachers themselves were not rejoicing. Their faces were serious and they looked worried, probably because snow was not on their schedule. The fact is that teachers cannot cope without their timetable; they become unhappy the moment it's upset, which was what was happening now. To begin with, the first teaching period had to be abandoned because there were so many latecomers, and then the planned movie show in the gymnasium had to be postponed. It was hardly an appropriate day to show a documentary on the burgeoning of nature in spring. It just wasn't shown. The children could not be expected to sit and watch trees budding, birds nesting, and caterpillars turning into butterflies while their ears still glowed from playing in the snow outside. It was decided to replace the movie by an hour of free drawing, from ten to eleven. That was of some benefit to the children, and, while the educational value was perhaps debatable, what they produced with their crayons was at least different: snowmen amid flowering rose gardens and sleighrides in a landscape of green fields and diving swallows.

Shortly after eleven the principal went round the various classes in person and told the teachers, "We've got to send the children home." The snow had not cheered him up, either. He looked just as dejected as the teachers. It was clear that a variation on the new saying had occurred to him: *Snow in May brings a holiday.* That was why his expression was so gloomy, of course: principals don't like giving days off, and a school with no children is like a pond with no goldfish, or worse, a pond with no water. So the children were sent home. It had just stopped snowing as they came out of school, but it was still clouded and the sky had the gray dampness of a freshly roughcast wall.

Bikkel had stopped to play in someone's front garden with a few boys from his class. There was a huge supply of beautifully white, untouched snow just waiting for them, and they had a terrific time. The snow was damp and easy to pack together, and a pitched battle soon developed into a regular free-for-all. At the height of the ruckus, they were ordered out of the garden by a grim-looking pasty-faced man. "Go play somewhere else. You're treading on all my primulas!" the old fogey shouted from the porch. Of course they had no idea what primulas were, but they understood that he meant the sugar-dusted plants in the trampled borders. When they showed no immediate sign of leaving, and Govert Geel even stuck his tongue out at the spoilsport, the man picked up the satchels lying by the porch and threw them over the fence into the street. That left them no choice but withdrawal.

"It must be after twelve. I'll be in for it when I get home," said

Bikkel, starting to run. He lived the farthest from school, opposite a factory where they made emery paper. His father worked at the factory and came over at twelve during the lunch break. If Bikkel didn't appear for lunch on time, he'd be in for a hiding, especially when they heard that he'd been let off from school an hour early. He wasn't so afraid of his mother. He could easily twist her round his little finger, but he was scared stiff of his father. He regularly flew off the handle. Everything about his father was rough: his face, his hands, his voice, his language—as rough as the paper he helped to make in the factory. After a while Bikkel stopped running. It made no difference now—he would be late anyway. And apart from that, all at once he felt terribly tired, as if he had been playing in the snow not just for an hour but the whole morning. He came past the French fries stand where his father had once got into a row with a loud-mouthed taxi driver. Farther up there was the shop where they had bought his bicycle last year; the shopkeeper had since died of cancer. There was a dead sparrow lying in the snow in front of the shop. He stopped and rolled the tiny corpse over with the tip of his shoe. He bent down to study it more closely. It was stone dead. Frozen to death, he thought at first, but that was impossible—it wasn't that cold. He put his foot on the bird and pressed it into the snow until only its legs showed, sticking up like two fruit-stalks. Then he trudged on into the Schansstraat. The snow creaked under his feet, like when he walked over the wooden floor of the attic where the dust-coated tailor's dummies stood beside his mother's obsolete treadle sewing machine. The floorboards up there made the same noise.

His face and hands were glowing. It was a strange sort of glow, not the familiar tingling and pins-and-needles sensation that was such a nuisance when you came into the warmth after playing in the snow with bare hands. No, this was completely different, more like the start of illness, as if he were feverish. There was a fierce heat coming from his insides rather than his skin and reaching up to his throat. It was almost as if his body had become a tub in which his blood was gently simmering. His neck hurt, too, as if it had been thumped. On the market square small dark heaps lay here and there in the snow, like piles of garbage. He walked past them, crossing the square diagonally, and then saw that they were birds, heaps of dead birds. He stopped in surprise and looked around. That's funny, he thought, so many dead birds. He'd never seen that before. He wondered if it were because of the snow. One of them was still alive, a black bird with a pink beak lying at the foot of the statue in the middle of the square. It lay on its side with its beak opening and closing as if it wanted to cry but couldn't. Bikkel felt sorry for it. He squatted on his heels beside it and watched curiously. It was a pitiful sight. He spoke to the bird. "Are you hungry? Or thirsty?" he asked. "Shall I take you home in my satchel?" He ran his finger carefully round the open beak. "Come on, say something." He stroked the downy feathers with the same finger. "Are you sick? Does it hurt? I hurt, in my neck, but you don't die of that." The bird no longer moved. Its eyes were closed, and its beak stayed open. It was dead.

Two men were approaching across the square, but they didn't look at the birds. They seemed to be in a big hurry and were busy talking. Bikkel, who was still squatting beside the black bird, caught the mysterious word that cropped up all the time in adult conversations and was charged with terrible meaning. An alarm word, like a red light. When used by adults it meant the same as danger, illness, death and destruction. It was a composite word made up of two parts which, when used separately, had entirely innocent meaning having no association with danger, illness, death or destruction. But when you put the two parts together and pronounced them in the same breath, you got a completely different word, the dreadfully ominous word that recurred constantly in the papers, on the radio—hey, see, on the radio—on the TV and in conversations between adults. Adults used a whole lot of words like that to indicate things you never heard mentioned at school—things which posed a threat to the life and happiness of the people on Earth. At school only constructive, uplifting, educational, and useful words were used: burgeoning life in nature, Holy Trinity, multiplication tables, honor and obey your parents. They were never composite words, but always simple and preferably of one syllable: fish, fire, bag, boat, horse, tip, feast, sea... words for things you could see, hear, smell or touch, never for things that hung in mid-air, things you couldn't possibly visualize. Those were the words that his mother and father used quite often—vague, ambivalent, blurred terms such as disgrace, pay raise, discard, credit, mistress, cancer, transfusion, and the notorious red-light word. While he was thinking about all this, Bikkel walked on. The pain in his neck spread to his shoulders and made his back stiff. He didn't feel at all well and would have liked to sit down on some steps, but he was afraid that his father might beat the life out of him.

At the Hoge Dam he met a woman crying. Her swollen red face was burned and covered with large blisters. She walked past him howling loudly with her head in her hands. He turned round and stared after her, his mouth hanging open. Evidently he was the only one surprised by this spectacle; the other people in the street took not the slightest notice of her. They seemed to be blind and deaf, as if they saw and heard nothing of what was going on around them. Something must have happened, thought Bikkel; everyone is behaving so strangely. There are dead birds all over the place, but either they haven't noticed or don't think it unusual, and no one bothers to look twice at a woman in tears and her face covered with blisters.

But immediately afterwards he found out why the people had ignored the crying woman. They had something else to look at, something more important. It had nothing to do with the woman with the burns. That was an individual case, whereas what was happening up there in the sky very probably concerned them all. Bikkel, in turn, looked up and saw the airplane flying low over the houses and leaving a cloud of white powder in its wake. The powder hung briefly in the air like fog and then drifted slowly down on to the streets. The plane banked and disappeared from sight. Bikkel remembered seeing something similar recently on the TV news: helicopters being used to fight a forest fire. That had worked in just the same way, with stuff being sprayed from the air. Well, they didn't need to worry about forest fires here. Where there were no forests you couldn't have forest fires. Was it possible that they had made the snow from that plane? Nowadays they could make anything they wanted artificially, even new faces. Uncle Karel, for instance, had been given a new face complete with moustache and false teeth. They had made fertilizer from the old one, the leftovers. They knew the art of making everything: faces, fertilizer, teeth (everything except making art, Uncle Karel said). But there was still something funny about the snow. What was the point of that? What was the use of making snow in the spring? Certainly not for the kids—not on your life, that wasn't it. They never invented anything specially for kids; they didn't bother with that kind of thing.

The people walked on, and Bikkel did the same. His satchel felt terribly heavy, heavy as hell. That was what Govert Geel was always saying, "as hell". Everything was hell with Govert: heavy as hell, dirty as hell, cold as hell.

God, the pain in his neck. And his legs—they felt strange too, as if they couldn't bear his weight any more. They were as weak as hell. He realized that in some way there had to be a connection between the pain and fire in his body, the dead birds, the crying woman, and the plane spraying powder—but he couldn't see it. Maybe the woman with blisters on her face was running away from a forest fire after all. He was too tired to puzzle it out.

From behind the houses, a loud voice blared at him. That advertising car was back again, with the voice from a loudspeaker. Sometimes it played music in between, at least it had last week. He stopped to listen, but it was too far away for him to follow what the voice said. For a moment he thought he caught the redlight word, but he must have imagined it. They'd never have commercials for that—what an idea! The commercials were always for nice, attractive, pleasant things. A convoy of army trucks approached from the other end of the street. Red crosses were painted on the cab doors so you could see at once that they were ambulances. But the men driving them were not soldiers, at least they didn't look like soldiers, more like astronauts. They were wearing oxygen masks and white suits that covered them up completely. They looked a little creepy. It was just like a convoy bound for the moon. Bikkel rubbed his eyes. Pretty weird kind of delivery, he decided. He stood mesmerized on the sidewalk and watched the trucks with their mysterious drivers. He was so stunned by the sight that he didn't even notice that the snow was beginning to melt. It was gradually turning into a muddy slush that splattered and spurted from under the truck wheels.

It's a dream, thought Bikkel, or a movie. Except that almost everything was real. His knees were giving way, he was that tired, and the heat and pain in his body had melted into one hot, glowing pain. The convoy had passed, but he was still standing at the curb looking at the tracks it had left in the slush. In the distance he could hear people shouting and cursing. They roared like wild animals. All through the town the cars with loudspeakers were driving around trying to drown each other out. They played no music but broadcast mysterious messages from other planets and the savage howls of animals which had caught the Earthlings on the other planets.

The plane flew over again, but Bikkel didn't look up. The pain in his neck was so intense that he could hardly move his head. He must get home as quickly as he could. He was sick as hell. By now his father would be raving mad (mad as hell!); but once he saw that his son was sick, he wouldn't beat the life out of him.

He was about to cross the street when someone grabbed him by the arm. He jumped and dropped his satchel. He was looking into an oxygen mask. The only living thing in there was the eyes, which spoke to him in a peculiar muffled voice. It was the eyes, not the mouth, that were talking to him. He couldn't see the mouth. The mask talked like a radio station that wasn't quite tuned in properly. He was receiving two stations at once and could understand neither. They merged into a senseless jabbering. Another man in an oxygen mask appeared at his side and spoke to him in the same way. Bikkel stepped back and was about to tell them that there were dead birds lying in the snow everywhere and that he was sick, but before he could say a word the masks pushed a wet cloth into his face. It smelt of acid drops and the stuff his mother used to take off her nail varnish. The masks took hold of his arms and pushed him forwards, off the sidewalk. He couldn't see anything, but he felt himself being lifted into the air by a pair of strong arms. Paralyzed by fear as he was, he couldn't say or do anything, couldn't even think any more. They made him sit down on a bench with slats, at least that was what he took it to be. The cloth slipped off his face, and he saw that he was on a beer truck. There were no kegs, but you could still catch a faint smell of beer. The long sides of the open truck were lined with rough slatted benches on which sat people with nodding heads, men and women and a boy who looked a few years older than Bikkel. They all had big heat blisters on their faces, like the crying woman on the Hoge Dam. But they were not crying. They sat with dazed expressions staring into space and nodding continually, as if in the distance they could see someone they knew approaching but were afraid to draw attention to themselves because they felt ashamed of being loaded on a beer truck like so many barrels.

A masked man climbed onto the back of the truck. He pulled up the tailgate with its chains and immediately afterwards the truck moved off. The mask came and sat next to Bikkel and put his arm round his shoulders protectively. Bikkel said nothing. He was scared, tired, and sick, and right now he didn't much care what the masks intended to do with him. The people on the benches were shaken from side to side, but they didn't seem to care much either.

They didn't look at each other or say "Sorry" when the truck swerved and they were thrown together. Their expressions revealed only a deadly apathy, and in one or two cases dazed astonishment, the look of a clockwork doll whose spring has been wound too tight and snapped. The boy had that look, just like a broken toy. Bikkel listened as the wheels splashed over the melting snow. It was like driving through the shallows of a river. On the banks sirens whined. My satchel, he thought. It had been left lying in the snow with the brand-new Atlas of the World inside. His father would go crazy! But was it his fault that the astronauts had taken him with them? What could he have done to stop them?

He looked weakly at the man sitting directly opposite him. His face was blistered and contorted with pain. There was one like a bubble blown from gum under his nose. It pulled up his top lip, revealing stained yellow teeth as in a skull. Bikkel saw him distractedly push his hand through his hair—he had beautiful curly fair hair—and so pull out a clump big enough for a duster. Instead of being rooted to his head, his hair seemed to have been badly glued on. The man looked in surprise at the clump he had combed out with his fingers. He could not take his eyes off it and sat with his mouth twisted in a grimace and stared. He didn't throw it away or let it fall to the floor, but kept it clenched tight in his hand like a precious relic for the rest of the journey.

Bikkel felt his stomach heave. He turned away and tried not to look at the man again. He watched the passing houses. He had just seen snow sliding off the roofs when the truck slowed, made a sharp turn, and entered a large gate. It stopped in a small courtyard, and they all had to get out. Masked men and women in white were waiting for them and they silently hurried towards the truck carrying stretchers.

It had not snowed in the courtyard, which smelt of sunny, undefiled spring. There were lovely red flowers in bloom, and green creepers had been trained up past the big windows to spread out under the roof gutters. That was as much as Bikkel saw before he was lifted up and laid on a stretcher. He was carried down a long tiled corridor, and the swaying motion made him throw up. The hot mush which had been simmering in the cauldron of his body all the time suddenly boiled over. Vomit ran over his clothes, the stretcher, and the corridor—but no one took any notice. They carried on without pausing and brought him into a big room filled with glaring light. When he raised his hand to shield his eyes from the glare, he saw those horrible blisters on the back of it, like gum bubbles.

Skilled hands undressed him, hands without blisters. He had to give his name and address and then he felt a prick in his skin, but it didn't hurt. He was barely aware of it. His skin was numb, soft and swollen like a sponge. Masks bent over him. Eyes stared at him from behind glinting portholes. It hardly ever snows in May, he thought, how was it possible? A red light went on and off under his eyelids. It jumped about on the switchboard of his imagination, like the lights on a pinball machine. A woman's voice spoke the red-light word, and as soon as it penetrated his consciousness it fell apart into its two components. They kept rolling back and forth inside his head, from one side to another, like marbles in a can or an empty jam jar when you tilted it first one way and then the other. His head was continually growing bigger, so each time the marbles had to roll farther to get back to one side. Then all at once there were so many marbles that you could make sentences from them, harmless sentences in which the big red marbles didn't stand out so menacingly. For instance, a sentence like: *Turn the radio down a bit.* That was one of his mother's sentences. And this was one of his father's: *At that age you're already less active.* When all the marbles rolled back together, or more or less all of them, that made: *At that age you're already a bit radioactive.* That was everyone's sentence. God's and everybody else's, because the composite red-light word was in it.

The marbles went on rolling back and forth inside his head until the evening. He was delirious and called out for his mother several times. She was holding the hand of a strange boy and taking him back home. He yelled and shouted till he was hoarse from the snow-covered front garden where he was held prisoner, but she never looked around. Now she had another, better-behaved boy, and she wanted nothing to do with him. A grim-looking old pasty-face came into the garden and said, "Hey, crybaby, I'll teach you to make such a hullabaloo." He opened Bikkel's satchel, took out the Atlas of the World and began to tear out the color plates one by one. Bikkel howled like a wolf. When the man heard him, he was overwhelmed by pity and was soon crying himself. As he did so, he tore great clumps of hair from his head and went on until he was bald.

A plane came over and dropped balloons with advertising slogans. Bikkel couldn't chase after the balloons because he was trapped in the garden. He fell to his knees in front of pasty-face and begged for a balloon, but the man shook his head and said, "You're sure as hell crazy. Those aren't balloons. Take a good look." Bikkel looked and saw that indeed they weren't balloons. They were dead birds. One of them, a black bird with a pink beak, fell into the garden among the plates torn from the atlas. It was still alive and Bikkel squatted down beside it. "Poor bird," he whispered. "Does it hurt? I hurt, in my neck, but you don't die of that." Pasty-face stood next to him and said, "Be careful, I wouldn't touch it if I were you. It might be radioactive." Bikkel didn't hear the warning. He stroked the bird's head gently with his index finger. "A little pain won't be the death of you," he said, and while he repeated this over and over, the garden and the man and the bird sank away from him, and he breathed his last.

Hugo Claus (b. 1929)

in 1950 joined the famous group of artists known as Cobra, already well established in the art world. Claus is not only a renowned painter but also one of the most prolific playwrights, filmmakers, novelists and poets of the Netherlands. His short stories belong to the type one might call satirical surrealism.

Everyday there is a fresh supply of old ladies in the marketplace, and sometimes you can lay your hands on a fairly good bargain there. Then it's advisable to make a quick decision, for a good second-hand old woman is soon sold out. Those gentle handmaids must be treated well, not only because it's humane, but principally for the commercial gain. Those who don't obey the rules must face the consequences with a vengeance.

The Birthday Present

Lola and her little brother had been back from boarding school for a week, and one morning, when their parents were out visiting, they decided to explore the neighborhood. They knew only Dark Street, White Street, Orange Street, and Wild Men Street. They wandered into Saxony Square and looked in amazement at the marketplace, at the one hundred identical houses all painted pink, and at the gravel and the rows of white-painted trees. To Lola and her brother, so shortly (only a week) back from boarding school, it was all very strange. In the middle of the square stood a gentleman without arms, tummy or legs, with a friendly look on his face.

"That is the King of Saxony," said Lola.

"He is dirty. The birds poo on him," said her brother.

They walked hand in hand past the pink houses and looked in through the windows, but it seemed as though all the inhabitants of Saxony Square had gone away, for there was nobody moving about.

Then they came to a store which, although it was broad daylight outside and the sun was shining brightly, was lit by eight electric lamps. There was a sign in the window: DAILY ARRIVAL OF OLD LADIES.

Lola read it out to her brother (he was only five) and stood on the porch for a moment before going into the store. Her brother, slightly afraid, followed her.

"Good morning, Madam," said the storelady. She was wearing spectacles with blue-tinted lenses. "Can I help you?"

Lola asked if any old ladies had arrived yet today.

"Of course," said Blue Spectacles. "They have been here since nine o'clock. Fresh every morning at nine."

Lola and her brother followed the store lady into a beautiful drawing room, with red plush chairs that had smooth gilt legs, like the golden legs of young maidens. And sure enough, there sat the old ladies, smiling at them as they came in. Walking around the circle, Blue Spectacles said, "Here they are, Madam, all fresh this morning," and presented the first one: "Mrs. Pitt, who can tell you all about the fourteen-eighteen world war." Blue Spectacles walked on. "This is Mrs. Robertson, you must not take her unless there are dogs in the house. Do you have any dogs at home?"

Lola shook her flushed little head.

"Pity," said Blue Spectacles. "This is Miss Julie, who dirties her pants twice a day, but she does it ever so nicely, she sings while she does it, so no one will hear, and she sings, oh, so beautifully, better than Thelma Wietnschatt or Jenny Lind, but that was before your time. It's all jazz nowadays, isn't it?"

Lola said she didn't know, that she was only just back from boarding school.

"You'll find out soon enough," said Blue Spectacles, "but remember this, Miss, there's nothing can beat the classical genre."

Lola was dreadfully disappointed that Blue Spectacles had suddenly stopped calling her Madam, but she bit her lip and followed the Spectacles down the line of old ladies. Her brother came closer beside her.

"This is Mrs. Anicet, who could give you history lessons, though I believe her view of history and geography is partial and therefore one-sided. It's because she was in a Japanese concentration camp," she whispered into Lola's ear, raising her eyebrows and briefly shutting both eyes.

"And that one?" asked Lola, pointing.

"No, I can't let you have that one," said Blue Spectacles, with an apologetic smile. "I keep her for my own personal use. She does the housework, you see. Even the weekly wash. And she eats—oh, hardly anything."

"I should like one," said Lola, "who is a good cook and who can do the washing and the shopping and tell stories in the evening. Because it is really for my mama. It's her birthday today, and I would like to give her a lovely, a really lovely present."

"That's not true," said Lola's brother. "It isn't Mama's birthday today."

"What do you know about it," snapped Lola. "You're only five, and I'm fourteen. And you can't even read and write yet.'

Blue Spectacles seemed at a loss. "I'm afraid I haven't got one today that would suit you," but she added at once, as if remembering something, "unless you take Mrs. Nerciat. But do you have a room with green wallpaper at home?"

"Can she cook and do the washing?" Lola asked quickly. "And tell stories?"

"She can do all those things to perfection," said the store-lady. "Do you know Sir Andrew de Nerciat? Well, she used to be housekeeper there, and if that isn't a gold mine of stories, I don't know what is. But she must have a room with green wallpaper or green paint. I can't explain why, you're too young yet to understand."

Lola's brother started to snigger, but Lola ignored him.

"I shall see she will get a green room," she said, and gave the store-lady her name and address and the number of her identity card. Blue Spectacles promised to send Mrs. Nerciat's contract to her parents the following day.

"Nothing doing," said Lola's father, a few days later, when the novelty of the present had worn off a little and the family had already grown used to Mrs. Nerciat and her immobile presence in the wicker chair, where she sat peeling potatoes, grinding coffee, cleaning vegetables, darning socks, and so on. "Out of the question, that I should put green wallpaper in one of my beautiful rooms. Have you gone crazy? How much do you imagine I earn?"

"Oh, please, Hector," pleaded Lola's mother. "Please Hector, do it for my sake."

"No," said Lola's father, and that was that.

Mrs. Nerciat said nothing, but she slowly began to waste away. After a week she had already lost fifteen pounds, more than two pounds a day.

"How can it be?" lamented Lola's mother, and she was most put out, because she would never again find an old lady like Mrs. Nerciat, especially not as a birthday present.

"I can't help," said Mrs. Nerciat feebly, "but I have to live in a green room."

One evening, Lola's father came home with a story his brother, who was a gynecologist, had told him. In a factory in Lyons, women working with photographic plates, and therefore exposed to red light, produced incredible numbers of children, but when similar women worked in a calm, green light, the number of births became normal.

"What does that have to do with Mrs. Nerciat?" asked Lola's mother.

"One moment," said the father, and the children were told to get ready for bed. They could just hear Mrs. Nerciat complaining: "But it says so in the contract."

"Contract my foot!" shouted the father. "Who is going to pay for it?"

In the following days, Mrs. Nerciat became ever thinner and more yellow. Lola and her brother were very upset, for they were kind children and quite fond of the old lady, who told them stories at night such as they had never heard before, about a certain Sir Andrew de Nerciat, who did the most astonishing things. Moreover, since Mrs. Nerciat had come to live with them, they were no longer locked up in the wine cellar when their mama and papa went to the movies.

One morning, and this could have been foreseen—or at least something like it—the bars of Mrs. Nerciat's window had been sawn through and the old lady had gone, with all her clothes. How Lola's mother wept! And Lola's father swore and shouted, until the third-floor neighbor rapped on the floor with a stick.

Lola and her brother were sent back to Saxony Square. But the old-ladies' store had meanwhile been taken over by a fishmonger who claimed not to know where the previous owner and the lady with the blue spectacles had gone.

"You miserable skinflint!" Lola's mother berated her husband who, predictably, took it out on Lola and her brother. They were very glad, therefore, when in August they were allowed to go back to boarding school.

Frank Herzen (b. 1933)

educated as an architect, tried to live off his writing and is now an editor at a publishing house. He wrote radio and TV plays and a great many stories, many of them pure Fantasy. There is a Future-Fantasy, in which the setting is moved to far-off planets, but there is also SF which is limited to our own Earth and mankind as it is known to us. Many writers have occupied themselves with the question: What would happen if a highly developed species of animal were to dethrone mankind? Jonathan Swift as early as 1726 dreamed of a horse-society. But plants, too, are living beings. In The Netherlands the sundew grows and it eats flies. The next imaginative step is easy to take.

And Sundays a Piece of Meat

The street in which the house stood was located in one of the suburbs of the city. It was the last of a row of bungalows, separated from each other by wide strips of land. Behind the houses stretched the polders which until now had been spared from the slowly creeping blanket of stone which covered plants and trees, until everything died, asphyxiated under the heavy foundations.

Sometimes, when the gardener hadn't been around for a while, the grass would try to creep out from under the tiles again. But it only reached into sunlight for a little while. Then came the hoes and the long scraping instruments which purify the sidewalks and steps and leave everything clean and regular again.

There wasn't a lot of traffic in Mr. Van Dormolen's street. Particularly at night, it was very quiet in this neighborhood. If one walked into the polder for a little way and then turned around on the old dike to look at the city, it was like an underground fire in the opening of a crater reflecting against the black sky. And each Sunday night, when there were at least the stars to look at, there was that sound. The soft tones of someone playing an harmonica. It was a somewhat unreal sound, and a little scary. Certainly for someone who by nature didn't feel at home with the sounds around him.

"In their own country, in Brazil, they can get much bigger," said the fat shopkeeper with the red face. "This is only a small one; she doesn't want to grow at all here, by the way. I think it's the climate. You can find them on the upper Amazon; that's where this one came from, too."

He bent forward to the customer and lowered his voice a little as if he were disclosing a great secret and didn't want to awaken his conscience.

"They're meat-eaters, holy plants; the Indians are supposed to bring them offerings. It's actually deadly dangerous—something like that in my shop."

He was panting a little, and his eyes became smaller. Then his mouth grew somewhat sad, and his tongue glided across his fat lips.

"Its Latin name is *oleandra carnivorum humanica*," he said softly. "I feed her dried flies and maggots. But it's quite a job to keep up with. And she doesn't want to grow much. Maybe I'm doing it wrong. It would be worth a lot to me to get rid of it. But who would want a thing like this?" He looked sadder yet and was silent for a while. The sound of traffic penetrated vaguely through the big shop window.

"Besides," the dealer said, "I am only borrowing her. An acquaintance who went on another expedition brought her here. If I would take care of it for a while. That was six years ago. And he never came back." The fat dealer shrugged his shoulders. "Well," he said, "as far as I'm concerned they can take her away for nothing. As long as I get rid of the bitch." He looked at the plant again, put his hand through his shirt in front and scratched himself for a long time. The nails scratched the flesh and the hair on his chest. "That piece of trash," he whispered, "it makes me itch all the time."

The customer looked at the small, light-blue plant which stood in the window of the flower shop. She looked most like a bromeliad, he thought. The tough leaves grew in a crown around each other from the sturdy base. The round opening the leaves formed in the center of the plant was closed off by a layer of white hairs like mold, the plant's mouth. When he bent over he smelled the sweet, nauseating scent that rose from the heart of the plant. It stimulated his mucus membranes as if he were thirsty. He rose again from his squat and looked at the shopkeeper. "I'll take her," he said pointing at the oleandra. "Maybe I can get her to grow bigger. I could try in any case. I have quite some experience with plants, you know." He nodded and rubbed his mouth with the back of his hand. "You have to have something to care for," he said, almost apologizing. "And in a good spot it might turn into something, I think."

The fat shopkeeper had risen from his sad position. He said nothing. Then he grabbed under the counter, took the plant from the window and put her carefully, taking pains not to touch the leaves, into the cardboard box which he closed and pushed over to the customer.

"Sir," he said, "there you go. I'll say she died. I don't have to take care of it forever, after all. I have something else to do, too. For you," he said, "no charge."

The customer picked up the box and already held the handle of the shop door in his hand when the fat man still shouted something after him.

"Only on Sundays, sir," he said, "I would always give her a little something extra. A few pieces of liver or a slice of pork kidneys. After all, you don't know with this kind, do you?"

The customer nodded his head. "I'll remember," he said. Then he closed the door of the shop behind him. The dealer watched him go while he pensively rubbed his underarm.

"Perhaps I'd have done better to tell him," he mumbled a little absentmindedly.

But the customer had already reached the streetcorner and did not look back anymore.

When he got home, the box with the plant clutched under his arm, he went around to the back. These last few years, Mr. Van Dormolen had always gone around the back way. That habit had grown over the years. Or, in fact, the years had made the habit grow. He would like to go in through the front door, but his wife didn't like him coming home with rubbish and going through the hall with it. She liked things tidy. That he brought things home, okay, but it shouldn't become a mess. When Mr. Van Dormolen walked by the side of the house, he heard her rummaging around in the kitchen. He should hurry. The table would have been set already, and he still had to wash his hands and clean himself up a bit.

Quickly he walked past the flowerbeds to the part of the big garden farthest to the rear. There Mr. Van Dormolen had his private sanctuary. It was hidden from the house by a row of small poplars and tall shrubs. Behind the trees a narrow tile path had been made in front of the shed, which was as wide as the whole garden. He had painted the front of it green so it wouldn't stick out. There were no windows in the front of the shed, only a door.

Mr. Van Dormolen carefully put down the box with the plant. Then he got out his keys and opened the door. He picked up the box, stepped across the threshold, and closed the door behind him with his foot.

124

The shed wasn't dark. Through large glass plates in the roof, the light shone almost as abundantly as outside. Particularly when the weather was very sunny. At night, when he was in the shed, he could turn on the big lamps fixed all around on the wall. Sometimes he would leave the light out and watch the stars.

The left side of the shed Mr. Van Dormolen had made, separately, into a large glass hothouse. There he practiced his favorite hobby, the cultivating of plants and flowers. In the hothouse, the various kinds had been arranged with neat name cards on little pins, stuck into the dirt next to the plant. A visitor could see at once that much care had gone into Mr. Van Dormolen's hothouse. And he was proud of it. He would guide them around and show them the different varieties. He knew how to impress them with his knowledge. One had the feeling of being in a botanical garden. There had even been a story about him in the local daily. That article hung framed between two glass plates, sealed by waterglass against the moisture, on the inside of the door of the hothouse. Everyone who visited had to notice. There was no way around it.

Mr. Van Dormolen put the box containing his new acquisition down on the cutting table. Then he put on a pair of thin rubber gloves and cautiously took the plant from its wrapping. He placed her in the soil in a large zinc tray, which he kept free of other plants. New acquisitions first went into this tray to get used to their new surrounding. Plants were like people in many ways. They, too, needed time to acclimate themselves. Mr. Van Dormolen had taken almost a year to get used to the idea that the shed was his real home. The house was his wife Helga's domain, all proper and pure. And in fact it was best this way. Nobody came to disturb him here. There was no irritating drone of vacuum cleaners. He was totally himself here, and he felt happy when he was at work in he shed.

Mr. Van Dormolen looked for a little shovel and dug a hole in the dirt of the tray. Then he took the plant and placed her lovingly in the hole which he then filled up with dirt again. With water from a little watering-can, he moistened the dirt a little. Then he took a step back. The oleandra stood just right. She would be fine like this. He thought she showed well, the pale-blue color of the leaves against the dark wall of the shed. He grinned to himself. This would become the showpiece of his collection. No plant had ever died with Mr. Van Dormolen. That would not happen this time, either.

Carefully, more carefully than before, he closed the door of the

125

shed behind him again. Then he slowly walked in the direction of the house. He washed up and sat down at the table.

"I have another new plant, dear," he said while he pulled up his chair and tucked an end of his napkin into his collar.

The extremely precious care with which Mr. Van Dormolen tended his nouveauté the first week pretty soon led to results. The oleandra seemed to repair itself as if from a serious illness.

Mr. Van Dormolen only kept partially to the advice of the plant dealer. He fed her fresh pieces of meat every day, instead of only on Sundays. He'd soon changed from liver and kidneys to pork, fresh pork, straight from the butcher. That was much better he found. And the plant fared well on it. That was clear. She grew more each day. Only the color wasn't completely pure yet. But Mr. Van Dormolen knew that he would manage to set that straight, too, if only he'd persist. Even at the office Mr. Van Dormolen was known to be persistent, a real worker. He was hardly at home anymore. Every evening when he got home from the bank, he would go to the hothouse first to see whether the plant lacked anything. The oleandra stood full and firm in the tray. The sweet scent hung always like an invisible haze around her. He ate hurriedly, hardly allowing himself the time to chew his food properly, and then he would disappear into the shed again for the rest of the evening. On the weekend, too, he was with the plant. His wife didn't say anything about it. Helga had never said much, by the way. Only that she didn't want that rubbish in the house. He should be able to understand that. A respect for one another's feeling and personal freedom were the first things that made a marriage healthy. She had the house, he the shed with the plants. They weren't in each other's way.

About ten o'clock the lights always went off in the house, except for the little light in the hall they left on. And he didn't have to disturb her when he locked up the hothouse and went to bed, either. They slept separately. Even when they furnished the house, fourteen years ago, Helga had wanted to have a lits-jumeaux in the big, luxuriously furnished bedroom. He hadn't objected. He had found it a little bit strange in the beginning, but later he got used to it. They weren't animals, were they, that did it every day? Mr. Van Dormolen had nodded. Good, Helga, he'd said, if you want it that way. They hadn't had any children.

When Mr. Van Dormolen entered his sanctuary that Sunday,

eight weeks after getting the plant from the dealer, he thought about these words.

Animals, he thought while he looked pensively at the plant, which now stood in the middle of the hothouse. He had given her quite a bit of space. He had rearranged the other plants a bit and made a red tile path around the tray, so he could reach it from all sides. He was very proud of the oleandra as she looked now. She had, in the short time she'd been with him, grown a lot. From the base to the line the crown of the leaves made, she was now already three-and-a-half feet. This enormous growth amazed Mr. Van Dormolen a bit. But on the other hand, he was glad that the result of his continuous care was so clearly visible.

He put the cage with the white mouse next to him on the floor and took off the black cloth which hung over it. With a gesture of habit he stroked his chin with his hand. I could have a try, he thought. Why wouldn't I do it, meat was meat, whether dead or alive. But fresher meat than this he would never be able to give her.

He put on the rubber gloves and took off his coat, which he hung on a nail. Then he bent over and picked up the little cage in which the mouse was locked up.

He was sweating. If this didn't succeed, all the work of the last months might have been for nothing. He would never be able to get the mouse out of the plant again without damaging her severely. Furthermore, he didn't much feel like grabbing around in the mouth of the plant with his bare arms. It would be like feeling the insides of a recently slaughtered animal. No, if his decision were a mistake, he could not start all over.

He thought of Helga's words again. We aren't animals, she'd said. In the muggy warmth that hung in the hothouse, the oleandra stood motionless, and waited.

Mr. Van Dormolen held the cage above the opening in the stem, and with one hand opened the little hatch. The mouse lost its foothold, and at first slowly, but then more rapidly, slid out through the opening. She wound up exactly in the middle of the layer of white hairs which closed off the mouth of the plant. She desperately fought for support, kicking her little legs. Then there was a short peeping, the layer of hair bent inwards, and she disappeared.

Then Mr. Van Dormolen heard the sound for the first time. Suddenly it was there. A dark sonorous grumbling which made the air above the plant and throughout the hothouse move. Mr. Van Dormolen stepped back. The sound was coming from the plant. It seemed to stretch itself. The leaves moved gently, and the tips curled themselves trembling. She changed color for a moment. At least that's what Mr. Van Dormolen thought. But it could have been his eyes. Or the sudden clearing of the sunlight that flowed in from above through the big windows and which enveloped the plant in a strange haze. Then the sound stopped, and it was just as quiet as before. He came slowly nearer. He stretched out his hand and touched the leaves. They felt rough and firm. The contact his fingers made with the leaf stirred up an odd excitement in him. As if he had eaten well and abundantly. Mr. Van Dormolen felt a strange happiness rising in him. The plant would not be bothered by the meat he'd given her. She had accepted it. Mr. Van Dormolen knew he had found a new love.

The oleandra had gotten so big now that she needed a new container. With sturdy oak planks he made a new enclosure a foot and a half outside the tray. He had dumped fresh dirt in it. Then, with the metal scissors he cut away the old walls. The roots were stuffed up so much in the tray that the plant itself pushed down the zinc as if able to choose her own space. The single mouse he'd given the oleandra the first time was not enough anymore by a long shot. Every day she now got a ration of ten. The pet shop had acquired a good customer in Mr. Van Dormolen.

The sonorous sound which the plant made each time he fed her did not scare him anymore. Only the intensity of the sound changed. It doubled, became almost a chord, as if someone were playing an harmonica softly. Each time he listened to it, he felt a strange trembling which groped in his insides like a searching finger: a signal which was lost in the complication of his thoughts. "You should see how big my new plant is already, dear," he had said to Helga. "I know it doesn't interest you, but you shouldn't miss this."

She had looked at him disapprovingly with her cold, sterile eyes. The frigid body stiffened and bent forward as if she wanted to push the words into his face.

"No way. In that dirty shed of yours? You should be ashamed of yourself to be rooting around in the dirt like a little boy and treating some filthy, stinking plant as if it were your child. It makes me sick."

Mr. Van Dormolen didn't reply. He'd expected an answer like this. That's why it couldn't hurt him. But the disgust was plain in his eyes, and he didn't talk about the oleandra with her anymore.

When the oleandra had grown so tall that it had become impossible to feed her from the ground, Mr. Van Dormolen had constructed a kind of scaffolding out of steel tubes. Around the crown of leaves, a wooden planking had been made on the tubes. A little ladder led up to it. The opening of the oleandra's mouth now had a diameter of twenty inches. The white mass of hair had thickened. It constantly swayed gently back and forth. It looked like grass at the surface of the bogs, flattened by the wind. The color of the plant had changed to a sort of cornflower-blue with purple ends at the tips of the leaves. The outside of the stem and the leaves had become hard, scaly, and a little flaky as if she had just gotten a new skin before losing the old one completely. He had solved the food problem by raising the mice he needed for her care. A large terrarium on the other side of the shed served as temporary housing for the mice. He supplemented her diet with large pieces of offal from the slaughterhouse, deposited in front of the shed by a messenger boy from the bank. After a while, though, the plant did not grow much taller. It seemed as though she had reached her limit. This phase, Mr. Van Dormolen knew, came just before blooming. But how would she bloom? He had no comparative material. In no essay had he been able to find anything about the oleandra. Possibly she would only change color. That occurred with certain primitive plants. And then there was the possibility that the plant would bloom only for a very short time, perhaps a night. If only he could be there then. He decided to pay still closer attention to the oleandra.

He thought about the problem while slowly climbing down the ladder to go into the house. He still thought about it after he'd undressed and was lying in bed with his eyes wide open, staring into the dark. She might need something else to get into bloom. What had the dealer said again? "It's a holy plant, the Indians bring offerings to it."

His thoughts whirled around. If he didn't move, he was able to hear Helga's quiet breathing. The sound attached itself behind his eyelids. In Mr. Van Dormolen's mind an idea gradually took shape. Vague still, but more clearly as the night progressed. He was awake for a long time. Chilly and alone in the tomb of the house.

In the shed the oleandra was waiting, as if making herself ready for her next feed. Her scent was stronger than ever. Large and mighty she stood in the diffuse light that fell through the windows.

That Sunday the lights in the house had been out for quite some time already when Mr. Van Dormolen closed the door of the shed behind him and walked to the back of the house. He turned off the light in the hall and tiptoed upstairs. Without making a sound, he closed the bedroom door behind him. For a few minutes he stood dead quiet in the middle of the room and listened to his wife's breathing. Then he walked over to the bed and looked down at her. From his pocket he took the bottle of chloroform and emptied it onto his handkerchief. Then he fell with all his weight onto her and pressed the cloth firmly to her face. His weight and the blankets on top of her body made her powerless. Only when he was sure she wouldn't move anymore did he take the handkerchief off her face and nose. He sat down on the edge of the bed and put the bottle and the handkerchief away in his coat. The night was clear when he walked through the garden to the shed with the limp body.

Mr. Van Dormolen stood on top of the scaffolding and looked down at the plant. The layer of hair in the mouth opening had closed itself and nothing indicated that the oleandra had accepted the offer.

Suddenly the sound came. But not soft as at other feeding times: full and heavy a dark chord rose from the inside of the plant. It was as if somebody was screaming in a tunnel inside a mountain and the echo was resounding a thousandfold against the walls.

But this was not the reason why Mr. Van Dormolen bent himself over the mouth opening of the oleandra. He was looking sharply at the layer of hairs. Then he saw it clearly: the hairs began to change color. At the edge of the circle a deep dark red was developing, as if the plant were filling up with red oil. The stain spread rapidly towards the center. The whole layer of moving hairs became one great red flower which gleamed in the light of the strong lamps like a large coral. An enormous drop of blood.

Mr. Van Dormolen had reached his goal. He stared fixedly and silently at the blooming oleandra.

The next day before going to the office, Mr. Van Dormolen visited the fat flower merchant. He looked well, he thought. He was

130

actually a very nice and sympathetic man.

"You should see her now," said Mr. Van Dormolen to him. "I succeeded. It was quite a job, but I did manage: Didn't I tell you? I have quite a bit of experience with plants." He smiled.

"I'm glad for you, sir," said the shopkeeper. "How did you manage?" he said, watching Mr. Van Dormolen.

He closed his eyes a little. Nothing but the joy of his victory could be made out in his face.

"I followed your advice," he said. "I give her a little something extra on Sundays. Every Sunday, a piece of meat. They're pretty big pieces now. She's grown quite a bit in the meantime. She's even blooming now. You never saw anything like it in all your life."

He reached inside his coat pocket and took out his card. He gave it to the dealer.

"You should come over," he said. "It's worth it. Come next Sunday. Then you can watch the feeding. I'm always home around three o'clock."

"I'll certainly do that, sir," the fat shopkeeper said happily, while he looked at the card. "I'd like to come by some time."

"See you Sunday, then," said Mr. Van Dormolen, and he went out of the shop into the street. As usual he was at the bank on time.

Kees Simhoffer (b. 1934)

writes in an ornate, sometimes baroque prose. He is a virtuoso with language, using original images and sustaining remarkable fantasies with his powerful imagination.

Many people don't agree with the institution of death. But nothing has been done against it. In folklore and Fantasy, however, many attempts have been made to fight the power of destiny. Everybody knows that the body disappears, but a man's soul or spirit is invisible and there's nothing against assuming it can return. Sometimes the soul, in the guise of a dybbuk, is not able to find a new body to inhabit, and occasionally the spirit is still bound to the place of dying. When this happens, it is a frightening sight.

Death's Hat

At four o'clock, I take off my coat and whistle for the dog. My father is standing in the doorway of the shed, feeding the gulls. I stand behind him and hear the white trash screech. They're bastards, actually. Pigeons are much more beautiful. The old man used to keep carrier pigeons. As a boy, you had to sit inside the whole day on Sundays to time the things. And my father would stand in the garden cajoling when one of them came back from the North of France again. Sometimes a discarded champion would end up in our soup. Nobody knew that I dreamed about it at night. That I'd eaten the wrong one. The holy ghost is also a pigeon. Gulls aren't. They are the devil's messenger boys.

"Father, you should wear a muffler when you're feeding the gulls."

The old man turns around. When I'm seventy I'll look the wrong way, too, of course. Old people never look at you.

"I'm just going to walk the dog; I'll be back shortly."

My father wipes the breadcrumbs off on his old sweater. Since the time of my mother's death, the greasy thing has been hanging on his body. She knit it. If you don't wash a thing like that, it'll last you for years. You only wear out dirt. When he's dead, I'll bury him in it. God has to be able to see who he has in front of him. The old man drags on mumbling ahead of me into the kitchen where the dog is waiting for me with trembling jaws.

"When you're pissed off for one day, that dog has to go out all day long. How many times already today?"

Grumbling he puts the collar on the dog. That's *his* job. I better not say anything. You never give old people the answer they want. We only keep in touch via the dog. When I open the front door, the animal jumps up against me. He already went out ahead of me, into the garden, so excited that the snow is blowing around. His leash is pulling a line through the snow. Then, suspiciously, he sniffs his own tracks from this morning. My father comes after me, dragging his bad leg. With a muffler. "You talk about me. You'll catch your death of cold in a minute. You'll follow your mother before you know it. You have her constitution. Here!"

It is his own muffler. I tie the thing around my neck. The dog is scratching at the garden gate. My father swears I should wash him better. In contrast with the snow you see how filthy he really is. I let him jaw. The times he takes a bath, it's as if he has a white rash. Wears the same underpants for weeks. They're just like dogs. You tell from the smell how old they are. I hope he'll die when I'm not around. When I have to take care of his leg at night, I hold my breath.

I have hardly gotten outside before the cold draws tears from my eyes. If they freeze at this moment, there would be ice flowers on my retina. Those tears aren't real, otherwise they would offer a nice bouquet of grief. I have hardly walked a hundred yards before my ears are numb. The snow crackles under my feet. It makes a sound as if someone else is walking next to me. My father used to accompany me. All of Sunday afternoon, walking where he wanted to go. Now he has a bad leg Sundays are mine.

The dog has left the street already. On that side stands the old gas cylinder. Like an enormous hat it lies in the snow. The kind undertakers wear. The gas factory was bombed at the end of the war. The shell of it was left. The town council doesn't do anything about it.

They should bury all the dead in it. Then it would be of some use, at least.

And then they could saw a huge hole in the top, from which the souls of the dead could be launched. They could use it to advertise, too. Your last resting place with a view of heaven.

It always puts the thought of death in me, when I look at that gray tank. You're better off living next to a graveyard. There the dead keep up some appearance, with all the green. As a child, when I came in the neighborhood of the gas tank, I was scared to death it would explode. But now it's empty, no doubt about it. There must be a lot of deposit money on the thing.

At the end of the street my dog is waiting. He never knows whether to turn left or right. Straight ahead, on the other side of the canal, is Death's Hat. A bunch of gulls are flying around it, like the ring of a planet. They sit down by the hundreds on the edges and then start shitting down the side of it. When you stand right in front of it, the thing isn't black but broken out in green and brown. Black is a bad color for death. It fades, or it breaks out in green. If you stare at it long enough, it turns purple. White, that's a mean color. I only have to look around me. As far as I can see, the whole country is lying under that sheet of death. The inundated pieces of polder have turned to ice. No cow can believe in it anymore. A little further wild ducks are sitting in groups on the ice of the moat, frozen solid. No spring will arrive there anymore. I grab the dog's leash. It has gotten entangled between his legs from the running. He never lifts the good leg. You always have to pull him down first. He is my mother's dog. An old beast. He can never run for long. Then his tongue hangs from his mouth like parchment. But he still hears everything. Or he smells it, for he only goes to something if it stinks. He doesn't have a name, we always say: dog.

When my mother would play with him, she became young again. That was shortly after the war. That whole rotten time before, she stayed fit. After the war she collapsed. I don't remember anything about my father then. To me he has always been an old man. I have never seen him give my mother a kiss. I must have known the difference between man and woman then, but I didn't know what they did with it. I think I have always used my mother as an excuse for the fact that I had a father.

Everything that according to the books can go wrong with your lungs my mother got. She asphyxiated, according to the doctor. I only know she was blue when she died. After her death she turned white again. White is the color of death, damn it!

That snow here hurts your eyes. The dog pulls me onto the ice of the canal with his leash. He smells the ducks, frozen to their own dung. But I keep the leash taut. If he goes for those birds, the spell would be broken.

Snow and ice mean something magical to me, always have. Even though it never freezes in the Bible.

With the dog I walk in the direction of the tank. If there's any gas left from the war, he should be able to smell it. Those Krauts must have been dead drunk when they had the gasworks bombed. They could have put the gas to good use themselves. You can still see it on TV now. All those lines of people going into death naked: A film like that is now worth a lot of gold. During the war I had a forbidden friend. No child in the neighborhood knew he was a Jewish boy, but from a certain moment he walked around with a yellow star on. Later I did not see him anymore. Not a child in the street bemoaned him. Me neither. But when a dog in the street had been run over by a car, the whole neighborhood buried the animal in a box under a stone. There were girls who wanted to burn a candle on the grave.

Here on the other side you can only come when there's ice. The few workers' houses on the road to the old factory have survived the war. They still look alike. The people who lived there were all of the same family, I believe. Behind one of the windows, a red cyclamen is showing off. The little houses are still alive. The snow has been shoveled. The steps are a clumsy mosaic of broken flowerpots and pebbles. Kids have pried the stones loose and made little holes. To play marbles, of course. How old would those kids be now?

There used to be a retarded child living there who wore Manchester pants. With old suspenders used as a slingshot, he shot birds that only he could see, and then he said goddamn... with a double tongue. And every five minutes he had to pee against the fence of the gasworks. But he never had more than a few drops. When he was older he walked around our neighborhood with his fly open. When he wanted to talk to you, he got the hiccups. He must have gotten stuck in those hiccups when the bomb fell.

The fence is now rickety and largely derailed. I can step over it just like that. The gas tank is so close that you can distinguish the colors in the black and count the gulls. Old rubbish is everywhere. Unrecognizably maimed by the layer of snow. My dog pulls me through a ruined city with his nose to the ground. There are footsteps in the snow. Behind the factory area a freight train thunders past. You can see it from here. Such a trail of gray coffins they used to transport the Jews in during the war. The train gets smaller, the noise softer. The war had yet to begin for me. I must have been somewhere else with my head, because all of a sudden my dog is loose and shoots over to the gas tank. But a little farther on, he gets stuck on something with his leash. He hasn't been able to bark for a long time now. It is a dry moaning without an echo. He is pulling furiously on something. I walk over to it. It is a rusty piece of tube that sticks up out of the ground. An old gas pipe. With my shoe I kick the snow away from around it. Then I throw a stone in it, but I don't hear anything fall. How deep is it here?

"Cool it, stupid beast. That's gas you're smelling."

When I free him he tears away again and disappears behind the gas tank. That tube is at least a foot and a half above the ground. The devil's periscope through which he spies on us. If there's a hell, they should modernize the equipment from time to time. I walk to the tank. The gulls follow my dog in a long line. Around the extremely rusty barrel, there's a little fence. You can look through the chink from which the gas used to come up through the gas container. My dog is nowhere to be seen. The gulls are coming back. They hang around my head. You can tell something from the flight of birds.

One of them lets himself fall right in front of me. His beak is like a bent bloody nail. He returns once more to show himself again.

"Get the hell out of here, you bastard! You already got something from my father."

Above me I see the iron handgrips go up. The ladder God mounts to talk to the dead through the hole of the tank. If you look for a long time, you get dizzy, you see visions.

There's the dog again.

"What have you been up to?"

He stands in front of me panting, his tongue all wrinkled up. And with eyes that have seen death at least. I grab him by his skin that feels moist.

"Come on, we're going home. Or do you still have to go?" He understands that. An enormous tree like this he's never had before. I stand before it, too. When I see somebody pissing, I have to go, too. When I was little, I had a hard time keeping my pants dry if the tap was running.

I aim the yellow stream at the chink into which it disappears without a sound. If that precipice were deep enough, and I could keep it going for a while, I would extinguish the fire of hell. I should have peed in that tube. The dog waits patiently for me to close up my pants, then it suddenly huddles up against me. He is afraid of something.

When I turn around I am startled by a man, suddenly standing right behind me. In that snow God could follow you unnoticed. But then he's weirdly dressed. I haven't seen such a crazy old man in all my life. Stands there grinning at me like an escaped lunatic.

He says something.

"Your dog wanted to jump up against me, but I talked to him."

The worn coat must have belonged to a rich man in another life. Perhaps it was his.

"Excuse me for bothering you on your walk, but could you tell me where the entrance to this synagogue is? I walked around it already, but I can't find anything." His language is more expensive than his clothes. He is as skinny as death. His face a grayish wad of paper. He's talking about a synagogue. Then he is a Jew, or he's nuts.

"There is no entrance. Only for Jews. If you're a Jew, where's your star? Jews have to wear a star."

He has to think about that. He isn't even aware that I'm kidding him, or he doesn't show it.

And who guarantees that he's not kidding me? Something is going on with the gulls today. Maybe that guy is Neptune or something. The Manchester pants that spiral around his legs are much too long and turned up at the bottom. He is not wearing a tie. I don't see a shirt, either. His neck is a transparent white. He must be perishing from the cold. He has a broad-rimmed hat, but I only see that when he puts it on and points upwards with a maimed hand. Not one finger is complete anymore. Then the man must be real. Something like that they can only manage to do in a camp. A traffic accident isn't as subtle. He stays like that pointing up a little while where the gulls are screeching around the synagogue. He stands immobile, a prophet caught in his holy fury. But his voice is soft and tearful.

"Have you seen the birds, too? You know, they aren't birds, they're my friends who are waiting for me."

He comes over close to me. I notice that he is not very big. The brim of his that touches my neck, when he whispers to me:

"My friends were naked when they entered the gas oven. I saw it through the gate. Now could you tell me where the entrance is?"

Of course, he's nuts. Or holy. The god of the gas tank. If they knew at all at town hall what happens here, they would fix things up. There are tourist guides to Dachau too, nowadays.

"The entrance is up there, by way of the ladder."

Now I'm starting to freak out myself. That's because of the snow. Snow can make you insane.

"That I didn't think of. Jacob's ladder. Of course the entrance is upstairs."

He walks over to the fire escape. He's crazy enough to climb up in this weather. I have to distract him one way or other. Where is my dog? Don't see him anywhere. Probably, taken to his heels. He'll find his way.

"Don't you want to help me? I have a hard time getting over this fence here."

The king of Jews is actually trying to get onto the ladder. Before he is upstairs, he'll freeze. Then the council will have their war monument at last. I have to take him somewhere where there's no snow that's driving people crazy. It is almost dark. The gulls will leave in a while.

"I'll tell your friends you were here. Shall I take you home now? You're cold. Take my muffler."

He lets me go ahead when I open his collar and tie my father's muffler around his bony neck.

"Come along."

Now I am his ally. The people in the street won't be able to see who's leaving. I have to give him an arm, that's how weak his legs are. When we want to go across the snowy fence, he stands still.

"It is very kind of you to want to take me somewhere. But I don't live here. I took a train here."

Then he takes the black rabbi's hat in his hands and walks across the fence. When he's on the other side, he beckons me with an expression as if he'd just made it across the Red Sea. I bend over and write in the snow: Moses was here.

When I look around, the swarm of gulls touches down on the roof of the gas oven. They went into the oven naked. When I was young, I was taught about some bird rising out of its own ashes.

I step across the fence, which gives like a diving board. "The station is that way," I tell the man, who has put his hat back on. Then I give him an arm. The station is not very far. It is behind the gasworks. All trains pass by here. Between the houses the snow has almost gone. And there isn't such a cruel cold. The whole way we don't say anything. We both stare straight ahead of us. Two nuts taking one another in. It only takes five minutes.

At the station a policeman addresses me. He doesn't trust this situation.

"Who's that man?"

While I talk with him, the rabbi walks on. He crosses the square. Wearily, as if he had to climb a mountain. Jacob's ladder. I quickly make up a story that I have to take an acquaintance to the station. I do know him. I'm not lying. I have seen that freight train with my own eyes, haven't I?

When I cross the square, Moses has already disappeared into the station. In the hall I see him take a platform ticket from the machine with trembling scarred hands and walk over to the checkpoint. I hurriedly look for coins in my wallet. The machine roars and spits out the purple thing.

On the first platform there's a train ready. The station master is just about to raise his signboard. I see the old man walk alongside the train. He tries a few doors that have frozen and refuse to open. At the end of the platform, he squeezes himself through a door that can still be opened halfway. But he loses his hat. And what is a Jew without a hat?

The train is already moving when the thing rolls over the platform and comes to a halt in the snow outside the entrance of the station. The long caterpillar of the train is rolling by me. Most of its doors bear a red sticker: out of order. They said on the radio this morning it would be freezing ten degrees. In the south, fifteen to eighteen. That's where that train is going. I walk to the end of the platform. I brush the snow off the hat and put it on. The train can't be made out anymore. It must have passed the gas tank already. The gulls will be flying after it. Those bastards.

With the hat on I walk through the checkpoint. Nobody stops me. The hat makes you invisible. Now I am one of the chosen people. The road home is as long as a person's age. The wild ducks pull a long line along the horizon, still aglow from Sunday.

At home I first take the hat to my room. I have to save it. In the kitchen I take the pot with salve. Of course there isn't a clean roll of bandage.

When I come into the living room, my father is sitting motionless in a chair in his long johns and the sweater. He undresses in stages at night. For a moment I think he's dead. He doesn't move. Not when the dog comes up to me, either. But sleeping old people look like death. A little later he opens his eyes.

"Are you back at last?"

I roll up his pants. Wind the filthy bandage around my hand.

"First I'll do your leg."

The wound is swollen and purple and has gotten bigger again. I should pester him into a heart attack. Or let the wound go its own way. That's what he's waiting for. Then I can live my own life. And at the funeral I could wear the hat and never take it off anymore.

Raoul Chapkis (b. 1936)

whose real name is H. Brandt Corstius, is one of the most prolific columnists of The Netherlands, disguising himself behind a dozen or more pen names. In his spare time he is a mathematician, specializing in the science of cybernetics.

The world in which we live is full of contradictions. Nobody knows how the madness that governs our destinies came into being and is able to maintain itself. Raoul knows the answer, however. It's all about a little key which opens the door to the secrets of our planet.

A Little Key

Are you familiar with Monopoly? A terrible game, although with the Dutch version, at least you can, as you wander around Utrecht, suddenly feel at home on "Neude", "Vreeburg", and "Biltstraat". Monopoly ends when all but one of the players have gone bankrupt. This player then owns everything, although—considering the game doesn't cover salt mines and slave camps—the winner can derive only a moment's pleasure from it; the game is over and everybody moves on to Parcheesi or Scrabble. There is a chance, albeit a small one, that the game never ends and that two players are left, continually staying at each other's hotels without going bankrupt. I have never heard of that happening; most often the game is over in an hour or two.

The capitalist system, on which Monopoly is quite clearly a take-off, doesn't end that quickly. People who foresaw the end of that little game, like Marx, turned out to be wrong. But it does seem as though all of the speculating, merging, investing and consolidating ends up just like Monopoly: one man who owns everything. Now, you could claim that there is also a non-capitalist sector, but in this article I don't wish to involve myself in politics because I fear I would readily have to make some criticisms of our capitalist system, and I really wouldn't want American marines on my street. My only intention is to bring forward some forgotten facts that will hopefully serve as a warning.

By the end of 2048, it had gotten to that point. True, it wasn't one *man* who owned the monopoly, but it was one individual, a woman, Mrs. Patricia Nelson-Smith.

Mrs. Patricia Nelson-Smith, we must hasten to add, was a nice lady who really didn't abuse the situation. The accident I am going to describe, the effects of which you are at this moment experiencing, is not on any account her fault but must be regarded as a grave misunderstanding.

Private ownership of everything simplifies everything. In this way, Mrs. Nelson-Smith owned all the shares in all the corporations, and the entire stock market, with all its fuss and bother, thus became superfluous. She was the only one to pay taxes, and the tax legislation was entirely aimed at her. But don't be mistaken: this was not a question of dictatorship. Mrs. Nelson was a true democrat, and the elections were just as open as at present. Except the government could borrow money only from her, could conduct business only with her, received income tax only from her. All the money was hers; for everyday trade, people had access to handy stamps that you got free with every purchase at her stores.

Everything was headed towards gratification, and the only sound of distress you could hear came out of the little throats of newborn babies. Don't forget, this takes place in 2048, and everything had finally been arranged: world peace, spacious homes for everyone, every man with a couple of good-looking women, every woman with a couple of good-looking men, sherry from the sherry tap, Bach twenty-four hours a day on the Bach station, lumps of cheese for the taking, and beds everywhere. It couldn't have been better. And now a holiday was on its way, as well. Mrs. Nelson-Smith was, thanks to medical science which hadn't stood still in all those years, going to celebrate her hundredth birthday. It was to be a grand celebration! It wouldn't take place until 2066, but years ahead of time the largest university in the world had already received several million sheets of stamps for a leisurely study on how this unusual birthday ought to be celebrated. Neither cost nor effort so Patricia had said, were to be spared. It was to be a celebration that humanity would always remember.

Ah, but how terribly that wish came true.

The intellectuals had a great time thinking up festive ideas. Turning the Earth into a cube, to every inhabitant a free pair of wings, alcohol in mother's milk, a general summer vacation lasting fifty years, boneless fish in the sea, making twenty-five-hour days— what would it be? It became an historical pageant. And naturally, one commemorating 1966, the year of birth of the great benefactress.

This decision was made in the summer of 2050, and compliance with it was directly and seriously taken in hand. First, detailed information was gathered on what life anno 1966 had really been like, since there was no one who could still recall that. Fortunately, however, there were historical studies, films, and television documentaries which portrayed rather well those peculiar times. Neither cost nor effort were spared to make everything just the way it was then. Enormous bungalows were torn down and replaced by confining slum dwellings. The Amsterdam metro was replaced above ground by ridiculous-looking little tramcars. So-called "automobiles", that had made the streets unsafe in those days, were manufactured by the millions. Only bicycles were allowed to remain, since they were already around in 1966. However, the speed-chargers were replaced by the old biwinged jets (not a single museum could locate a working sample of the propeller-driven planes). Atomic plants were replaced by coal plants, the electric mole by the electric train.

At first, some wanted only Europe to be remodeled in the old style, but inhabitants in other areas of the world were so envious that Mrs. Nelson-Smith made a particularly noble gesture: she had all her capital, that is, the whole world, including all personal and real-estate property, made available. What a lot of hard work was done in those years! For the people, who had been put out of work by automation, it was a delightful change.

In Africa and Asia, especially, a lot had to be removed. Where there were cities and parks, they now rebuilt the jungles and deserts of 1966 with great care. The people didn't spare themselves, either. In fits of laughter they dressed themselves in rags, and even stopped eating for a time in order to develop that truly starved look. In Europe and America as well they dressed themselves in historical costume: the women covered both breasts, and the men wore "neckties". You know how wonderful it is to go camping and make do with minimal comforts? That's how people gladly huddled in their measly little houses, let themselves be pelted by snow and hail, descended into long-forgotten coal mines, breathed extremely toxic exhaust fumes—everything, just to make it seem like the real thing.

To stretch absurdity to its limits, so-called national governments were reestablished, and in a few countries that in 1966 were still monarchies, even kings were put on their thrones. In Holland there were quite a few pretenders to that role, but the person who was a direct descendant of the queen ruling The Netherlands in 1966 was chosen.

By 2065, the exterior of the world was just as it was in 1966. In the last year before the birthday, people ransacked all the libraries and destroyed everything concerning time after 1966. At the head of the movement stood the Minister of Psychological Warfare, Mr. Duinstee. In the course of 2065, this Mr. Duinstee got an idea that can certainly be called a stroke of genius. An historical masquerade, even if it took place on a world-wide scale, was naturally amusing; but wouldn't it be much more fun if the people who had jumped on the band wagon were really taken for a ride... I mean were true believers? The techniques of psychological propaganda had developed to such an extent that this was possible. Don't forget that Mrs. Nelson had all the means of publicity at her disposal. Patricia found Duinstee's idea marvelous and that very same month she bought up all the advertising space in all the newspapers; the editorial sections she already had. In this space she had the papers printed like those of 1965. At first, everyone really had to laugh at this whim of "the Old Lady", as everyone affectionately called her. Duinstee, however, perceived his work well, and by the end of 2065, there were only a few among us who knew that the world in all certainty was operating in the twenty-first century, that these crazy circumstances had been organized only in order to have a birthday celebration, and that the day after Patricia's birthday the whole world would reappear from underground hiding places. For, of course, we hadn't burned the valuable inventories, but had concealed them in hiding places that only a few insiders knew about. These shelters could be opened by only one little key. And that little key naturally resided with Patricia Nelson-Smith.

Everything had been organized so well that in May of 2066 all the inhabitants of the Earth were convinced that it was 1966. Nothing would, come the twenty-ninth of August of that year, keep Patricia the birthday-girl from seeing the world again as it had been on her day of birth. The true spirit of the celebration, so she thought, is not this successful masquerade, but the happiness of my people when they realize that it is a hundred years later and that the misery in which they are now is just a joke.

And she saw to the final touches in the country cottage where she had been born, now reconstructed stone by stone.

At the beginning of August, 2066, Patricia didn't feel well. She called a doctor who had unfortunately regressed to the 1966 level and who could, therefore, do nothing for her. "You are getting yourself too excited," he told the Old Lady, and when she went on about the wonder-serum that had kept her alive for so long, he thought she was rambling, gave her an aspirin and left the house. That same night she died. The little key fell out of her lifeless hand into a crack in the imitation bedstead.

That's why everything now is the way it is.

Isn't there anyone who can remember that it was a comedy, a woman's whim? Certainly, other than myself there are others who know it. But we are a small minority. No one would believe us. The others have remained silent because they don't want to end up in a loony bin. Some of the more clever ones have been employed by oil corporations and always drill right into a reserve of natural gas. No wonder, since they hid that gas there themselves. I will not remain silent, but speak the truth in this inconsequential little book. I could give more evidence, but why should I? You wouldn't readily accept the idea that you are playing a role in historic dress in a historical pageant. And if you do believe it, it would only increase the general dissatisfaction. For, it is one thing to have it bad because of stupid and backward ancestors, but it is much worse to have to blame one's awful environment on oneself. There's nothing to be done about it. The little key is gone.

The worst thing is, I think, that if our imitative labor is in fact good, and if the world we now see around us is exactly the same as a century ago, then in 2066—or rather in 2166—the same causes will lead to the same results: there will be yet another birthday, and yet another historical pageant. This article is really intended for those who are going to be organizing it: gentlemen, do think about what you have just read. You can take it to be true or not, but in either case: a little key like that can get lost easily, so have a few copies made.

Anton Quintana (b. 1937)

is a pseudonym for Anton Kuyten, who has earned a reputation as a writer of numerous TV plays, filmscripts, and hard-boiled thrillers.

A mirror is the entrance to an inverted world. Left and right change places. A man has only one body. But in the mirror it looks duplicated. Sometimes one is inclined, by regarding oneself in a glass, to wonder how many selves there may be and which is the real one. But what is real, when you think about it?

Reflection

It was one of those evenings when he wished he was someone else. His own thoughts bored him, and the books and magazines failed to grip his attention. Without interest he had watched the last TV program to the end. There was nothing going on in the world that he could get excited about. A war here, floods there, an epidemic in Asia, and a song festival in England—none of it meant a thing to him.

He lived his own dull life, buried in his books day after day, translating one bulky scientific study after another without enthusiasm. He was solitary by nature. There were days when he never left the apartment. Then he would putter around without changing out of his pyjamas and dressing gown—a middle-aged, unworldly bachelor with a pale, rather pasty face and myopic eyes. That evening he took a careful look at his face in the mirror.

He rubbed his unshaven cheeks and pulled the loose skin under his eyes tight. He had been young once, but no better looking, so there was little to grieve over. Despondently he drew his index finger down the brown scar on his right temple. As long as he could remember, it had always been there. As a child he had fallen against a hot heater, but the experience could not have been traumatic since he did not remember the incident. That was how he had got the scar, a straight line of brown wrinkled skin. He sighed and turned away from his reflection.

He was discontented with his face, himself, and his whole life. But he lacked the energy to do anything about it. In fact, he wouldn't have known what he did want. He wandered through the immaculate modern appartment and tried to listen to a record of a piano concerto he used to enjoy. But the music now seemed hollow and flat. In the end he switched the record player off, and then felt as if he were sinking into the cushioned silence, the result of double glazing and soundproof walls. He needed to be able to work undisturbed, but sound from outside would have been welcome now.

Uncharacteristically, he obeyed a sudden impulse and opened the sliding glass door that led into the garden. It could hardly be called a garden, since it was devoid of natural greenery. An artificial oval pond shone dully in the moonlight amid carefully grouped blocks of stone. The pastel-colored gravel beside the spotless paved walk had been meticulously raked.

Now he could hear the rustle of a summer breeze and the noise of traffic in the distance. His slippers flopped on the paving slabs as he walked to the marble seat by the pond. A dry leaf from the poplar beside the road blew over the high garden wall, which was decorated with glass fragments set in cement. It landed silently on the black water, making a circle widen across the surface. The single leaf bothered him. He bent down and picked it up. As he did so, the last trace of haze slipped from the moon. His reflection appeared surprisingly clear on the calm surface, as if it had suddenly floated upwards. He started, without at first knowing why. Then he realized that the reflection was grinning at him. It was a light, mocking grin.

What was the joke? He touched his face in surprise. Yes, he was grinning. Or was he? He looked down and saw his own perplexed expression. This was embarrassing. What was wrong with him tonight? He slapped at the water in annoyance, making it splash up. At once he felt ashamed of such uncontrolled and childish behavior. In a bad mood he went back inside and closed the glass door.

But, then, it had been an exhausting day. Tomorrow he would have to go on with a particularly demanding chapter on disorders of the nervous system in fresh-water mussels. He yawned and shivered. Had he gone outside without putting on a coat? The perfect way to catch cold. He would make sure to drink a cup of hot tea before going to bed. He felt more like coffee, but that always kept you awake.

He put the kettle on and brushed his teeth while the tea brewed. Then he sat down in his leather chair next to the gas heater, the china cup held delicately in his hand. Just as he was about to take a first sip, he saw his reflection, small and trembling, in the cup. He thought he detected that teasing grin again. Nonsense, of course. It must be the effect of the ripples. He'd blown at the tea first, hadn't he? Or had he? Why couldn't he remember? For a moment he stared gloomily into the golden brown liquid, then quickly raised the cup to his lips. The evening was definitely not proving a success. Why should that be? He didn't normally keep seeing his reflection all over the place: in the hall mirror, the pond, and even in a teacup! It was very strange. Had he been overworking perhaps? He didn't fancy any more tea and went to bed in low spirits. Lying in the dark, he fretted about the translation of a sentence he wasn't happy with.

"Some aspects of the morphology, ultrastructure, and histochemistry of the nervous system of the *Anadonta Cygnea*", he muttered.

He was almost asleep when he heard light footsteps on the gravel in the garden. He wanted to sink deeper into merciful unconsciousness but the crunch of footsteps kept him awake. All at once he was fully alert and lay listening. Silence. Had he really heard something?

Crunch, crunch. The footsteps on the gravel continued and came closer. He lay as if paralyzed. What was going on? There was someone in the garden! How was that possible? He had waged a long, exhausting correspondence with the building inspector before obtaining permission for that high wall round the garden. He must have his privacy. And now... there was someone out there!

He sat up in bed. Outraged and frightened. The footsteps stopped at the glass door. Had he locked it? This was what happened when you broke your normal routine. He never went out into the garden after dark. He couldn't have forgotten to lock it—surely!

He was straining so hard to listen that his head seemed to ring. Silence. And then the sound of the glass door sliding slowly open... Oh, sweet Jesus! He gulped for air. What should he do?

The footsteps crossed the wooden floor of the living room, agonizingly slow and menacing. He pulled the blankets up to his chin and shuddered.

This was no good. He had to do something! But he was no longer capable of moving. His eyes were fixed on the doorknob, barely visible in the dark. The footsteps stopped. The next minute seemed to go on for hours. Then he heard the door knob move. The door opened...

He tried to scream but could make no sound. He drew his legs up until his bony knees were almost under his chin and pushed himself back against the head of the bed. His face was contorted into a grimace of disbelief and horror. The door now stood ajar, and a white hand felt along the wall and found the light switch. Click.

The bedside lamp came on. It was enough. A high-pitched squeak came from his wide-open mouth. The man entering the bedroom was wearing striped pyjamas. He was middle-aged with thinning hair and a light grin on his pasty face.

It was as if he were looking in the mirror again.

The man was himself.

A moving reflection, one that had come to life and seemed to lead its own independent existence. The man stared at him coldly. Then he stretched out his hands like claws and approached the bed...

Now he screamed and managed to scramble out of bed. The man laughed, sat on the edge of the bed, and swung his legs over it. In one movement he was on the other side. His hands were unnaturally strong. Clumsy and awkward, he struggled with the man, but could not stop himself being slowly but surely forced out of the bedroom, into the living room, and on...

They fell against the heater, which fortunately had been cold for some time. To his own surprise, he tried to grab the poker, but the man kicked it beyond his reach with a laugh and dragged him past the open glass door into the garden.

All the time he was screaming for help with his voice breaking, but privacy proved to have its disadvantages. Nobody heard him. Now they were wrestling on the gravel. What did the man want with him? The other who was himself! The man just went on grinning, making his pasty cheeks quiver. The scar on the side of his head was brown and wrinkled like a withered leaf.

He lost his balance and went sliding through the gravel. With a chuckle the other followed and gave him a firm push while he fought to regain his footing. He tumbled over backwards into the water with his attacker on top of him. The man kept holding on to him. He panted and gasped as he struggled to break free, but the weight of the other dragged him down under the water once and then again. He screamed and swallowed water, but the white hands would still not let go. His back was pressed against the bottom of the pond. He saw the moonlight refracted in the swirling surface of the water and then the face of the other—*his* face, *his* popping eyes. The large head blotted out the swollen moon and everything went dark. He felt himself sinking with a last startled thought: I'm breathing water!

The first thing he felt was the chill that crept through his whole body and brought him back to consciousness. Why was he so cold? He reached for the blankets and touched his sodden pyjamas. At once he began to cough and shiver terribly.

He opened his eyes and saw the moonlight in the black pond, a couple of feet from his face. He was lying with his cheek in the gravel. He sat up in surprise. The soaking pyjamas clung to his shuddering body. He remained on his knees for a while. Slowly the realization sank in that he was alive and had not drowned. The garden lay silent and deserted. No trace of an intruder.

He must have dreamed it. A nightmare. And of course he had been sleepwalking, straight into the shallow pond. He got to his feet, feeling embarrassed but above all relieved. He hurried back into the apartment. A hot bath and a cup of strong tea with a sleeping powder was what he needed. His bare feet left wet marks on the parquet floor. He would have to polish it tomorrow, he thought with annoyance. What a ridiculous situation. He looked at himself in the bathroom mirror while the water ran. His scanty hair was smeared over his forehead. He looked thoroughly shaken. Just as long as he hadn't caught cold. He looked for a moment at his white face. There was something... something to do with the nightmare. But he could not put his finger on it, like an incomplete thought or a word that escaped him. Still shaking his head, he got into the steaming bath.

It was amazing what a hot bath could do for you, and the strong tea took care of the rest. He noticed that he was slurping the tea and felt something like affection for himself. What terrible manners! With a smile he looked into the antique cup and saw his reflection in the golden brown ripples. Motionless, he waited for the ripples to stop, the china cup held at arm's length. Then he saw it clearly and sat with a fixed stare while a cold shiver started at his toes and slowly crept up his back to his neck. The liquid moved again and the reflection was distorted, but now he had seen it. He knew now what had seemed odd about his reflection. Slowly, fearfully, he raised his hand and touched his right temple with the tips of his fingers. The skin felt smooth. The wrinkled brown scar was gone.

Then he touched his trembling fingers to his left temple. There he felt the scar.

The china cup smashed to pieces on the tiled floor.

Gerben Hellinga (b. 1937)

*has made a solid reputation for himself as a writer of thrillers of the Lew Archer
private-eye type. He is also one of the best-known playwrights in the Netherlands.*

*There is a story about a child, born of poor parents, who is destined to become
king of eternity. Nobody knows the truth behind this mysterious event, but it is still
regarded by many as the most important moment in history. It is commonly said
that history repeats itself. Hellinga's story deals with a recurrence of this birth in a
far future.*

King

The captain raised one hand, at which the sergeant who was riding behind him turned around in the saddle and issued a command
to the patrol. The men reined in their horses, spoke to them, and
patted their flanks until the animals stood still. The captain turned
his horse to face his soldiers, sitting erect in the saddle. Twenty
men, each of them twenty years old. The sun, which had risen
above the misty countryside only minutes ago, glittered on their
lances. The men, boys still, looked stonily and unruffled at the plain
that stretched below them in the depth, but the captain knew from
experience that this was an outward lack of emotion and that the
restlessness of the horses was due to their riders, who sat in the
saddle trembling with excitement. Before starting to speak, he exchanged a meaningful look with the sergeant, whose lips displayed
the hint of a smile.

"Bare your swords," said the captain as he stuck his sword in the
air, "and repeat after me: we, sons of the Human Race!"

"We, sons of the Human Race!" repeated his soldiers.

Their voices were echoed by the mountain sides surrounding the
plateau. E-ONS-F-E-MAN-ACE!

"Swear that our actions and thoughts in the land of Taboo..."

Again he waited until the soldiers had repeated his words and
continued:

"...will be born out of the will to defend the Race..."

"Defend the Race..."

"...and to keep it pure. The offspring of the War are beings we
neither hate nor despise. But we shall be merciless should they
threaten the Race."

"Threaten the Race."

EATEN E-ACE.

The captain sheathed his sword and swung his horse around. A command sounded and the squadron began the descent to the Land of Taboo.

The Human Race that lived in the mountains did not know how long ago the Big War had raged. Their ancestors had burnt all written records. For writing, knowledge, letters, and words had led to that total destruction, hadn't it? The Human Race, a nation of a couple of thousand souls, descendants of mountain people who had escaped the nuclear explosions and the fall-out rains that had destroyed the world, had returned to the essential things of life. They grew wheat and vegetables, raised sheep, chopped wood, and reproduced themselves. And they were soldiers. All able-bodied men were available to defend the Race at any minute of the day. They manned the watch towers along the borders—the points where the mountains passed into the plain—and every suspicious movement in the land of Taboo was reported. The whole country could be mobilized within minutes. The mutations were not agressive, but at regular intervals there would be nomadic tribes from distant regions trying to find protection in the mountains and the highlands also held a great attraction for mutated animals. Patrols were sent out periodically to gauge the mood in the plain and punitive expeditions were undertaken now and then. From their twentieth year, all male members of the Human Race were required to take part in these patrols. The captain and the sergeant had already led three generations through the Land of Taboo, and it no longer held any secrets or terrors for them. It was a different story for the young, inexperienced warriors. With pale, drawn faces they looked at the first mustard-gas rat that crossed their path and on seeing a charnel tree—a shrub composed of human skeletons clappering in the wind—a few soldiers had to vomit.

Towards midday they rode past a small lake. The captain brought the group to a halt and pointed at the mirror-smooth gray water.

"What's that?"

"A lake, Captain! Water, Captain!" There would always be a couple of boys who wanted to outshine the others.

"What can you do with water?" asked the captain somberly. Their enthusiasm wearied him.

"Drink it, Captain! Swim in it, Captain! Wash yourself, Captain!" The men laughed.

The captain signaled the sergeant, who had already prepared his crossbow. He aimed it and shot down a flying cow. The creature, no larger than a little dog, dropped at the feet of his horse. The sergeant took his lance, stuck it into the fat little body and lifted the animal. Some green fluid dripped on the grass.

"Have a good look," said the captain.

The sergeant immersed the lance in the water. The lake instantly started to foam. Small fountains spurted up, whirlpools churned and a voracious slobbering was heard. Thirty seconds later you could hear a pin drop. The sergeant raised the lance. A picked-clean little carcass was hanging from it.

"Predatory fish?" asked one of the soldiers.

"Carnivorous plants?" offered another.

The captain shook his head. "Carnivorous water."

Late that afternoon they reached the ruin of a castle. Behind the six-foot thick, crumbling walls lived a female mutation with seven or eight children, which she had received from roaming mutations. For over twenty years now, the captain and the sergeant had called on her on their trips and they had never observed the children to grow any older.

The female mutation spoke the Language. That was the reason they spent the night beside the big house a couple of times a year. They got information from her about the events in Taboo.

After the tents had been raised, the horses cared for, and the watches had been arranged, the sergeant rode to the ruin where the mutation was awaiting him. She was sitting on the ground in front of the entrance, a scaly, shapeless lump with a green face full of noses that always had a cold. Her children, some of them feathered, others with scales like the mother, all of them small and going about on four paws, were playing in the sand.

The captain, who had remained behind in the encampment, watched the sergeant being greeted with great delight by the little monsters as he threw them a handful of carrots and went inside with the mother mutation.

He did not return for an hour, when night had already fallen. There was a glow of excitement on his face when he entered the captain's tent. The captain was lying on his sleeping bag.

The sergeant squatted down beside him and said:

"Odd news."

"Bad?"

"Odd. She says: A child has been born."

"So?"

"A son of the Human Race."

The captain sat up and scrutinized his subordinate.

"In the interior, three days from here, two mutations have produced a child, she tells me. The baby is perfectly formed, without deviations, hale and hearty, with blond hair. 'A son of the Human Race,' she says."

The captain didn't speak for a while, rubbed his nose and asked: "Two mutations?"

"Third degree, I imagine, from her description. The mother is part-scaled and the father is a quadruped. He's got hooves and paws, but he speaks a few words that are related to the Language."

"A son of the Human Race?"

"And that's not all. He's a king, she says."

"A king?" The captain got up, threw aside the flap of his tent and walked outside. The sergeant followed him. "She told me a long tale, hard to follow, about a prophecy. A son of the Human Race would be born. A king who will reunite the people of Taboo."

The captain chuckled, but the sergeant's face remained grave. "She says that pilgrims from the farthest corners are traveling to the child's birthplace and they will change the world under his command."

The captain bit on his lip. "Madness," he said. His voice sounded unexpectedly hoarse.

"She says that everyone in Taboo has been talking about the impending birth for years, and tonight this prophecy has become a reality."

"Why didn't we know anything about it?"

"She says that we never asked her."

A soldier jumped to attention in front of them, saluted and stammered: "...C-capt-..."

"Not now!" But he saw the fear in the young man's eyes and asked: "What's up?"

"That sound..." said the soldier huskily.

The captain looked towards his men who had been lying around the campfire but had now leaped up, drawn their swords, and were peering into the dark night with every muscle tensed.

There was a noise closing in on them from afar. Creaking, grinding: crushing everything underfoot. An invisible mass was bearing down on the campsite.

"Walking trees..." murmured the sergeant. "Put out the fire!"

The soldiers beat out the fire with their coats. A brief silence fell, then the noise crawled away in a different direction.

"Walking trees?" asked the soldier.

"They can grow to a height of seventy to eighty feet. Stagger on their roots. When they're old, they turn suicidal, look for canyons and fire." The sergeant dismissed the soldier and turned to the captain, who was staring at the ground, frowning.

"What'll we do, Captain?"

The officer raised his head. "Can we find the location where the child was born?"

"We merely have to follow the mutations."

The captain nodded.

"And then?" asked the sergeant. "Kill him?"

The captain shook his head. "If it's a mutant, there's nothing to worry about. But if it's a son of the Human Race..." He made a magic sign, drew his sword and cleaved the air.

"When do we strike camp? Now?"

The captain glanced at the soldiers, huddling together in the darkness. "They're still too inexperienced for riding at night. Tomorrow morning."

The female mutation had mentioned a three-day journey, but she probably had hobbling and crawling mutations in mind. The sergeant calculated that they would arrive in a day and a half. En route they passed nomadic tribes, smaller groups that lived as one family and lone travelers. In the long run, the soldiers got reasonably accustomed to the moss-grown monsters, and all that still shocked them were the exceptional absurdities.

It struck the two officers how calm the mutations were. Normally they were always fighting among each other. Also, they were unarmed, whereas at other times they were always equipped with sticks, steel pipes and rocks. They sometimes produced a rhythmical buzzing that made the soldiers burst out in jittery laughter.

The patrol spent the night near a place where the mutations camped. After the tents had been raised and the duties shared out, the captain and the sergeant visited the improvised camp of the pilgrims. They had settled themselves among the remains of a small town. The female beings were preparing the evening meal, the children were playing between the ruins and the male monstrosities were sitting around in groups. No quarreling anywhere, no fighting anywhere. Just the sound of the rhythmical buzzing here and there. Flying cows circled over the site, lowing plaintively. The two officers walking their horses through the camp were ignored. "They're ignoring us," said the captain. The sergeant's mind was elsewhere.

"It would be better to kill the child," he said. "Whether or not it's a mutation."

The captain shook his head. "Think hard, Mato," he said.

He seldom called the elder man by his first name, except on very rare occasions.

The sergeant looked up, surprised.

"A mutation can never be king. Let them have their way. In a few days time, they'll bash his brains in anyway. Or a few years from now. But if it's a son of the Human Race, created through a regeneration process... Perfectly formed, unblemished, blond-haired... Do you believe in that prophecy?"

"A king who will change the world?" asked the sergeant. His lips creased into a dim smile. "No."

"I do."

They simultaneously reined in their horses and looked at each other.

"If the child is a Human, then the first part of the prophecy has already come true, that's why..." The captain tapped his sword.

They didn't speak for a long time. Finally the captain broke the silence. He pointed to the East where the sky sparkled with a golden hue. "A volcanic eruption."

The sergeant sniffed a couple of times and nodded.

"The wind tastes of sulphur."

By the next morning, they reached their destination. The lines of mutations had come together to form an unbroken flow, which ended in a winding valley, possibly the bed of a dried-up river. Some moss grew here and there, there was no sign of other vegetation. The mutations had burrowed holes into the rocky soil, and the female beings and the children looked for protection in them from the icy wind that cut through the valley. The male versions had gathered in groups around smoldering charcoal fires. The rhythmic buzzing resounded everywhere. The patrol, traversing the campsite, was completely ignored. The burrows were placed in straight lines, at regular distances from each other. Down the center of the valley ran a wide road that separated the camp into two parts. The

156

captain had never encountered a similar systematic construction among the mutations before. He cursed, yelled an order, and made the patrol break into a gallop. The squadron pounded and thundered down the central pathway. A few mutations, who hadn't been in time to jump aside, were left behind on the gravel, trampled. The path ended at a structure made of rocks that had been stacked on top of each other. It was fairly big, sixty feet long and about twenty feet high. Neither the captain nor the sergeant had ever seen such a house built by mutations.

The sergeant issued a command. The horsemen dispersed and surrounded the house. A second command sounded. The soldiers swung their horses around so that they had their backs to the house, took their lances in their right hands, stretched their arms, and froze in their saddles.

The buzzing had swollen to a vibrating hum that drowned out all other sound. Mutations crawled out of the burrows around the house, and a crowd started to collect. The soldiers stared impassively at the hazy, blue hills in the distance. Despite the overwhelming, numerical majority of the monsters, none of the men was afraid. After all, they were the defenders of the Race.

At the entrance to the house a feathered, possibly very old, male mutation made his appearance. He beckoned the captain. "Officer! Come!" He spoke the Language.

The captain and the sergeant jumped from their horses. The mutation pulled aside a hide hanging in front of the entrance and the two representatives of the Human Race went in.

At the end of the sizable interior, which was lit by a number of fires and filled to the brim with squatting figures, was a dais with a male and a female mutation on it. They were surrounded by a number of feathered, scaled and hairy monsters and a couple of quadrupeds that the captain took to be animal rather than human mutations.

The being that had called them in led them to the dais and uttered some sounds. The bystanders replied.

The male figure on the platform was a quadruped, with hooves and paws, but his face was identifiable. The woman had scales, the fairly sound face lacked eyes. She was wrapped in a blue piece of cloth that had a strange sheen in the wavering light. By their feet, in a wooden bin, was a baby.

The sergeant extended his hand, speechless with surprise. The captain held his breath, and his right hand slipped to his sword.

The child was absolutely perfect. He had ten fingers, ten toes, a little penis, a well-formed skull, even the earlobes weren't grown to the head. His eyes were closed. He nibbled on one thumb and kicked his legs.

It had grown deadly quiet. The sergeant drew his sword. "Let me do it."

"Stop!" cried the captain. The sergeant reluctantly stepped back.

"Are you the father?" the captain asked the male mutation. He recalled that the creature spoke the Language.

The being shook his head and said, fairly clearly:

"Nobody is father."

The captain pointed at the female figure.

"Is she the mother?"

"She is mother."

The bystanders mumbled. The baby bounced.

The captain drew his sword and took a step forward. He lowered the sword, let the tip rest on the wooden bin and hesitated a moment. Maybe straight into the heart? Just then, the child opened his eyes. He looked at the captain, smiled, carefully took hold of the sword and pushed it away. The sergeant cursed, but the captain looked at the child for a long time, and the child looked at him, then he lifted his sword and returned it to its sheath.

"When was he born?' he asked the male mutation.

"Two nights. Three days," barked this being.

"He can already see," said the captain thoughtfully.

"Could always see. From start," answered the quadruped.

It hadn't struck the captain until now how big and fat the child was. He had chubby little arms, rotund with lots of creases, and his legs resembled well-filled sausages. The face was framed by several double chins. The captain leaned forward, lifted up the child, moved him up and down and tried to estimate the weight.

The baby crowed and made a grab for his nose.

"How much does a newborn child weigh?" the captain asked the sergeant.

"Six or seven pounds," came his gruff reply.

"Feel this." He handed him the baby. "This one weighs some twenty pounds, at the very least. Don't you think so?"

The sergeant nodded and passed him back without glancing at the child.

158

"He can see, what's more." The captain wiggled his finger. The baby crowed and made a grab for his hand.

"You see? He looks at me. He can smile. This is a one-year-old child." He walked up to the mother and sat the baby on her lap. The child crowed again and said quite clearly: "Mommy."

"There you are!" said the captain. "He can talk and smile, he's as fat as a pig, and he was born three days ago. Stop worrying, the creature has nothing to do with the Human Race. First degree mutation, I presume. God knows how they managed to get it."

"You've got a beautiful child," he cried to the parents.

"King," replied the father.

"Yes, king," chuckled the captain. The sergeant smiled.

Things weren't to his liking, but he knew that the captain had never been wrong yet.

"We'll give it a present," said the captain.

He drew his sword, cut a gold button off his coat and placed it in the child's little hands.

The baby smiled. "Mommy," he repeated. The mutations shivered.

"Wise man. You," said the father.

"We wish you lots of luck," said the captain. "He's going to be a fine boy."

"King," said the father.

"Yes, king." The captain turned and walked to the exit.

The sergeant followed him. The mutations humbly made way for them.

"Grisly thought," said the captain while mounting his horse, "that a mutation can so strongly resemble a son of the Human Race."

The sergeant growled something and screamed an order.

The patrol left the camp at a gallop.

The king in the house crowed and accepted his dominion.

Paul van Herck (b. 1938)

is a purebred SF writer. His novel Sam, or the Pluterday *(1968) has been published in the United States, England, France and Germany. His SF radio plays have met with remarkable success.*

The mysteries in the Bible might be logically explained if we assume the existence of parallel worlds with changing time-schemes. What happens when the rain will not end and a man comes along who wants to buy your dog? You can smile about it, provided you don't know another story about a long, long rainfall many centuries ago.

Rain

It was seven o'clock in the evening. Dark clouds had been gathering all day, and the threat of a storm had hung in the air. There had been a distant rumbling since about five. Now the storm broke violently. Fierce gusts of wind tugged from left to right, making the telephone wires sing. Then the rain came. It fell at an angle, lashing into the eyes. Pools of water began to form; the flooded drains could swallow no more. Cars passed with their headlights on and sprayed huge clouds of muddy water on the pavements and each other.

At nine it was still raining.

Winters switched off the engine, wondered whether to chance it, and sprinted to the front door without locking the car. He rang the bell. When his wife answered, he was already drenched. He stood in the hall looking woebegone and watched the water drain off him to form a dirty puddle at his feet. He took off his coat, dried his hair with a towel, gulped down three aspirins, and gratefully drank a cup of steaming coffee.

"Not fit for a dog," he remarked when he was feeling himself again. "Any mail today?"

"No."

"No one came for me?"

"No. The office called. Nothing special. And..." She smiled. "Actually, someone did come. About half an hour ago. Wanted to buy our dog."

"What?"

"Yes. He offered two thousand dollars."

"The guy must have been out of his mind," said Winters absently. "Why?"

"No idea, I didn't ask. I got rid of him as soon as I could. He looked funny. Sounded like a foreigner and he was dressed very oddly. Oh, yes, and a beard. I didn't trust him for a minute."

"You watch out for these weirdos, dear."

"I know."

"Didn't leave his name, I suppose?"

"Yes, he did, yes. Noah or something."

Outside the rain poured down incessantly. The water was now halfway up the doorstep.

Jacques Hamelink (b. 1939)

writes in a carefully constructed style with remarkable flights of imagination. His stories can scarcely be brought under a general heading. Everything he touches is enhanced with the power of dreams in which every event assumes a symbolic importance.

In the land of fancy, called Glamorrhee, people lose their tails, shrink when they die, or participate in a game of unadulterated murder when the nights get longer and the mood darker. The horrors of Glamorrhee, however, are made more palatable by Hamelink's subtle irony.

Glamorrhee's most beautiful Woman

She is indisputably the most beautiful woman in Glamorrhee and in the whole world. Her body, barely clad, is faultlessly proportioned. Her legs are long, her back arched. Long golden hair dances around her face like fire. Exceptional are her breasts, superb her hips, everything about her is as perfect as an archangel. Her facial features are classical, severe, and yet arouse a hint of inexhaustible lascivity.

Only one small detail flaws an otherwise perfect appearance. On her left cheek, near the nostril, she has a small brown wart. Actually, it's not such a small one; in fact it looks like a rather large insect that has decided to settle down for good. That wart, that little thing, lends her face color, something cunning and wary reminiscent of witches and indeterminable age.

And once you have got that into your head, it also suddenly strikes you that her neck has wrinkles and is shorter and less aristocratic than is desirable. Her nose, her whole face, though especially her eyes focus cross-eyed on that wart. She *is* cross-eyed. The wart has also distorted her mouth; it grimaces a little. Is it because of the wart that her hair looks dirty, unwashed, peroxide blonde, like straw? Her bosom is cumbersome, a double bulging mass of fat. She has no hips, or ass, or thighs, she's made up solely of fat. Her stubby legs are crooked, she can hardly walk. When she speaks she lisps and spittle flies from her lips.

Cramps constantly wrack her face and entire body. It is plain to see she suffers from a horrible disease. She is a wandering, wobbly tumor, a pathetic sight. They say that when no one is looking she spits blood into her handkerchief and stinks from her mouth like a sewer.

To give herself allure she smokes, with awful distaste, a thick cigar rolled from geranium leaves. Her teeth are rotten.

She is a whore who stands on street corners baring her crack, wiggling her ass-like boobs for the benefit of a bunch of raunchy, jeering, scared-stiff boys. She swears like a sailor, and her foul mouth causes toadstools and cattails to sprout. Mushroom clouds billow wherever she walks. She is a witch, a monster.

She is, if you look closely, the ugliest woman in Glamorrhee and in the whole world. The strangest thing is that a second later you start having serious doubts.

The Man on the John

"Glamorrhee", I heard a man scarred by grief say, sitting on a pink porcelain toilet bowl in a presumably unbounded area, a hideously twisted, fleshy drainpipe joined to the small of his back, and discharging into infinity, "Glamorrhee", and at that moment his voice even sounded like infinity, "is the city in the shape of an ornament you can wear in your ear and through which you can hear the entire world. It is the city of violent, unsettled, doomed dreams. A flophouse for the homeless and for cyclofrenetic flights of fancy, as well as a roof for the night for tramp semen, de-braining experts, and other hard cores.

"Glamorrhee is the boiler room of the Devil. It's built out of nothing, out of sawdust, menstruation blood, leftover brain scraps. It is no simple Sodom. Glamorrhee is the greatest soap bubble human degeneration can still grasp. But it is merely a stage in the mental illness of the grandchildren who, at present, are being extorted by their mothers. And it is religion and nonsense, nonsense and religion, and beyond that nothing is known."

I heard him out; I knew what he said was the Truth and was deeply saddened by it.

Excessiveness on 491st Street

The most eye-catching thing about 491st Street is its excessiveness. What a waste of energy, say those living in the surrounding neighborhoods, what a power drain!

The people on 491st Street think otherwise. That's just the way we are, they say smugly, we are as we are; happy. And they give their houses mottos, such as "Here Lives the Happy So & So." All over the place, you find inscriptions like "This Is a Happy Street", "Only Happy People Live Here".

But that's excessiveness. It's just too much, it's overpowering.

Take a funeral on 491st, for example. It lasts at least three months, often five. People weep and weep and just do not stop. The preparations alone are incredibly elaborate. Apart from the funeral attendants, there are special masters-of-ceremony who also find themselves in a maze, groping along in an attempt to create order by reading at the top of their lungs from old law books or just plain newspapers.

Every regulation, each stipulation, thrives on excessiveness. Those on 491st Street cling to every part of the ceremony as if their lives depended on it.

Not until weeks after someone's death does anyone start making burial arrangements, but then excessiveness immediately asserts itself. One corpse is not enough. There are still so many leftover tears. And so members of the deceased's family are killed as well as their neighbors or someone who happens to be passing by. Then they start the whole preparation procedure from scratch.

In an orgy of remorse, their houses are torn down or burned. Each and every funeral oration goes on for days. Then the male company of mourners pays their traditional visit to a whorehouse, where the respective bonds of friendship are tightened. While in the brothel they actually take up residence.

During this period the women occupy themselves with the preparation of the mourning feast. This lasts for weeks and consists of, among other things, entire theatrical productions. The participants' hunger and desire for pleasure are insatiable. Yes, and then they must sleep, and their slumber is just as pervasive and violent. They sleep, to be exact, until another death has taken place, at which time they hurl themselves into the same frenzied degree of unbridled activity.

Where the dead are, in the meantime, is a question that cannot be easily answered. In any case, they are left behind during all the hustle and bustle, sometimes in churchyards, and are often put up in inns. If they run accross their neighbors, they are quickly wrapped up in cardboard and trotted off to the nearest free grave where the interment is held in all privacy and outside the confines of 491st Street. The excessors have better things to do.

Yet something else might be behind this all-pervasive excessiveness. What? Is it nothing more than sloppily concealed forgetfulness? I'm merely raising a question.

A Funeral

A funeral procession, and by no means a short one, makes its way down 666th Street, Glamorrhee's most prominent thoroughfare. Almost the entire city, young and old alike, follows with dejected faces as the hearse is being drawn by four horses adorned with mail chink and braided manes. Everyone is wearing his Sunday best, mourning attire that is, glistening black.

Halfway up 666th Street a scrawny white dog crosses the road— one of those obnoxious garbage can scavengers no one ever succeeds in locating the owner of. Right in front of the horses, he scampers off into an alley. In the horse's eyes, just discernible despite the black blinkers, the white lightning of panic flashes. All four of them rear at once, jerking the wagon as they make off at tremendous speed. The dazed procession stops dead in its tracks in front of the unbridgeable abyss which is opening before them.

The people scream, arms are waved. In doing so, one should remember how people are in Glamorrhee: Where is our welfare now, our dignity? These are considerations that precede or accompany public conduct. What is to be done?

The horses race, galloping madly towards Axinghead Square, but before they reach it the left-front axle of the carriage, which juts out quite a way, catches on the cornerstone of the last house before the Square. The bridles snap. Frothing at the mouth, the team of horses thunders into the Square.

The carriage flips over. The black shrouds fly into the air—the coffin smacks to the pavement, tumbles over, and in doing so the lid flies open. Those attending the funeral, who have since rushed to the scene, want respectfully to avert their eyes, but they are curious. Their stealthy sidelong glances glide towards the box.

Their eyes suddenly take on a staring expression. They turn

away from the coffin and gaze at absolutely nothing. Not a soul dares look at his neighbor. The eerie consternation which arises does not foster communal feeling. On the spot, the inhabitants of Glamorrhee become gripped in the throes of an unspeakable shame. Their deepest secret lies bared in front of them. Glamorrhee will never again be the carefree Fun City it was. The stench of disgrace suddenly smokes through the streets. People want to lay blame, to inveigh against, but cannot find the words.

The coffin contains no revived case of suspended animation. The coffin is empty. And the people of Glamorrhee know: their city, with all of its gateways and towers, is built on deceit and atrocity. Sweating in what are now highly uncomfortable clothes, blushing a fiery red, their eyes downcast, they clear out as quick as they can, slipping into side streets and alleys.

With sirens wailing, two fire engines come rushing to the scene. Anonymous, helmeted men bury the coffin, yank the wagon upright, gather the horses together who are grazing in a public garden, and take everything with them. Not ten minutes later, it's as if the whole thing never happened.

Such things happen often in Glamorrhee, but you cannot talk to anyone about it. A day later no one remembers a thing.

Shrinkage

Yet the average cause of death here is much more trivial, and for example in 900th Street, where I was born, not a single drop of blood is shed. In view of this, it remains to be seen whether you can actually speak about cases of death. That's how you can go from one extreme to the other.

It is common knowledge that old people start to shrink. People in Glamorrhee mature early, often in one day. So it follows that shrinkage starts early and advances rapidly. Body volume and height of adult Glamorrheeians begin decreasing quite visibly. They dry out. They shrivel up. Every slight breeze can crease, break, or blow them away—if they are not careful (which they seldom are: they don't say ''The older you are, the more you want to roam'' for nothing in Glamorrhee). If you cut them open, you'll notice they consist of a dry yellowish powder, like ground-up bones. They don't know what pain is. They have no desire to eat and drink and often lie motionless in a corner for hours where no one can step on them, or on a mantelpiece for example.

It is difficult to distinguish them as living human beings; something even close family members do not often succeed in doing as their disappearing bodies begin strongly resembling dried tobacco leaves, knitting needles, and the knotted ends of woolen thread.

My mother (one of my mothers, a coarse fool—which mother in Glamorrhee isn't one?) brought her fast-shrinking parents home so as not to lose them. Poor old Grandpa and Grandma! Within a day, they had slipped through the space between the floorboards and were not to be found, no matter how long my mother kept poking around between them with her darning needle.

In the end, however, she was successful, by virtue of her insane tenacity.

One day she did indeed scrape out a pair of frazzled balls of fluff with stems, which quite plausibly may have been my grandpa and grandma.

As is usually the case in the street where I was born, they were ceremoniously placed in a vase on the window sill among the other remains of a bone-dry past, in plain view of passers-by. Having intact ancestors enhances the family's respectability on 900th Street. This is probably the case because a heavy tax is levied on the vases that have something valuable in them. Only the well-to-do can allow themselves this luxury.

The common man just loses track of his shrunken ones, or at best packs them away in some forgotten corner among dead memories and dusty bottles. Death does not require many tears in Glamorrhee. Mourning and the clamor for funerals remain superficial. The dead are referred to with everyday expressions as rubbish or useless, though still somewhat decorative bouquets of old, dried flowers.

Bob van der Goen (b. 1940)

was also first published in Morgen. *For him, however, his debut was synonymous with a temporary end. When the magazine ceased to exist, Bob couldn't find any outlets for his ideas. Magazines can be useful.*

Life is getting noisier and noisier, and sometimes musical merit is judged by its volume. Silence is becoming a costly affair. Everybody wants a ruckus, but there are always heretics who want to live life against the grain. Nevertheless, heresy is dangerous—always, everywhere, no matter what the reason.

Sound

Korver hit the table with his fist.

"That's it, enough!" he shouted. "If you don't quiet down now, then..." A deafening drone made the rest of his words incomprehensible, even to the children sitting in the first row. It was the thirty-second airplane this hour to fly overhead. This time it was a Domberjet, one of the fastest planes technology had been able to produce, and recognizable by the penetratingly shrill sound that accompanied the drone.

"Eh, what?" said Rial, the pupil at the foremost desk, cupping his hand demonstratively behind his ear. The whole class burst out laughing. Rial kept on looking at him with his deceptively trustworthy eyes. He was the ringleader of the class, with the most innocent pair of child's eyes in the world. The calmness and matter-of-factness with which he perpetrated his escapades endowed him with the sort of natural authority over the class that Korver, for one, was sadly lacking.

He felt his rage ebb, making way for the usual dull resignation that was becoming second nature to him of late. Dutifully, he wrote on the board in big chalk letters:

I am	*We ams*
You am	*You ams*
He am	*They ams*

Ansje, sitting in the last row, raised her hand. Ansje, again.

"Yes, I know, Ansje," said Korver wearily, "at the other school you learned 'you were,' and 'he is.' But here we say 'you am' and 'he am.' To make it less difficult, since..." Fortunately, there was number 33 to wipe away his explication. It was difficult enough to make it clear to an intelligent child (the only one in the class) like Ansje, who had just recently come to live in the neighborhood, why he was satisfied at this school with merely succeeding to teach the children to talk a little and to put a few scribbles on paper—it didn't matter how. This just happened to be a school in the vicinity of the notorious X72 runway—although it had stopped being notorious long ago.

Several years ago there had been enough of a to-do over it, but afterwards everybody had had to put up with the inevitable. In the environs of the airports, houses had become cheaper, and so the workers recruited from far-off countries had moved into these residences. Opposers of this trend accused the authorities of forming ghettos from cheap foreign labor forces that were, on top of this, beginning to show signs of all kinds of psychological disturbances because of the constant noise going on night and day, while their children were mentally stunted to such an extent that they couldn't comprehend even the simplest things.

In using this argument they had forgotten, according to others, that these people had come of their own free will, that they had been rescued from starvation by our society, and that their children would otherwise not have been able to enjoy any education at all. It was a shame that their homes had to be fenced off with barbed wire and watchtowers, but unavoidable since these people displayed an abnormal aggressiveness. Fair enough, this might well have something to do with the unbearable noise; but, then again, they did travel by plane when they went on vacation once a year to their homeland, didn't they?

With his pointer, Korver indicated a pupil to read out loud what was written on the board. The one indicated, however, stared at him with an asinine grin on his face and started to bleat like a sheep. The only thing Dodo had ever learned was to imitate all sorts of creatures, and he let this be heard at both the right and the wrong moments. His classmates roared with laughter and thumped on their desk tops by way of approval. Encouraged by this, Dodo allowed himself to fall out of his desk and crawled on all fours in the aisle while uttering hoarse barks. And then he actually sank his teeth into another pupil's leg. Unhappily enough, this was Rial.

For a split-second, the classroom was unnaturally silent.

"Rial..." Korver started and not knowing what else to do, stuck out his pointer in Rial's direction as a warning. In a flash, the latter had torn the pointer out of his hand and was stabbing towards Dodo's face with it. It wasn't by chance that an eye was encountered by it, but—Korver was certain of it—it was the result of an intentional act. Dodo threw his hands up to his face and the blood dripped between his fingers. His wails had stirred the class into a state of great excitement. If anybody had an accident, the children considered it to be a kind of party, a welcome interruption of the lesson, from which they wanted to gain the greatest possible benefits. Since the unfortunate Dodo was now unable to defend himself any longer, the entire class threw themselves on top of him, shrieking. Korver jumped off the podium and kicked and hit the attackers wherever he could reach them. He grabbed Dodo and maneuvered him out of the classroom. In a glance, he saw the way Ansje was crying in the middle of the screeching children.

"That child doesn't belong here," he thought as he led Dodo to the first-aid room. Here he entrusted Dodo to the school nurse, who daily treated two or three pupils, victims of the aggressive bouts of their classmates.

Before he went back into the classroom, he spied through the barred window in the door (a simple safety precaution to avoid walking into an ambush). A few had gotten out their transistor radios from under their seats and were letting them blare at each other. The stations to which they were tuned replaced their music with an on-going, high-pitched sound, and the game now was to find out whose radio was the loudest. A sudden reluctance restrained him from sliding back the double bolt on the door and reentering hell. He snuck away to the faculty room at the end of the hall.

"Well-well, Korver, free so soon?"

It was his colleague Brukers, who was reading a newspaper in the faculty room. Korver emitted a hoarse sound and pointed upwards as a jet went over.

"I can't take it any more," he almost whispered. These words were naturally inaudible, but Brukers had acquainted himself with lip reading. He was a remarkably well-rounded person. Not only was he head and shoulders above the other faculty members at the school where education and literacy were concerned, but he was also the only one who had succeeded somewhat in keeping order in the classroom—this last without the use of force.

"I think you're good and ready to take a look at my invention," he said.

Korver rested his head in his hands.

"Thanks, but even with the best intention in the world, I can't get interested in anything whatsoever any more. At night I take my pills and then at least I'm deaf to the world."

"In this, you can," Brukers said with conviction. "Come with me to my place. I promise you it's something special."

Brukers lived on the twentieth floor. Before opening the door to his apartment, he looked around to make sure no one was there. A moment later, Korver knew why: his colleague had furnished his bachelor apartment rather strangely. To put it a better way: one couldn't talk any more of apartment, nor of furnishing for that matter. Bewildered, he kept standing in the doorway. All the walls had been torn down, leaving one space. In the center hung an enormous steel sphere on cables that linked the colossus with the corners of the room. Without saying anything, he followed Brukers up a rope ladder and stepped through a trap door into the interior of the sphere. Inside, a wooden table with an open book lying on it and a couple of chairs were all there was to be found—nothing else. Korver involuntarily sought for a steering lever with his eyes. It was obvious that his colleague had taken leave of his senses and in all likelihood now thought he had built a spaceship.

Brukers appeared to have read his thoughts.

"No, we're not going to Mars," he smiled. "We're staying right here."

He closed the trapdoor carefully and looked directly at his companion. Korver began to feel stifled. When the trapdoor was being shut, an almost unearthly change had come over the atmosphere, which he couldn't name but which coursed through his entire body. It had something to do with the calmness Brukers was radiating. Had Brukers hypnotized him? All at once, he recalled a moment in his childhood when he had gone to a church with his mother and the smile on her lips as she kneeled in front of the altar in the deep silence...

"Brukers!" he shouted. "It is quiet, it's quiet, goddammit!"

He embraced him and sobbed it out—like a school boy.

When he had pulled himself together again, Brukers brought out a bottle and two glasses and talked of how it had taken him twenty years to build this sphere. Everything had to be done with the utmost secrecy, since it wasn't allowed to make even the slightest alterations in the apartments, and he had no illusions about what the authorities would think of his experiment. After numerous failures, he had finally—together with an engineer friend—in the course of many nights, fashioned the sphere from a particularly sound-repelling material. He had managed to smuggle the colossus into his apartment in chunks. And now he was enjoying the absolute silence. Even the piercing sound of the Domberjet couldn't penetrate the sphere. He was a happy man.

When, after some hours, Brukers opened the trapdoor once more to let his guest out, a ghastly, piercing whistle bored into their ears. He immediately replaced the door again.

"You can't go yet," he said. "It's the penalty alarm."

Korver knew what this meant. Occasionally, as when an apartment manager had been beaten up by the tenants, a whole block would be subjected to the engagement of the "penalty alarm." To this end, the government had installed a kind of loudspeaker system through which tones intolerable to the human ear could be sent out. The tenants spun on the floor like bluebottles from which a child had plucked a wing, and screamed out as if they could neutralize the tones with the sound they were emanating; others lost their reason and threw themselves off the balconies.

When the penalty alarm was over, Korver went home and he felt so refreshed that he hummed to himself. His new friend had told him he could come back as often as he wished.

The nightmare appeared so fearfully like reality that he threw off his blankets and got up. He wanted to reassure himself right away. Over his pajamas he put on a pair of trousers and rushed out the door. The wind blew down the back of his pajama top and he shivered. The moon was mirrored a thousand times in the windows of the apartments. His friend lived two blocks farther on.

The door stood ajar...

The space was full of people. The sphere exhibited a gaping hole, and a couple of men in overalls were busy making the hole even larger with blowtorches. Brukers lay near the rope ladder. He lay on his stomach, and both the lenses in his glasses were shattered as if someone had stepped on them. A trickle of blood came out of his ears. Like a sleepwalker, Korver stretched his arms out to a man who was disinterestedly leaning against a wall smoking a cigarette. He looked as if he were supervising. The man looked at him. (The same open-hearted, childlike look as one of his students. Or was it he? Grown-up already?)

"You have destroyed the last of the silence," said Korver. "I will inform the police."

"We are the police," said the man.

Ton van Reen (b. 1941)

is not only a writer of novels, stories, and radio plays, but also a publisher who wages a courageous fight against the powerful conglomerates.
Witches have connections with the devil, and they belong in hell. Any woman who looks different is a candidate for a witch in the eyes of the watching mob. There were times when they were burned at the stake or drowned in water. Witches have disappeared, but the mobs are still watching.

Stars and Stripes

Alice had dozed off.

Her head lay on the base of the sewing machine. She was fast asleep. Now and again her shoulders shook, and the top and bottom halves of her false teeth clacked together.

No one else could have slept like that, but Alice could always sleep at the strangest times and in the most impossible places. Not so long ago she had nodded off on the subway. She was shaken awake at the end of the line by the men who cleaned the cars. They'd had a good laugh at her. The swine wouldn't even let her just go. They threatened to report her to the police. Then they got really nasty with her; Alice was afraid of the police.

Most of her experiences with men had been lousy. They always assumed they had a right to rage and curse at her. When she was very young she had wanted to get married one day, but that turned out to be a vain hope. Men treated her like dirt once they'd decided she was too ugly to occupy their bed on a regular basis, and after that she more or less gave up the idea of marriage. She could get along perfectly well without a man. She knew all too well that if she did ever get one, he was bound to be the type that would drink or beat her up from time to time or smash the place up.

But here, in the comfort of her own room, no man could bother her. She was free to drop off to sleep on the sewing machine if she felt like it. This was her own little world. No one else was allowed to stick his nose in here.

There was a sudden loud crash in the street outside. Alice jumped. Her head slid off the sewing machine base, and her chair nearly tipped over. The jolt made the bottle of oil for the machine fall to the floor. Luckily it did not break, but the oil poured through the neck and formed a puddle. Alice picked it up and threw a cloth on the puddle of oil. She was suddenly fascinated by the marvelous colors in the bottle. The light drew a sallow band through the oily glass ending at the red cork. Alice put her hand behind it. In places the red glimmer of her hand turned the yellow liquid orange. Through the glass her fingers looked thick and heavy, although she had lovely hands. She knew that. Any movie star would have been grateful for hands like hers, not to mention that cardboard girl in the Coca-Cola poster on the billboard across the street. She had often studied that girl's hands. She had fat, stubby fingers, as if the painter's brush had slipped when he was finishing off her hands. He'd made a much better job of the rest of her. Beautiful long hair, teeth like pearls, curving backside, huge breasts, and long legs. But the feet hadn't really come off, either. Her toes looked like chunks of sausage.

It was warm in the room. She was still a bit dizzy with sleep. She was often shaky after a nap, a bit feverish. She would have liked to go to bed but knew that would only make her feel worse. It was too hot to sleep. She could feel the sweat on her brow and wiped it away with her handkerchief.

A small spider crawled along the wall at eye level. Alice watched its progress. It climbed into a corner just under the ceiling where she could vaguely distinguish a web. Scores of small yellow spiders hung in a jungle of threads. She thought about destroying the nest, but she didn't feel like it at the moment. After all, she had nothing against spiders. They didn't bother her, which was more than she could say for people. So she decided to leave them alone. She wouldn't like it herself if people intruded on her territory.

She still didn't know what had caused the crash that had woken her up, so she went to the window. Passing the mirror, she glanced quickly at her face. A glimpse of white skin covered with speckles. She drew her head back sharply, as if startled by the sight.

She pressed her forehead against the window. So nice and cool. Glass was always cool. She could think better with her head against the window, follow things more clearly. The people on the street resembled animals with blinkers and feelers scuttling past each other. There was nothing very special to be seen, and indeed it was a perfectly normal weekday. An everyday mood prevailed, and there was little cause for agitation.

Except for the two men whose cars had collided and who now stood cursing furiously at each other. They went on yelling about damage to bodywork, the level of insurance premiums, and who was at fault.

175

Alice went back to her sewing machine. She had made a dress from the Stars and Stripes. The pattern came from a fashion magazine. She had tried it on at least ten times before she was finally satisfied with it. Sewing was something she knew all about. For years she had worked at a garment-maker's, doing all kinds of different jobs. She had worked at the cutting-table and later at the press. Each day she pressed a whole stack of pants. If she'd had a man, he would have had enough pants to last the rest of his life with what she pressed in a single day.

The dress was beautiful. The top half was striped and the bottom half spangled with stars. But she was worried that it might not suit her. There weren't many colors that went with her pale complexion.

She wanted to know what people thought of her dress. She put it on, made up her mind, and went out. The reaction was less pleasing than she had expected. People seemed to start when they saw her and walked past quickly. She felt they were running away. She wasn't hurt. She had long got used to the idea that people were shocked by her appearance. She didn't mind. No one bothered her, and these days that suited her perfectly. She didn't at all like people any more.

She turned the corner at the end of the street. The people coming towards her on the sidewalk turned their backs to her. They pretended to be looking at shop windows or went out of their way to give her a wide berth.

Two policemen on motorbikes came down the street. They wore helmets and leather jackets and were armed with pistols and night sticks. When they saw Alice, they halted and called at her to stop. They got off their bikes and came over to her.

"You know you're not allowed on the street like that," said one to Alice.

"Why not?" she asked in surprise.

"You're walking around wearing the national flag. It doesn't suit you."

"Lots of women wear clothes made from the flag." Alice tried to defend herself.

"That's true, but this is different," said the cop. "It's not so much the dress itself; it depends who's wearing it. In your case it's just not right."

"How come other people can wear this kind of dress and not me?"

176

asked Alice in amazement. "What's the difference between me and other women?"

"Well, other women mostly look like women, see? It's not a national disgrace to have pretty women walking round in the Stars and Stripes, but you—well, are you trying to kid me that you're a woman? If you want to know my honest opinion, you look like the devil to me."

The other cop laughed. People stopped to watch. There must be something special going on the way those cops were enjoying themselves laughing.

"I just made this dress today. I just finished it," said Alice. "I'd like to wear it."

"You'll have to take it off," said the cop. "We can't have you desecrating our flag."

"I'll go home then," said Alice sadly.

"No, you've got to take it off now."

"I can't undress in the middle of the street!" cried Alice indignantly.

"I don't see why not." The cop laughed nastily. "I'm ordering you to get that dress off immediately. If you don't do it right now, you'll be guilty of disobeying a lawful command. And you'll regret it."

Alice saw that he meant it. She didn't understand. The police were supposed to be there to protect people, not to make them look ridiculous!

"No," she said firmly. "I'm not taking it off. I'm going home."

The cop snapped his fingers. His colleague reached for his nightstick.

"Are you still refusing to take that dress off?" asked the cop.

Alice didn't answer. She made a run for it, but she didn't get far. Someone stuck out a leg and she tripped and hit the sidewalk. She screamed with fright and pain.

"Pull the dress off her!" The cop shouted in rage. "We can't let her wear the Stars and Stripes! Look at the way she crawls along the street. Like an animal. And screaming like the devil!"

The other cop opened his knife and cut the dress from Alice's body in a few strokes.

"Will you look at those tits!" yelled a man in the crowd. "She's not even wearing a bra! That shows how depraved she is."

More and more people stopped to watch the show. They pressed together in a circle around Alice. All she could see was their legs. Creases in pants. Shoes.

"OK," said the cop with an air of satisfaction. "Now you can go home. We've done our duty. Don't you ever dare sneer at our country again. Next time we won't let you off so easy."

They left her lying on the sidewalk, got on to their bikes, and roared off.

Alice tried to stand up. It wasn't easy. She was in pain and felt she would die of shame. When she was almost up, they kicked her feet from under her. She cried. She had no idea how to stick up for herself against these people. She had always felt embarrassed in public. Now she was lying in the street practically naked she wished she could sink through the ground or die on the spot.

"We can't have this slut wandering the streets naked," said a man. The crowd agreed.

"Now if she was a movie star," said another laughing, "a good-looking twenty-year-old, like that Coca-Cola broad on the wall there... but an old hag with boobs that size! It's revolting!"

The others roared with laughter. Alice looked for a gap through which she could escape, but their legs formed a stockade around her.

"What about our kids?"

"What if they saw the shameless old tramp on the streets? We can't have that!"

"She acts like a pig."

"Look at the way she rolls her eyes!"

"It's a serpent! It's the Devil himself!"

"We should get hold of a priest," said a woman who was crossing herself continually.

They fetched a priest from a nearby church. He wore a black cassock under a stole of coarse white material. He blessed Alice and sprinkled holy water on her.

"In the name of God and the Holy Church, I call on the Devil to leave this wretched body," he said loudly.

Alice cried. She couldn't understand what was happening. She'd never had anything to do with the Devil. She had always done her religious duties faithfully, and had never committed a mortal sin. Every Sunday she had gone to communion, even though the parish priest had objected at one point. After that she had worn a veil in church and he had not said any more. Now she tried to speak to the priest, but she was crying so hard she could only stammer.

178

"The Devil won't leave her," said the priest, who could make nothing of the noises she made. "There's nothing more I can do. Maybe she is the Devil himself. Let us thank God for making him visible to us so that we can punish him." He turned his back on Alice and went off.

"You heard him," said someone. "The priest says she's the Devil, and we must punish her. We can't leave the Devil among us. We've got to fight him. That's what the Holy Church teaches."

"We'll have to kill her," said a man, rolling up his sleeves.

"Yeah," said the woman who kept crossing herself. "She must die! She's not part of Christ's mystic body that died for us!"

"Yeah, let's kill her!" screamed the crowd. Most of them seemed to find the idea fun.

Alice couldn't hear what they were saying. They were yelling so hard she couldn't understand. She had nothing to dry her tears with so she wiped them with her hands, leaving grimy marks on her cheeks. They made her look even uglier.

"Shouldn't she be tried in court first?" asked one of the crowd hesitantly.

"Are you crazy?" the others shouted angrily. "That's a waste of time. The courts only deal with secular cases. What's at stake here is our spiritual welfare. It's a religious matter. It's our Christian duty to drive out the Devil. You're not siding with the Devil by any chance, are you?"

The man was shamed into silence.

"If the Devil's inside her, she's a witch," said a woman.

"No. There ain't no witches anymore," said another.

"Sure there are. You'd be surprised. They got thousands in England!" the woman shouted.

"Maybe she's British," said someone else.

"Hey, are you British?"

Alice said nothing.

"How do we find out if she's a witch?"

"We'll have to give her a test."

"She's a witch. You can see that from her face. Witches are marked by God."

"Ask her if she knows the Devil personally."

"Hey, do you know the Devil personally?"

Alice shook her head. She had nothing to do with the Devil. What did they want from her? Why wouldn't they let her go? She wanted to go home, to be back in her room where she was alone and nobody bothered her. Why were they standing around her? Why were they yelling this way? She hadn't done anything to them!

"She won't answer," said the woman who kept crossing herself. "That's clear evidence. We should put her to the test, the way they did in the old days. We'll throw her in the river. If she floats that means that God is with her, and He'll spare her life."

The crowd yelled their agreement. Men grabbed Alice's arms and legs and carried her to the bridge at the end of the street. The woman crossing herself called on God to be merciful to them and to protect them from strange influences.

It became a regular procession. The news that they were going to drown someone spread like wildfire. Nobody wanted to miss the show.

The procession halted at the bridge. The men tied Alice's feet and hands. When she saw the water, she realized at last what they intended to do. She started screaming, but that only made the crowd wilder. She struggled and bit one of the men. So they tied the ropes tighter.

"Now you can see she's a witch!" screamed a woman. "She's trying to escape God's judgment. She's fighting like that because she knows she's guilty."

"Guilty of what?" asked a man who happened to be passing and did not know what was going on.

"Only God knows that," said the woman. "And it's a good thing that he keeps that secret from us. What kind of a life would we have otherwise?"

The men pushed Alice off the bridge. She hit the water with a thump and sank. She surfaced once but no longer moved. Then she sank out of sight for good.

The people went on staring at the water for hours.

Peter Cuijpers (b. 1944)

is a sociologist by profession. He made his debut as a writer of futuristic stories in the magazine Morgen *with the story* Hands washed in innocence. *Since then his reputation has grown.*

Cuijpers, too, is fascinated by the possibilities of the parallel principle in the technique of story writing. One moment in world history has been looked upon by millions as the most important event since the creation of man. And travelers in time will want to return to that moment, to find out how it all went precisely. In Cuijpers' version, it does not turn out to be a stimulating experience but for a different reason than one might expect.

Hands Washed in Innocence

There was prosperity on Earth in those days, and plenty of everything that body and soul could desire, following thousands of years when the sun, with its increasingly dangerous rays, unnoticed for ages at first, had decimated the human race. Women, and more often men, became sterile and died young without having procreated. The many millions who fled the solar system in despair, even less protected than they would have been shipwrecked on a raft, did not count anymore. The end of the human race had already been in sight, when at last the neutral gas that could be added to the atmosphere to absorb the deadly radiation was found and produced. It took three generations before enough of this gas had replaced nitrogen, and many centuries after that a last sterile remainder of mankind had struggled for its survival.

But that struggle was forgotten. Two thousand years had passed, two millenia in which a handful of strong, dark people enjoyed the possession of a small number of beautifully located cities and the wealth of a whole, nearly untouched planet. Even the joy in the possession of a great many daughters belonged to the past again. In a comfortable, peaceful existence Man explored the continents and the seas until nothing was left to discover anymore. He investigated the stars without ever feeling the urge to leave the comfortable Earth and he probed ever deeper the mysteries of his mind, until this, too, started to seem boring. But he stayed peaceful, Man, for he thought that it was supposed to be like that.

Certainly, there was prosperity and plenty for everyone; there was knowledge and safety. But in expensive living units Man was wasting away.

Then Eckmar II invented time travel. During his lifetime a statue was erected in his honor and within a few years the world knew a pastime—a hobby to one, a sport to another, a passion to a third—that spoke to everyone: traveling in time.

Eckmar II and especially Ina Rb wrote profound essays about the paradox of the anteriority of posteriorities and about the course of history as a result of infinitessimal probability calculations. Ina Rb, too, deserved her statue, for *Prolegomena to the Traveling in Time and the Heuristic, Mathematical and Logical Implications Thereof*. But in this peaceful time, among these pigeon-soft and tactful people, there was one person so impolite as to dare admit to not having read this magisterial work. A statue is of course a civilized solution in a case like that, but in the meantime the great majority of the time travelers knew no more than was to be read in the directions of their portable timeliner:

Thou shalt not kill;

Thou shalt not leave behind artifacts from thine own time;

Thou shalt not make thyself known as a time traveler;

Thou shalt not go into either the near future or near past (limit: at least two thousand five hundred years);

Thou shalt not procreate in a different time, nor respectively, be impregnated thyself.

Not a few had difficulties even with these simple rules already; but fortunately the last rule, which in practice was of course by far the most important one (because of the state of pharmacology at the time) was easily observed by men as well as by women.

Zeppo I, Groucho I, and Harpo Mx, three old friends, who, like so many people in those days, lived exclusively for their own sexual pleasure, were among the first time travelers. As a matter of course, they had heard of Eckmar II and also of Ina Rb—especially since not a single man can overlook her statue, so perfectly lifelike, in their place of residence—but for the rest they were not encumbered by any knowledge of importance.

One day they decided to travel twelve thousand years back in time to a country on the Proctor side of the formerly Catholic Middle Lake. Thanks to their convenient little language converters, they knew within a few hours that they had wound up in the province of Galilee of a large empire, called the Roman, and that the local population wasn't too happy with those Romans. There was an extensive series of fun to be had, and therefore they stayed.

Zeppo I, Groucho I, and Harpo Mx had learned one thing extremely well from their previous trips, and that was that the little primitive peoples from prehistoric times were almost without exception extremely crazy about the metal aureal, which they called gold or goud or money, a metal which the city laboratory could supply you with whenever necessary, free, and in any quantity required. So our threesome had brought masses of the stuff with them, in the form of vague coins with an eloquent weight, and discovered once more that almost all women, girls, and boys could be hired or even bought at a certain price. The three sprightly men amused themselves therefore supremely well, but this aspect is not to the point here any further.

Now they were lucky that towards the end of their stay in the capital of the area, Jerusalem, a public amusement took place. In their clothes, no longer too new-looking, and armed with the invisible language-converters (which had been applied surgically, by the way), they could easily pass for native merchants of comfortable means. Their gold took care that they needn't spend a night without company. Groucho I bought three women at the same time and still breakfasted alone because the ladies were too exhausted to get up; Harpo Mx had a satisfying relationship with all his boys, be it that he restricted himself to one at a time, but Zeppo I, with his preference for blond women with big breasts and long legs, was less happy because that type did not exist here.

Naturally he amused himself in spite of that, but still a feeling of dissatisfaction gnawed at his heart constantly. In the daytime he drank too much, and towards the end of his stay he even started to mix himself with local politics. Hormonal matters have been known to drive men into politics before, but, however it may be, it was a political issue that gave Zeppo I the idea he had been looking for and which would make his presence in this country and in this time somewhat more memorable.

On the day of their departure, there was to be a mass meeting at the marketplace in front of the temple. The area's governor would give a speech and who knows what else would happen? Zeppo I prevailed upon his friends to attend this local event with him. Countless superfluous gold pieces, which were of value here but not at home, burnt in his pockets, and he wished to spend them appropriately. Groucho I immediately agreed, yawning, and Harpo Mx stared dreamily into the distance, without even noticing that he was being asked something. But after Zeppo I had explained three times what he had planned, even the reserved Harpo Mx became pretty enthusiastic. He could always appreciate a good joke, particularly one as pronouncedly subtle as this one.

The governor's name was Pontius Pilate, and he gave a moving speech in which he announced his willingness to liberate one of the prisoners, after the free choice of the present crowd. Then he went on with an extensive argument for the liberation of one whom he called "the King of Jews", and against the liberation of an infamous tramp and murderer. Zeppo I nudged his friends, whereupon they joined the crowd, each separately, with a bunch of gold pieces within reach.

"Whom do you want to be free," Pilate asked with a broken voice, at the end of his passionate speech, "Barabbas or Jesus?"

The hundreds on the square had no doubt and didn't even listen to the strategically placed high priests among them, who expressed a different opinion.

"Jesus of Nazareth must be free," they called out, as one. "Let Jesus free."

Here the prank of Zeppo I and his comrades began. Generously they gave away gold pieces—dozens, hundreds—aided in rapid tempo by the high priests. Again and again they repeated the same exhortation: "Ask for Barabbas! Ask for Barabbas!"

Within five minutes the shouts for Barabbas prevailed, and a few minutes later the name Jesus could not be heard anymore.

Grinning, Zeppo I, Groucho I, and Harpo Mx went to the edge of the city to return to their own time from a quiet spot.

"And what should I do with Jesus, the King of Jews?" they heard Pilate call despondently in the distance.

"Crucify him! On the cross with him!" the crowd jeered.

And they weren't even paid for that.

Eddy C. Bertin (b. 1944)

has been writing horror stories, Fantasy, and Science Fiction since he was very young. In a short time he made a name as the most prolific, boisterous, and fanatical fantasist in the Dutch language. He has published collections of stories and two novels which have been well received by the critics. He has also contributed to American magazines and anthologies.

Everybody knows that our world is not meant for eternity, but nobody knows, of course, how long it will last. Many people think we'll end in a big mushroom cloud, but even that's not certain. It's just possible, on the other hand, that at a certain moment a shabby, fat little man will pop up in some run-down bar with a mumbled message of doom. No doubt he will be mocked by all who hear him. Beware of fat little men. They might be more dangerous than you think.

Something Ending

"You don't exist," was the first thing the ugly little fat man said to me as I entered the pub. He was seated on a barstool which was much too tall for someone his size, and his short stubby legs in their wrinkled trousers dangled freely without even touching the floor. He could hardly be called an attractive specimen of homo sapiens. His face looked like a sponge, with flabby cheeks and slobbering thin lips. His deep-sunken eyes were blurred by the amount of strong drinks he had had, and in these he showed an amazing appetite for variations, as indicated by the outstanding series of different empty glasses in front of him, and which he refused to let be taken away. The barman was eyeing him with open hostility and annoyance.

He looked me over once more, nodded satisfied at his own reflection in the mirror, and repeated with more intonation: "No, you really don't exist." Satisfied with the approval of his mirror-image, he ordered another drink. There was no other place vacant, so I took the stool beside him, and since he made no gesture of buying me a drink, I ordered my own.

"You seem very certain of that," I said. Not that I cared very much what any fat drunk muttered to me, but I hate just sitting and drinking. I had been obliged to spent the evening in town, with no friends I cared to see, and no movie worth going to, either. In fact I had been preparing myself for a quiet evening at home with a good novel or maybe a rock-show on the tube, and a couple of good Napoleon brandies, when Vodier had called me on the phone, asking if I were at home that evening. This had immediately resulted in my stating that I had to rush off to an urgent press-conference in a couple of minutes, and wouldn't be home till the next day. Vodier was a nice chap, but he had the irritating habit of hanging around till the early hours of the next morning, and his conversational habits were limited to one single subject: himself. Since I knew Vodier was liable to drive over anyway, just in the vague hope that my conference had been cancelled at the last instant, there was only one thing to do: get out as fast as possible. Which I had done.

Maybe this weirdo would bring some amusement in an otherwise dreary evening, and since there seemed to be no free female companionship available in this pub, I might as well make the best of it. Ghent is a nice city to live in, but it hasn't much to offer as night life, compared to Brussels or Antwerp, and I didn't feel like driving another couple of miles to find another more interesting café.

The stranger shook his head pityingly, murmuring: "Poor, poor chap, so utterly convinced that he really exists, that he has real life, and what is he in fact? Phut. Nothing. Zero. A hole. A vacuum."

"Can't say I ever thought about myself that way," I said grinning. "Maybe my reasoning is a bit confused, but I feel my hands here, flesh and bone, and here a head on top of my body. *Cogito ergo sum*, I think therefore I am. More, I FEEL that I am. Seems quite logical to me."

"Bloody nonsense," he said angrily. "You only BELIEVE that you exist; there's quite a difference between believing and being. You have no real proof of your existence. You're just a dummy; you may as well believe me. Knowing the truth about oneself always makes one happier, or so I've been told."

I laughed. The funny chap had his voice remarkably under control, but he clearly was completely stoned. You don't meet them often that way and still able to talk.

"All right, I don't exist," I grinned. "So what next? What makes you so goddamn sure anyway? If I don't exist, then why are you speaking to me?"

He looked me over with what surely must be the special look he reserved for people asking insane questions. "I am speaking to you because I want to," he said. "Because nothing exists except me and what I want. You are here because of me, you exist because I want you to exist here and now. I would have thought that was very simple to see, don't you? Oh, go to hell! One can't talk with someone of your kind. You understand nothing, accept nothing, bah."

He rose and dropped himself from his high seat of judgment. He threw some money at the barman and walked away, without saying as much as good night. I concentrated on my drink and had two more, still thinking with amusement of the words of the funny madman. Then I drove home, got out and walked straight in the arms of a grinning Vodier, who had brought a crate of beer with him and kept me up till four o'clock in the morning.

The second time I ran into the funny-talking fat stranger was at quite a different place, at a charity ball of all things. It was one of those dry and hot evenings, which reassures you in advance that it will be raining like hell before the evening is done. The heat was unbearable in the dancing hall, and the fridge of the bar had chosen that exact evening to break down, so they had no ice cubes for the warm drinks. I decided to get a breath of fresh air on the terrace. And just guess who was standing there, his small hands on his back, staring up at the night stars? Yes, you got it right the first time. Mister You-Don't-Exist himself.

He looked over his shoulder as he heard my footsteps approaching and smiled amicably. He seemed sober this time.

"Hello, Mister Dummy," he said as a matter of greeting. "Made your mind up yet about whether or not you exist?"

"One day or other you're gonna get punched in the mouth if you speak to anyone like that," I said. For a moment I considered whether I should turn around and just walk away. After all he was no more than a bizarre but harmless weirdo. Still something about the fat little man intrigued me, and I decided to stay around for a couple of minutes. But he had already turned away from me and contemplated the night sky. He spoke again, this time more to himself, as if it where totally unimportant whether I listened or not.

"Nice shining stars up there," he said. "Specially the great sparkling one over there. You know, if I could stand up high enough and stretch my arms, I could just pick them right out of the sky. That specific star as well as all the other fake ones. It might convince you that I'm not crazy. And maybe then I would find out what's on the other side of that sky."

I shrugged. "Then why don't you just do that?"

He grinned. "It doesn't work," he said. "I tried it a couple of times, but they're faster than me. As soon as I stand on my toes, they just raise the sky a bit higher, out of my reach."

"So?" I asked. "First I don't exist. Now the sky is a curtain where you can pick the fake stars from. You do hold some pretty cranky ideas."

"Cranky?" He seemed shocked. "Wasn't it Shakespeare who said that the world's a stage? Or was that someone else? Not that it matters that much who said it, he or she surely had some idea about the truth of existence. But why am I bothering with you? One can't talk sense into an empty head. You're nothing, go away, shoo!"

"So, I am nothing. Well, just feel this hand. Feel the flesh, the muscles, the bones? That seems real enough to me. And you do hear me, don't you? So I can speak too."

He smiled, all sympathy. "You got me all wrong, Mister. I am not talking about your material body. Of course that exists, just as this terrace and these stars exist for the time being. A window dummy exists, which doesn't means that he IS. The ego, the mind, the 'I' which you call 'me', that doesn't exist. The material body you have, the street over there, they are for real, too, but only temporary. They're make-believes, stage settings, just as the whole neighborhood. As soon as I'll be gone, they and you will stop existing. It's all here, because I am here. There must be air for me to breathe, there must be a terrace since I can't be standing here floating in empty air, and since I feel like talking to someone, you are here. If I decided to go to China now, this Europe would cease to exist the moment I left it. It would no longer be needed, since I would have left it."

This was just too much, and my laughing exploded in his face. It wasn't very polite, I admit, and it even might have been dangerous. You never know with a crazy; he didn't look aggressive, but you never know. But then, I was bigger than he, and I was certain that I could handle him if he tried to attack me. But he didn't.

"That's a good one," I said after I had stopped laughing. "Well, let me tell you that I know very well what I've been doing those last weeks, and I don't recall you being with me then or being in the neighborhood where I was."

"Artificial memories," he shrugged. "They're very good at them. They just put them inside your head so that you would be able to play your part as true-to-life as possible."

"They did, huh? And the rest of the world, all those other countries? I suppose they don't exist now since you aren't there?"

"Quite right," he said as if stating an indisputable fact. "They're just illusions, make-believes created to convince me that the world does exist. Tell me, were you ever really there? In China or Australia, in India or in Hungary?"

"Well no," I said. "I haven't been there. I wouldn't know why I should go there. But there are photographs, films, libraries..."

"Nonsense, it's all fake. You know only that small part of the world or even of this country in which you are, here and now. All the rest you know only by hearsay. I tell you, there is no world, no other countries, not even a real sky. It's just a stage curtain. Humanity as such is a dream. The only reality is my own being, and the stage they erect wherever I go. And of course all the dummies like yourself who only come into existence whenever I am near. People like you, and taxi drivers, and barkeepers, and cops, and traveling salesmen and housewives... people..."

I gasped at him. He couldn't mean that, could he? If he did... well, I had met quite some weirdos in my life, but this one was really too much. He was ready for the men in the white suits to come and drag him away.

"The truth hurts, doesn't it?" he asked innocently. "But don't worry about it, Mister. After a while, you'll get used to being a third-rate character in the play I'm performing."

With these words, he turned and disappeared into the crowd inside.

During the following months, somehow or other, my thoughts often returned to the crazy little fellow. Strange how some crazies manage to sound too utterly convincing and logical, even while they're talking absolute nonsense. Like when he spoke of those other faraway countries which only existed on films and photographs or just because others tell us they do exist. But, then, in the little man's mind, all those others were no more than animated showroom dummies themselves, so it hardly mattered. Must be quite a frightening stage in his own mind, I thought, a world-wide theater in which performs one fat little ugly performer.

History tends to repeat itself, as they say, and so does this story, because when I met the stranger the third time, he was stone drunk again. It was in another bar this time, one which had chairs small enough for him to sit on with his feet on the ground, which was as well, since I doubt if he would have managed his balance otherwise.

189

I sat down in front of him, his eyes seemed more hidden below the ridges of fat than before, and he had to look three times before recognizing me.

"Oh, yes, it's you again," he said. "My own Mister Nothing. They must think quite a lot of your character for giving you three stage acts. Have a drink with me, since you're here anyway."

He seemed preoccupied and moody. We had a drink and then another one, but he didn't brighten. He did talk, however.

"I'm scared," he said in an appropriate stage whisper. "You see, I've started doubting my own existence. Suppose, just suppose that I, too, don't really exist? What if I am no more than one of the dummies, a walking-talking-singing-drinking doll with a set of false memories? What sense would the world have then if it wasn't made for me? What if it is made and kept in existence for someone else? I couldn't bear that thought. If I was sure, I would have to hunt and kill that man or woman. But who knows? Maybe I would then cease to exist completely, as well as the rest of the world."

"That would be some problem indeed," I agreed.

"And it's not that fantastic at all," he continued. "I know, I have always known that I exist. But how can I prove it to myself? There is only one way to go about it: catch them! CATCH THEM AT IT! But how? I've tried everything possible so far. I went somewhere and suddenly changed direction. I bought a ticket to Africa and to London. But they're so fast, by the time the plane got there, they had built Africa and peopled it, complete with animals and tourists, just like in the traveler's catalogues. And when I got to London, they had already gotten it ready, except for part of the Tower, but they had their explanation ready: the Tower was being repaired just then. Everything turns out to be exactly as in the movies and pictures. They're good all right! It's almost as if they know in advance what I intend to do, or else they're just too damned fast and good at stage-building. They're smart, and they know I'm trying to catch them."

"THEY," I said." You're always rambling about THEM. Who or what are THEY?"

"Isn't that clear yet? The builders, the owners of the stage, of course. They who hide themselves behind the sky-curtain, they who have built this world-theater and put me here in their play. You see, I think this is something like those intelligence tests they're always supposed to be doing with rats and mice and guinea pigs. They put them in a maze, and the food is at the other end of the maze. The guinea pig has to find its way through the corridors of the maze or it'll starve to death. Since the guinea pig has no gun to burn itself a straight way through the maze, it has to search, but at regular intervals they change the corridors of the maze, so the guinea pig has to adapt all the time in order to get to the food and survive. See, that's what I think I am. A rat in a maze, and they control the corridors. But I am more than a rat, I know they're THERE, and I intend to find out about them. I'm gonna burn myself through that maze in a straight line!"

"But why... would THEY go to all that trouble?"

"I don't know, but I have several ideas," he whispered. "Maybe all of this is just THAT: an experiment with a lower animal. A kind of reaction test. Maybe they just want to know how I'll work it all out, how fast I react to stimulations. And maybe... they're afraid of me. It isn't that silly, there must be a very logical reason for my being that all-important to them, to go to all that work and trouble. Maybe this is some kind of prison they've put me in, and they've taken some memories out of my mind, so I can't remember who I am or why I'm here. Maybe it's some kind of mental symbiosis: maybe they only exist because I exist, and MY being is their only reason for being. Maybe I'm a psychotic god, a lonely god, who has built a neurotic wall around himself and is now trying to get sane again. Maybe I even created THEM myself, so they could put me in their own play! As a snake eating its own tail. Maybe I am the one and only center of the universe, and therefore they—as my creations—are afraid of me."

He took a sip of his drink, and wiped his mouth with his sleeve. The drink was getting to him, his speech was becoming less clear every minute.

"But it'll be over soon now," he whispered. "I'm not that stupid, you see. I said I would burn my way through at them in a straight line, and that's what I'm gonna do. I've found the way to get them, the bastards!"

He ordered new drinks and bent lower so that I had trouble understanding his words. "I'm going to them damn stars," he whispered. "Sounds like nut talk, doesn't it? I don't look like a scientist or a spaceman, but I'm going anyway. Right through those fake stars, and then let them try to make a universe for me. I've been thinking about it for some time. I can't make a space ship, but if I'm that important, then there must be other ways for me to get out of their maze. I've built a ship. Well, no, not exactly what you could call a spaceship. It's no more than just a hollow sphere with a chair in it. I can seal it airtight from the inside, and I'm taking oxygen tanks, food and drink. Probably I won't even need any of that, if the powers I've tapped inside my mind work out as I intend them to. Because I'm going to do it with my mind and nothing else."

He patted his head, grinning. "Yeah, ol' man, inside my head, there it is. Inside my brain, all the power I need to get at them. I've been reading up on such things as telekinesis, the transportation of matter by mental powers. Enough to lift the sphere and myself up to that damn sky, and burn through it. If there is only one really existing mind, which is mine, then that mind must possess those powers. I'm getting out of here tonight. You're the only one who knows now, and you're just another dummy, after all. Now once I'm through their sky-curtain let them try to keep up the illusion. Let them try to create real space, real stars, out there!"

"It's crazy." I said. "You need a real spaceship for that, engines, computers, technicians. It's an absurd idea!"

"Course it is," he agreed. "That's why it's genius. They'll never think of it before I get there and see for myself! You don't think I'm doing this without some preparations, do you? I've been testing my mental powers for weeks now, lifting tables, opening doors without touching them. Then other things, more heavy. Then giving them speed, always more speed! Oh, yes, I'm certain it'll work as I planned it. I just... FEEL it. I set my starting date for next month, so of course I'll be taking off tonight! I'll catch them all right when they're totally unprepared for me. But I thought I'd have a couple of drinks first, to test my courage. It may turn out to be a long trip if they try to create the universe when I'm coming, and I'm pretty sure they'll try. Even if I manage to drive my speed up towards the speed of light, it's still more than five light-years to the closest star, Alpha Centauri. But I may encounter them sooner than that."

When I left him, he was still drinking and muttering to himself how he'd finally get them, the bastards.

About eleven o'clock, I saw his sphere rising from the center of the city where I knew he lived. It was just a small, dark ball, which rose hesitatingly above the buildings, but then suddenly picked up speed, floating faster and faster towards the skies. It looked like a toy balloon, getting smaller and smaller, but it moved in one straight line up. He was going to burn his way through all right, just as he had said he would. He had left earlier than he had said, but I had expected that, too.

I waited till he had left the atmosphere, calculating the orbit he would follow to get away from earth and then the trajectory he would be following in the years to come, beyond the outer planets and into the void beyond, towards Alpha Centauri. I had already set the apparatus, and the projections of the outer planets and the stars would pass off satisfactorily on his eyes. There would be no errors. I still had time enough to catch up with him before he reached his destination. After all, I would have to be on the meeting committee.

"Boy, do your best," I thought. "You've wasted thirty-seven years down here: you should already be in the second-stage for a long time. Why doesn't your mind work faster, better?"

It wasn't my fault, nor my symbiont-wife's; our genes matched perfectly. Our getting a retarded child was just one of those things, it happens sometimes.

But now he HAD to succeed. He had left the nursery now, and was speeding towards the kindergarten. By then he would have figured it all out, he would have to! If he didn't he would be considered a total failure. I would be allowed no more children, and he... he would be erased from existence. The committee didn't lose its time with the unfit for the universe. They will be waiting for him, when he gets there, at Alpha Centauri, and I will be among them, unable to help him. He'll have to make it on his own, my son. And, though retarded, he hasn't been doing too badly after all. It was fortunate that they had at least let me work on the nursery years.

He has made a few errors and misjudgments, of course. What infant doesn't? He had drawn the wrong conclusion also when he had said that the world doesn't exist. When I do something, I do it well. There IS a real world. Now I'm beginning to tear it down.

Julien C. Raasveld (b. 1944)

like Bertin, lives in Belgium and has played an important part in the SF movement
of his country. He has published numerous magazines in which he printed his
blood-curdling stories under so many pen names that even he no longer remembers
who was who.

Explorers of the future are still marveling over the mysterious life of insects.
Bees, ants, and cockroaches may well survive the annihilation of mankind, and
there will be plenty of time for an interesting experiment with those small, industrious and well-organized creatures. Spiders are seldom mentioned in this respect.
But why couldn't they be the next reigning species on Earth?

Braggin' Harry

I tell you I'm not crazy. It's Braggin' Harry you want. He can
confirm it – maybe he'll even take you for a ride in his Wonder Car.

Yes, yes, I'll repeat it once again, but this is the last time. How
many times have I told you, Doc? Seven, eight? Yes, yes, I understand – everything must be checked and checked again. It's not that
I'm rebellious, Doc, but I'm getting tired, so tired... You got a cigarette? Yeah, I know I mustn't – I've been told, but I would like a
smoke. My story, oh, yeah... Well, as I said before, it all started at
The Pint, my favorite bar. Also Braggin' Harry's favorite bar. A
well-known person, that Harry – not a bad guy, but can he brag,
man, brag! Well, that's why we call him Braggin' Harry, you see.
You know, the sort of guy that has the best of everything, can do
everything better, and knows everything best. Mostly we take his
yarns in our stride – we had many a good night with them. But the
last time... no, then he went too far!

First there was his new car. Wonder Car it was called. The first
time I heard about this brand. At the time I thought it was something foreign – Japanese or some such; those guys throw all sorts of
things on the market lately with a name that sits better with people
here. Well, Harry was braggin' about his little car, man. Oh, admit-
tedly, it was a nice little thing. Brightly red, all rounded with small
wheels and a glass dome that opened so you needed no doors. I remember someone saying it looked just like a flying saucer. Which
made Harry laugh and started him off on his theories about
U.F.O.'s. According to him, those things were real and came from
Outer Space to observe us. I decided to put a stop to his drivel.

"Soon you'll be telling us there's little green men in them, Harry," I told him.

194

"Possibly, but not necessarily so. Why couldn't beings from Outer Space look just like you and me?"

"You're dead right," I grinned. "I happen to come from Venus. Where are you from, Harry?"

He looked at me strangely. The boys were softly sniggering.

"You don't believe me, do you?" he said.

"But I do, my boy, I do. In fact, I know you're not really Harry, but a spider in disguise from Vega IV or somewhere in that neighborhood."

It was too much for him, you could tell. He was silent for the rest of the evening and poured beer into himself at a rate that should have made him see green-red elephants dancing a cha-cha-cha the next morning.

So it was a surprise when at closing time he proposed to drive me home. At first I tried to get rid of him, seeing as how much beer he must have had sloshing around in his body, but he insisted so persistently and looked so sober that I at last agreed. In the beginning everything went well – he rolled through the streets at a moderate speed and I'd already decided to make up to him by complimenting him on his little car, when it suddenly dawned on me that we weren't taking the right way home.

"Hey, Harry," I told him, "you're going in the wrong direction, boy."

He shook his head and explained, "This is a short-cut."

"You're crazy," I said. "Do you think I don't know this little town like my own backyard – you're driving in just the opposite direction."

In the meantime we'd left town. He turned into a dark country road and stopped. I started to be decidedly uneasy. Had he taken my little joke so badly that in his drunken state he wanted to give me a beating?

"Harry," I said with shattering teeth, "what in the name of heaven is wrong with you?"

His face was dark, darker than I'd ever seen it before. His eyes were two fiery black holes staring in my direction.

"Joe," he said, "how did you find out?"

"Hey," I stammered, "what...??"

"You don't have to beat around the bush. I know you know and you know I know you know, hmmm, so... start talking!"

"I don't understand. Are you feeling ill, Harry?"

At the time I couldn't have cared less if I'd had to walk ten miles to get out of Harry's Wonder Car. I was convinced he'd gone out of his mind. I shut up, sweated and hoped he wouldn't become dangerously aggressive.

Harry grinned.

"You refuse to talk? Very well, then I'll have to hand you over to the authorized people. We can't risk our presence here becoming known."

Then he did something to the dashboard and hop! We shot into the air. At that moment I must have lost consciousness, because the next thing I remember is that we raced at an enormous speed close to some stars. Stars bigger than our sun and frighteningly near. I tried to scream, to move, but found out I was held paralyzed in some way or other.

Harry didn't deign to look at me. Apparently he needed all his attention for the dashboard. While the stars flew by us, I again lost consciousness.

How much later I came to I don't know, but it seemed we neared the end of our voyage. A big, purple-colored planet, circling around an enormous sun, came up at us. A little while later we landed at something that was probably the local space-port. The dome opened, and Harry pointed a thing that looked like a weapon at my head.

"Get out," he ordered.

Apparently I wasn't paralyzed anymore. I decided to play it safety first and obeyed. We walked in the direction of a big spherical building and a circular opening appeared in a wall. I went inside… straight into the claws of two giant spiders!

It's becoming monotonous, I know, but well… when I regained consciousness, I was laid out on something that probably served as an operating table. I couldn't move or open my eyes, only listen. Well, no, not exactly listen, because there wasn't a sound to be heard. Apparently I picked up thoughts!

Something I recognized as Harry said: "Are you sure, Doctor Tssklt?"

"Absolutely, Ttksst. The Earthling knows nothing. Why on Pprrfss he said that is something I don't understand. We've registrated it, but there is no rational explanation for it. Apparently this is caused by an emotion we don't know about and so falls outside our scale of references."

"*Wit*, of course!"

"What?"

"That's what they call it. Sometimes they say or do something that is completely unreasonable, and then they laugh, which means they pull their faces in strange contortions and make some noise. They also call it joking. I've been there so long, but I still don't understand it."

"No wonder, such an idiotic life-form, and primitive, too. Hopefully the spiders on their world will have evolved in a couple of million years, then we can at least have civilized contacts."

"What'll we do with him? Will you keep him for dissection?"

"Well, no, not interesting enough. Bring him back, they won't believe him anyway."

How he brought me back, I don't know, but apparently they were right, Doc, because I can see no one believes me. You don't believe me, do you? Why don't you try and find Braggin' Harry? No, I don't know where he lives – no one knew. Ask around at The Pint. No Braggin' Harry known there? Liars! He was there every day! It's a plot! Maybe they're all agents for the spiders! Dirty spiders, you don't want human beings to find out, do you? That's why you keep me here! But I won't give in, I'll escape...

Aw!

Let go! Let go!

No! No! Not the electro-shocks again! Not the electro-shocks! I won't do it again, Doc, never again! Aw!

Please, Doc! AW! OUCH!

DOC!!!

Jaap Verduyn (b. 1945)

is a journalist. His first SF story appeared in Morgen. *Many writers who have since become known found the opportunity to make their debut through* Morgen. *Verduyn as well. Afterwards, in 1975, he published the novel* The Pentagram in The Tower.*

Time travel really is more difficult than you think. H.G. Wells, its inventor, had an easy time of it. Others have had a harder time. A time traveler, having altered only the minutest trifle in the fixed course of things and returning a thousand years later to his own time, may find his intervention has caused colossal changes because of an accumulation of sequential effects.

Timetravel is harder than you think!

"The thing works perfectly," explained Joris Fonteyn, not without pride, as he showed me the glittering, chrome-plated time machine in the workshop beside his house. "Yesterday I had a ride on it, and, as you see, I returned in one piece."

With expert fingers he uncorked a bottle of cognac, and before my eager gaze filled two glasses.

A sheepish look on my face, I stared at the machine that looked like a motorcycle without wheels equipped with a comfortable leather seat and a large number of improbable buttons, handles, indicators, small screens, and a mass of strange protuberances neither knob nor lever.

"Don't bother trying to understand any of it," said Joris.

He led me to his living room where he deftly made a fresh bottle ready for consumption.

"It was only a two-hour trip in time," he continued, "but now I know the thing works, I want to go a bit farther away next time."

"To that party last year? I wouldn't mind going to that one again myself."

Joris grinned at me amicably. "Well, brace yourself," he advised and then went on: "As you may remember from school, a few hundred years away from here lived dear old Rembrandt who, but this is purely my personal opinion, perhaps reaped more fame than he justly deserved. Just have a look in the Rijksmuseum: which painting receives the most attention from the public? Exactly, *The Nightwatch*; and *The Steelmakers' Guild* has cornered its share of the interest. I don't object to that at all; on the contrary, why shouldn't I try to get in on this tremendous admiration for Rembrandt? That man's works are now worth ten thousand times as much as they cost then."

Finally, through the haze of cognac, it occurred to me what Joris meant. I gulped a few times for air and drank another mouthful to get over my emotion.

Then I regained enough control of my faculty of speech to declare: "You... you mean you're going to go back to Rembrandt to commission a painting, and when the painting's done, load it on your time-traveling steam-cycle and then pawn it off for a cash-in-hand sum in the twentieth century?"

Joris nodded blissfully. "Precisely," he confirmed with satisfaction. "I imagine that Rembrandt van Rijn, for a handful of gold pieces, will do a nice bit of brushwork for me. Now, is that business, or isn't it?"

Well, it was business indeed; nothing could be more straightforward. You could say what you wanted about Joris Fonteyn, but he certainly could think! I, therefore, proposed a healthy toast to the success of his undertaking and felt a little giddy a minute or two later as we headed toward the workshop animatedly discussing the capital to be earned.

Joris was talking a blue streak as he threw his leg over the seat of the apparatus and cautiously adjusted the indicators on his instrument panel to the mid-seventeenth century: "It will take me some time to find Rembrandt at a moment when he's not engaged in a project, and once I've set him to work I have to move up to the moment when the work of art is done. But you don't have to worry about that. I will set the coordinates in such a way that I, regardless of the time I spend in the past, turn back at the very same moment I left. And now: farewell. I'll be right back, complete with an authentic Rembrandt." And with an expectant grin on his face, he pulled the handle of his time machine and at the same instant disappeared from my field of vision, for all eternity, amen, never to return.

For, something went wrong. Despite the fact that he had assured me that he would be back right away, his disappearance was not followed by the immediate reappearance of a satisfied Joris, with or without a spitting new Rembrandt on his baggage carrier. Before my incredulous eyes, the place where the time machine had been was entirely empty and has, during the three weeks which have

199

gone by since then, remained empty. In the beginning this didn't bother me much. "He might have set his indicators off a little and will probably pop up again in a minute or so," I thought. But the minutes became hours and the hours days, and I was beginning to worry. "This can't be a result of inaccurate adjustments any longer," I realized. "There's something wrong, but what? Has his time machine broken down along the way and is he now trapped between centuries, or did he reach Rembrandt but can't get away for one reason or another?"

With the best will in the world, I couldn't imagine what happened to Joris Fonteyn, and for three full weeks I racked my brains over this question.

But now, at last, thanks to an unexpected brainstorm, I have found the answer. For, this morning, when I was already half a bundle of nerves, and was pacing up and down Joris' workshop as I had been doing the past few days for lack of anything better to do, the thought suddenly struck me: "Damnit, that's it! If any trace of Joris Fonteyn is to be found, it must be in the work of the man whom he was going to see, the work of Rembrandt."

The next step took barely a minute. I dove into a taxi, and allowed myself to be driven with lightning speed to the Rijksmuseum. The driver looked slightly surprised when, in my haste, I let him keep all the change, and the doorman had a lucky day as well when I stormed through the turnstile after overpaying on my way to the Rembrandts.

Naturally, I had no idea if my sudden brainstorm would produce anything, and being nervous, I first ran to *The Nightwatch*. However, except for the usual throng of tourists, there was nothing to be seen there, and, to be honest, I began to feel a bit silly when the rest of the Rembrandts, including *The Steelmakers' Guild*, didn't offer me the slightest lead concerning the fate of my friend. I sighed deeply with disappointment and was about to turn around, crushed, when I suddenly stood stock-still in front of a remarkable painting. Hesitantly I took a step closer, and, as horror and satisfaction alternately struggled to get the upper hand, I started, absurd reaction, to chuckle nervously. For, Joris Fonteyn, God rest his soul, seemed to have succeeded all too well in his intentions to have Rembrandt paint a new canvas.

Except, no matter how beautiful the painting may be, I still cannot believe that—ever in his life—*The Anatomy Lesson* (in which under the interested gaze of a number of seventeenth-century students the already half-cut-up corpse of Joris Fonteyn stared out at me with dead eyes) was exactly the kind of work that the poor fellow had in mind when he was making his plans.

Patrick Conrad (b. 1945)

is a poet, prose writer, draughtsman, and filmmaker. He writes in a refined, somewhat archaic style and is a master of the shock effect.

The puppetmaster who inspires his own creatures with life is a well-known theme. Anybody who believes that a doll is a desirable woman must be mad. But what happens when his madness leaves a tangible product? A good story does not reveal the whole truth.

Allegria! Allegria!

July 4th

Antoine Depaepe closed his office window. As he did every evening, the 63-year-old office executive had been hanging around a little longer than the other clerks in the monumental room of the Ministry of Finance. It had been a busy day, and at a quarter to four there was still a long line of waiting people stretching out to the sidewalk of the Lange Nieuwstraat, in spite of the wind blowing among the high buildings and pushing dark gray thunderclouds across the city.

That day, however, Depaepe left a little sooner than usual, almost elated. For it was Musidora's birthday, who was turning thirty, the age women shine like ripe, juicy fruit, like perfect knick-knacks in their apartments, and they would celebrate that this evening true to tradition, dinner for the two of them, candles, a bouquet of tea-roses (her flowers) on the table, silver, and perhaps tangos on the radio, and afterwards he would undress her slowly and seriously on the velvet couch, carefully carry her to bed, and quietly lock the door of their bedroom. He reached the Meir, by way of Eikenstraat, where it was less crowded than usual, since many inhabitants of Antwerp were on vacation.

He'd seen very expensive boots at Cecil's, in yellow leather (her color), in the most beautiful material in the world, the softest. He could already imagine how delicately they would contrast with Musidora's black nylons—her little calves will just sing, he thought—while the shopgirl curled the ribbon around the long box with a pair of scissors.

On the way home he stalled for a moment in front of the windows of Innovation. Young men in white shirts and bare feet were busy changing the window display, deliberating with broad gestures, and the brightly lit, messy spaces were full of naked, bald manikins without nipples. "They should see Mus (he sometimes called her that in moments of great tenderness) some time," he thought; and in the glass of the window he saw his own lips move, although he never talked out loud to himself.

Antoine Depaepe had been living for years in a small apartment in Otto Veniusstraat, Number 7. A façade without style and windows that stubbornly keep the sun from entering. An elevator like a cage and on the walls, in every room, the same yellow-flowered wallpaper. Excited, he closed the oak door behind him, and as a rule he would have mechanically opened the windows a little to chase away the stale air from the dark room; but that night he went on tiptoe straight to the tall mahogany armoire in the bedroom, opened it carefully, and in the mirror at the back of the closet door the room swerved away and there she was silent, impenetrable, waiting, more beautiful than ever, Musidora, his love and his life.

Carefully he took her in his arms, stroked her yellow waving hair, kissed her long on her mouth, on her nose, on her forehead, whispered in her ear that he had bought a surprise for her and then carried her trembling to the front room, one hand between her thighs around her little ass, the other one around her neck, and put her down on the yellow-golden sofa next to the sideboard, arranging her evening dress, placed her right arm in the deep valley of her hip, and the way she was lying there, bestial and full of mystery, she was exactly the portrait that Romero de Torrès painted of her in 1921 in Madrid.

"Look, darling," he said, almost without a voice, and with his heart beating he showed her the yellow, supple boots, his old gaze full of hope. Will she like them? Yes, he could already catch a gleam of her deep, warm eyes. She appreciated the present; she beckoned with her eyelashes, and he knelt down in front of her, took her left foot by the heel, took off her light-green plush slipper and slid the new-smelling, crackling bottine over the nails (painted dark red) of her little bent toes, stroked her knee, kissed her thigh a little above the knee through the fringe of her dress and his wet cheek touched her hand, and it was as if she stroked his gaunt skull with her rings.

Antoine Depaepe had never been married. He had known two women in his life, Annemarie and Ursula, but his adventures had never lasted longer than one or two weeks. Ursula, whom he'd met through an ad in the newspaper in May 1938, he'd been in love with, he had even asked her to marry him rather quickly, one Saturday afternoon, while rowing in the city park; but she disappeared from his life noiselessly. Ursula was not what one would call an attractive woman, but Depaepe feared and hated loneliness. To have some company anyway, at night after work, he'd kept a gray varan for thirteen years, a beautiful, drab reptile, which would stare at the paneling of the ceiling, regal and motionless. One morning—he was about to feed the cold, lusterless animal its monthly live rat—it was dead, perhaps already for days. He had rolled the hard bastard in a piece of brown paper and threw it down the garbage chute, and immediately decided to realize his old dream and to order Musidora from America for $ 300. Three weeks later he had got a notice that he was to pick up a package at customs. It was the Fourth of July, and after carefully closing all the curtains at home, he had opened the crate feverishly and there she lay: smooth, undamaged in her black, tight-fitting suit, the black muse, Musidora, listening to the Invisible, the delicious vampire with the satanic, deadly look directed at Depaepe. It was like a birth, and he'd knelt down for her. This would become a habit later. He had shyly mumbled something, excusing himself vaguely for his shabby outfit, for the mess in his apartment, for the stale air that hung in the furniture. He had promised her with a deep blush in his cheeks that everything would change, that he would treat her like a queen, a star, that he would live in her shadow, serve her in silence, would obey her most outrageous orders.

The first week Depaepe did not undress his mistress.

The "Musidora doll", made out of a springy foam-plastic material as delicate as the finest oriental skin, was a miracle of imitation and automation. The eyes followed the moving object in the room, so that Depaepe, wherever he was, met her gaze, the gaze of Jeanne Roques, the gaze he'd met so often, when the Cineac had still existed in the basement next to the Century hotel, where he followed from week to week the series of vampire films: *Feuillade, Le Cryptogramme Rouge, L'Evasion du Mort, Coeur Fragile, Satanas*, and especially *Les Yeux qui fascinent*; he'd stayed three times around to see that, the most beautiful one of all, he thought. The doll's breathing could be adjusted from a distance, normal or panting, and in bed she panted with breasts rising like dunes and she moaned like a girl dying of pleasure, and her mouth opened then and the tongue rolling back and forth discharged a sweet, perfumy liquid tasting of anis. Hidden in a triangular, kinky black garden between the broad white thighs, the darkbrown stretchable vulva, and languishing therein, the gleaming tube, the oiled, scarlet clitoris.

In the folder it said that she was twenty-four years old then, and in the six years he had been loving her desperately, he only had to replace the tongue once; the muscle had dried out, become crumbly and dusty; but for the rest Musidora offered complete satisfaction.

Antoine Depaepe demanded little of his love, by the way. To dress her, to undress her, to wash her, particularly her little ass, and then to lift her body gleaming of soap and lather from the steaming bath, and wrap her hurriedly in a bright yellow bath towel, to brush and comb her locks for hours, to make up her face, her nipples, to paint her fingernails, and then every night to kiss and stroke the mountains and valleys of her body, to press himself safely to her warmth and to go to sleep with his skinny hand on her breasts or in the clutch of her thighs and to cherish the simplicity and the restfulness of this perfect happiness. He had not been able to copulate with Musidora for a year and a half now. They had celebrated his last erection with lobster and champagne, as if both of them had sensed that it would be the last one. He could, however, still satisfy her with all sorts of little games. His yellowed fingers were still deft, and every night Musidora moaned before he closed her eyes for the night. By way of exception he asked her that evening, after dinner, to keep on her new shoes in bed, and around twelve-thirty he fell asleep, his head pressed blissfully against the shiny tips of her little feet in yellow boots. He had drunk too much wine, or was it only the intoxicating joy which had deceived him, it was hard to tell; but when he had undressed her he had noticed how firm and heavy her breasts were and how his wife had been as it were changing shape for some time now, almost invisibly.

July 5th

With a gummy taste in his mouth and a severe pain in his joints, Depaepe awoke. He had been lying in bed naked all night long with the window halfway open. Musidora had slept deeply again, she had hardly moved as always after they'd shared a bottle of Burgundy.

She had only lightly, instinctively opened her legs a little and the balmy zone in between trembled like dewy moss in the faint, early sunray that penetrated the waving tulle curtains.

At the Ministry, while the pastel-colored forms were stacking up on his desk, he sat dreamily thinking about her breasts for a long time. The two suns had not only increased in volume, but had also become firmer, fleshier; and the nipples, he could have sworn, were stiffer and fuller than normally, like minuscule, dark-brown mooncraters. It had not said in the directions that her breasts would yet swell up more; that was actually unnecessary, as they were broad, tender, and milky white, and—within the slightly rough nipple area—showed a small, hard nipple. They represented to his eyes an unmatched, almost perfect degree of harmonic balance.

If her porcelain udders had swollen up more, however, he would have written to America, not to order a new doll—one does not exchange a woman one loves, and Antoine Depaepe was crazily in love with Musidore—but just to inquire as to whether they might not be able to help him out with some cream or salve.

August 29th

About nine-thirty that night. The annual vacation was just over and Depaepe had not left home—he couldn't leave Musidora for three weeks behind in the armoire, could he, and besides what else could he desire than to care for her night and day, to watch over her—when he discovered, while he perfumed her armpits with opopanax, that her body had changed again, more clearly suddenly, and he broke out in a sweat and he shivered and he brought his hand to his mouth with a jerk, as if he wanted to suppress a scream of horror, joy, and despair, and with wide-open eyes he stared at the sensual, unique body of his pale doll, the animal with young, that was stretched out shamelessly on the couch. There was no more room for doubt: Musidora was pregnant.

He stumbled and fell down on a chair: it was clear to him suddenly that if his wife were expecting a child, he could not possibly be the father, and after giving her big belly an incomprehending look, nodding dully, he threw himself onto the sun-bathed street, bustling with ignorant, gaping tourists with cameras and melting ice creams.

September 9th

The first week Depaepe could not make a decision. He did go to the office every morning, but he had twice caught himself opening his window ten minutes late. In the evening he shuffled home through the streets, making a detour that increased each day, stared at the shop windows still and empty, and once went even to the café "Telefonneke" in the Lange Nieuwstraat to drink a glass of gin. He, who longed so much for his apartment, because he found Musidora there each night, innocent, vulnerable and so terribly beautiful, was now startled each time he put the key in the lock of his front door.

He avoided her fixed gaze, walked without any sound back and forth among the furniture, from room to room, rearranged little statues and objects he otherwise never touched, spilled the milk that, in spite of everything, he'd warmed up for her after dinner, hid silently behind the paper he'd bought three days ago and which he already knew by heart, and she lay there, breathing deeply, banal and provocative, swelling up like a balloon.

September 10th

But he could not go on reacting in such a cowardly way. He would talk with her, at first gently and graciously, after that without pity, he would force a confession out of her, the bitch, the slut, his Musidora who never wanted for anything, who got the most expensive perfumes, the softest nylons, the supplest boots, the yellowest roses from him; but no, he stammered with his hands, and with his whole body, he could not find the words, and it was as if the gap between them grew wider and wider, and the silence in that gap became more pressing all the time.

October 25th

When he pushed her into her closet that morning, uncombed and not made up, he could not close the door anymore without his wife getting stuck; her belly had the shape of the earth. "The pain will be unbearable," he thought, "if I close her up the whole day in that narrow space. And besides, she should lie down and rest a lot."

207

Jeanne, who came to clean the apartment twice a week, would discover her; not that Depaepe was ashamed of Musidora, but he'd never spoken about her with anyone and now it was too late, no one would understand him, certainly not in these tragic circumstances. So he wrote a long, friendly letter to the old woman, asked her not to come for a while because so to say he had to go on a business trip, and he locked himself up definitively in his tormenting despair, his impenetrable loneliness. From then on, without informing anybody, he did not go to the office anymore.

November 1st

Depaepe had read some time ago about a man in a London working-class neighborhood who possessed a marble crucifix that regularly bled from its hands and feet. Something like that was acceptable, of course; miracles do happen. What was happening to Musidora was perhaps also a miracle; but this he had a hard time believing, for as he knew her, she had little of the holy virgin about her. Yet she was clearly pregnant, he had seen her belly move lightly, the child was kicking; and when he pressed his ear to her navel, he could hear a vague life tossing around in her.

November 13th

Thousands of times already he had asked himself the same questions, sitting at the same table in the café "Telefonneke", without finding a solution; and when he came home at night, after having roamed around the wet streets of the harbor, he was usually so drunk and tired that he was unable to make a decision anymore and would lie down helplessly, damaged, in his moist raincoat, on his bed and go to sleep immediately. Musidora, who would probably deliver next month, lay neglected in her pains on the floor next to the couch.

December 9th

Antoine Depaepe was fired by his bosses and now lived off his savings, which didn't amount to much, since he had spent almost everything on presents for Musidora. During his long autumn walks, he had settled that Musidora could have betrayed him with either of two men: the window cleaner—a Turk who'd seen her once when Depaepe had forgotten to put her in the closet after a wild night, and his neighbor—a writer who had come to borrow a salt shaker one Sunday when the shops were closed and Depaepe had been dozing in his armchair, with Musidora on his lap, her skirt pulled up so high that one could make out, like an almost extinguished sun, her yellow lace underpants in the dusk. Naturally he could go over and talk with those gentlemen, but what good would it do? They would laugh at him and the way he looked—fatigued, wasted, and dirty—they might not even let him in; and furthermore he did not even have any proof against them. In his hollow sleep their sneering laughter kept resounding.

He could not call the police, either; they never understood anything, and he would not be able to bear the humiliation of their stupid, mean questions. He was at the end of his strength, a man without a past, without a future, exhausted and betrayed by life, and already so close to death that its unrelenting scent of decomposition was already hanging in his apartment.

December 25th

Never before had he felt so lonely. It was nine o'clock in the morning, and he sat in the muggy heat of a café the name of which he didn't even know, straight across from the Fine Arts museum in a neighborhood just as rundown as he was himself; and suddenly he thought of Ursula and he cursed her, and he cursed all the women he knew, all the women he didn't know; and he cursed his mother who had as they say given him his "life"; and he cursed Musidora, the Annihilating Beauty, The Holy Whore, Destruction Itself.

Depaepe paid for his warm wine and made his way to the Steen over the embankments, where he scattered bread for the gulls. This was a new habit. He had, no matter how, to demonstrate his love, it didn't matter to whom, and the white, screeching birds that swerved closely around his head, daily gave him a few moments of happiness and peace. On a bench on the walkway, he remained staring aimlessly; but it was cold and the wind penetrated his thin raincoat.

In the uneven streets behind the warehouses, shapeless old women were making themselves up by the red neon light of their display windows, and Depaepe spat at the glass when one of them invitingly beckoned him, sliding the little pink tip of her tongue over her painted lips. Then he decided to make an end to his misery as soon as possible, and in a squalid little store in Zirkstraat he bought a long, razor-sharp butcher knife with a deep blood groove and a pale yellow handle with three iron screws in it.

December 31st

It had started to snow—fat, floating flakes. The sounds of the city were muffled, and it stank horribly in his cold apartment. For months he had not cleaned anymore, and the windows were shut for good: the silence there was just as dull as in the streets and on the squares. In the disarray of the living room sat the guilty mother, the monster, the bursting breasts like two blisters hanging on her belly; and he looked straight into her ever seductive, black eyes, dark almonds in a face full of pretended innocence and love. Depaepe was particularly sober that night, relieved of the torture of a slow, aggravated hesitation; what he would do now was premeditated, foreseen, wanted. According to his calculations her baby could be born today or tomorrow; he should not waste anymore time, furthermore it was New Year and on New Year's Eve everyone celebrates. The whole afternoon Depaepe had been taking Musidora's clothes and shoes to the cellar to burn them in the incinerator. Eighteen hampers full, and a crate with make-up articles and seven wigs. A fortune. Then he had washed and shaved, set the table and once more lit the candles. A festive air prevailed in the room. The half naked Musidora was lying on her couch again, legs spread wide apart, her knees pulled up high, adorned in her most seductive underwear: a lemon yellow, almost transparent bra through which her fat nipples stuck like pupils, panties with diamonds and orange tufts over the cunt, a yellow hose belt, yellow stockings and then her fine boots, his last present. Her face was twisted with pain. He thought: "The contractions must have started."

At the supermarket of the Grand Bazaar on Groeneplaats he had bought cold turkey and red currants, and around 7:30 he sat down at the table and ate his feast meal greedily. He only now noticed he was torn by hunger. The last weeks he'd lived on sandwiches and bags of French fries.

In the afternoon he had found one more bottle of Burgundy in the cellar, covered with a thick layer of dust and cobwebs; and when the bottle was empty he staggered to the kitchen where he unrolled the new knife from the worn newspaper.

The radio was broadcasting continuous variety programs. Dizzy and panting Depaepe looked at the blade shining in the bleak neon light. First he had to catch his breath. He heard his heart beat in his throat. Down below in the street, a group of girls walked by noisily; odd how cheerful people are always when yet another year of their life has gone by. Then he walked calmly, mechanically to the sitting room, obeying a secret and fatal power, knelt sobbing down in front of Musidora, kissed her lips once more, her towering breasts, and then blindly plunged the knife in her belly. With an incredible force, the steel penetrated her flesh, a bit below her left breast, and with a jerk, screaming of exertion he cut her open with a slanting stroke down to her groin. The dry wound opened slowly like a giant shell. The stink became unbearable, and retching with grief and disgust Depaepe watched how dozens of slimy, white worms came crawling out of her torn body, a teeming, bubbling mass of blind vermin, fattened up with the decaying food in her plastic stomach; and the animals began to spread rapidly over the floor, under the carpets, between the plinths. Depaepe crawled hallucinating onto the table, bumped his head against the brass chandelier, so that the shadows in the room came to life, cut his thumb on the broken glass of the wine bottle. Some of the worms were twenty yards long. Desperately the old, destroyed man looked at the body of his maimed wife. She had a strange, cloudy expression on her face, and he remembered Musidora's face in the role of Allegria Detchard, dying in *Pour Don Carlos*; and with a broken voice he called out, while the tears were streaming down his wrinkled cheeks: "Allegria! Allegria!"

And from Musidora's left ear a shining stream of dark red blood began to flow slowly and heavily, which disappeared in the yellow velvet of her couch like a blurred rose.

Karel Sandor (b. 1948)

made his debut as a futuristic writer in Morgen, *and until now only a few of his stories have appeared here and there.*

There are a great many ways in which men can make life impossible for one another. There are immediate means of breaking others down, and slower-working means. Pollution works slowly but probably just as effectively as a nuclear weapon. We dump our garbage in the oceans if we don't bury it in our neighbor's backyard. Of old the blessing came from above. But what is above depends on the recipient.

Of the Blessing which would come straight from Heaven

The priest of the Yaka people looked out with his natural sonar senses over the dreary, soft, rolling hills.

Not so long ago agriculture had been a way of life here, stretching out for many miles, but no more.

The natural overgrowth had disappeared, too. Erosion now produced slow streams of stinking, bluish mud, which made the valley below impenetrable. Now the ground could only be used as a play area for a group of kids in pressure suits.

The priest remembered how, a little over a year ago now, the first case of incurable illness had been brought to him. The doctors had been powerless. The body had not wanted to absorb any more food.

There had perhaps been a silent hope that he might beg for a miracle. However, even before he had been able to finish his prayers, he had had to switch to the last rites, prayers that he'd had to repeat so often in the period after that he knew them by heart now.

The food had turned out to have been poisoned by chemicals of unknown origin. People had succeeded in purifying the food. But no matter how hard they'd tried, it had proven impossible to grow uncontaminated food anymore.

The next disaster which had swept down over the country still hung there: the breathtaking mist. In this case there had been no possibility of a solution, either, for getting around the threat, though people had succeeded in extracting oxygen from the atmosphere too poor in oxygen for breathing.

Everybody could now collect his daily ration of oxygen at Town

Hall. The houses had been insulated in the meantime so that no oxygen could escape when you had connected your cylinder to the circulation systems.

Yet there wasn't enough oxygen for the cattle and the wild animals. They'd had to die..

But who cared?

People were already glad enough that the Yaka people themselves had kept their chances for survival.

Animal food might thus be unimaginable to future generations, but the survivors among them would be able to eat vegetable food from the uncontaminated hothouses.

It would be a hard existence.

Nobody knew where the pollution had come from. It was a problem to which no reasonable answer had been found. People could only see it as a punishment from the gods.

More and more penitents had united in new sects to pray to the gods for generosity and to relieve the people of this existence, which was hardly worth living anymore.

Many connected the pollution with the flying balls and cigars which since a year and a day ago had been observed at a height of ten or fifteen thousand feet.

Formerly, however, no one had believed in the stories dished out by hysterics and fantasists about mysterious unidentified flying objects. Recently they were listened to more eagerly.

There were also more and more people who claimed to have received heavenly sounds on their sonar organs. A group of the most fanatic religionists had climbed the fifteen-thousand-foot high volcano. At the top some balls and cigars had recently been observed and heard. According to the climbers, the gods lived in the volcano.

They had called themselves the chosen and believed they would be saved by the cigars.

Of course they had died of a lack of oxygen and suppression. The atmosphere at fifteen thousand feet was much too thin to sustain life.

With doubt in his heart, the priest turned away from this sad view and entered the old temple. His lungs were squeaking. He needed oxygen quickly. The priest went to have a look at the outside often, and each time he doubted more and he was more inclined to agree with the new sects.

Always he had believed that the gods were good gods. But why then these plagues? Which sin was so large that a people must be punished for it so severely?

The Susan Scott was a small freighter.

The helmsman looked out over two cargo holds which were now closed by heavy iron cover hatches.

Captain Williams was already past sixty. He was used to his orders being followed blindly, as he used to follow orders blindly before he was a captain, and as he now still went where he was sent by the shipowner.

Captain Williams had remained healthy. Not only physically because of the pure air which could only be breathed two thousand miles away from the coasts of the polluted continents, but also mentally because discipline had always been his guiding principle.

But now, with the safe harbor of his pension ahead of him, he felt again the same insecurity he'd felt when he had stood on the bridge as third mate for the first time.

Deep in thought he ticked with a ballpoint against his teeth. Unconsciously, he had pushed away the papers in front of him.

Suddenly, he started at a knock on his door. Uncertainly, Captain Williams waited until there was another knock and then immediately said: "Come in."

Neil Stamfort was a recently graduated ecologist. He looked like many people his age: long hair, an uncultivated beard, a jeans suit.

Williams had wondered before whether this outfit was a fad of rebellious youngsters or a sign of permanent change in society.

Stamfort had a book in his hands.

"Yesterday you didn't believe my story about those traces, do you remember?"

Williams nodded.

"I found a book in my luggage. Look here, this picture."

Stamfort pushed the opened book across the table to Williams. He had to look for a moment before he could make out the regular traces on the somewhat underexposed photograph.

"Not that we should attach science fiction-like conclusions to this, but they do resemble shoes a bit. It is a fact that the ocean is bursting with life," Stamfort remarked.

The traces on the picture were rectangular wells. As if a biped had done its best to put its two feet as precisely as possible in front of each other.

"At what depth did you say they'd been found?"

"Twenty-five hundred fathoms and deeper. They have been found in many deep seas around the world."

"I have to admit it's an odd picture."

The priest was just leading the service in a prayer totally directed to redemption from the misery. His voice sounded lamenting. Sentence after sentence the eager crowd took over, a crowd which the priest thought perhaps believed even more strongly in the higher powers than he did himself.

Fortunately he managed to continue to make his voice sound convincing. So an interaction with his believers was created. That led to the prayer sounding more and more hopeful. The priest let himself be swept away. The enthusiasm in his voice was received like a wave of inspirational life by the mass moving up and down rhythmically. A mass which had been pretty much thinned out, by the way.

This prayer had to be heard by the gods. In the priest's soul, belief was blooming again. The gods would bring relief. He was convinced that his people had suffered enough. He was convinced that it had never been the gods' idea to make his people extinct. The people's voice across from him did not weaken as usual during a long prayer. On the contrary, the believers repeated after him more and more quickly.

But suddenly the priest was taken from his concentration by a scratching sound. His voice halted. He looked up disturbed.

Everybody's eyes now were directed to the quiet temple and to some cheeky street urchins who had dragged a large crate into the temple after themselves. They looked at the priest timidly. His fury ebbed away upon looking at the little ones. He knew their faces. He had often seen them playing in their pressure suits in the mud, where formerly there had been green fields. The priest had already forgiven them, although they had left a stinking trace.

"Don't you want to sit down?" he asked kindly.

The biggest of the group now came forward. He pointed at the crate behind him.

"This fell from the sky, and more of them have fallen and more of them are coming. We thought you should know, we thought that..."

The priest made a gesture and looked long and silently at the crate. His heart started to beat faster as a notion grew in him.

"You did right, kids," he spoke then. Their skinny faces gleamed and took on a little color again.

Slowly the priest walked up to the big crate. A joy welled up in him. Didn't it say in the Scriptures that salvation would come straight from heaven? The miracle must have happened, the prayer answered.

For a moment doubt still clouded his soul. This could also be the bad powers' definite reckoning. But no, it was not reasonable to suppose that. If it had been the gods' idea to make the people suffer still more they would have continued the process of pollution and reduction of oxygen from the atmosphere, until even the equipment wouldn't be able to draw oxygen from the atmosphere anymore. No, this looked like a present. He had to have confidence. It was clearly the idea that the crate should be opened. He should obey that. His sonar eyes directed themselves to the strange signs and the oddly shaped head on the crate. An image of the gods?

The crate was so strong they had to use a drill. The strongly concentrated poison gas escaped to do its job of murder, sparing no one.

Captain Williams commanded the drivers of the four-ton cranes and let the heavy hatches be closed again by the roaring winch. He did not dare look Stamfort, who had come to stand next to him, in the eyes.

Stamfort was a member of an ecological action group which had gotten the shipowners to the point of sending someone along who would see to it that they indeed used the indicated spot.

Williams took his eyes off the sea but before his eyes hung the image of the skull and crossbones painted on the crates.

For the first time he longed for his pension. Then the time would come for others in his place to dump poisonous gas here above Mariana trench, 35616 feet deep, and other trenches.

Bob van Laerhoven (b. 1953)

is a Flemish writer who, by the age of 21 had already published four novels and several collections of short stories. He has a job in the advertising business in a small town in Flanders but he is rapidly on his way to becoming a full-time professional writer.

The last man on Earth is a familiar motif. In this setting the solitary hero's struggle to survive becomes synonymous with the struggle to perpetuate the species. What happens when the hero is granted a single brief excursion through time? Time plays a cruel joke.

Unlucky Fellow

Wildly, Perche looked around him. Because of the black porridge-like substance all around him in the air, his view was limited. As always, the tide had the crooked whisper of an eerie hustler: a provocative, slimy sound.

Somewhere in the sky, between the yellow, green and dull brown strokes of a giant, mad painter against the enormous canvas, the sun was still shining, glittering as a far away, unreachable *centavo*. Perche knew that the palm trees had to be somewhere in the neighborhood, but he did not see them. The winds had dumped their daily, and growing, load of cieto into the whole South Sea… and into this little island.

Perche was a slender, bow legged little fellow. His upper body rested, short and small, on relatively long, crooked legs. His bony head was very big, and it was crowned with blue-black, lanky hair. He was completely naked. A rather sizeable penis dangled like an easy-going mouse between his legs.

Yes, Perche was the last living person on Earth. His round jade-colored eyes had witnessed, about an hour before, the death-struggle of his beloved mother. After she died, he had fled her body, crying, completely out of his wits. Now, he did not know his way back.

Somewhere, somewhere in the thick, burning mist, there had to be the last rotting palm trees…

His mother had been a professor at the University of Mexico, and—when the *cieto-maelstrom* had started its career before the West coast of the United States, and when the seas circling England began to show corrosive properties, when strange shiftings of the soil started to extract their terrible toll in North and West Europe, when the corn harvest of China, Russia, and Hungary had become completely poisonous by the activity of a strange enzyme—then his mother had bought two plane tickets to Honolulu.

Perche had never asked her why she did this. He never doubted the infallibility of his mother's decisions, and he had always been content being with her and with his books. Perche's mother was a resourceful woman. Not only was she a scholar, a specialist in biology, and anthropology, but she was also a splendid adept in the art of surviving.

From Honolulu, they went by a small boat to an almost unknown, small island, one of the smallest of the group. They had lived there for almost ten years. They had seen the tourists leave; they had heard fewer and fewer broadcasts about the disasters that plagued the world. And each day they had seen how the overlayer of filth on the waves had grown thicker and thicker. About five years ago, the first real *cieto-clouds* had reached the island, floated above it. For years, they had tried to hold out against the strange chemicals and pollution in the sea and the air—eating away the palm trees, poisoning the fruits, and killing the sea life.

And now, Perche was alone, totally alone. The last man on Earth: the convenient position of the island, and the strong winds had produced a more lasting life for it than for other parts of the world. But this Perche did not know nor did it interest him.

Each breath he took, made pain shimmer in his chest, but the loneliness in his heart was even more painful.

He materialized in a big city. For about one minute, he could hold on to the vision. Thousands of cars, and—at the brink of the city—the clouds of the chemical plants... Perche wanted to cry out his lonely hate and destroy... But his grip on time had run out, and again he sat lonely on his island.

He was furious and emotionally shocked. He beat with his fist on the slush that was the ground. With his back, he sat against a rotting palm tree, and without really seeing anything, his burning eyes stared at the slimy waves rolling lazily onto the muddy beach. The day was rather beautiful: the sun had the same effect as a lantern would have underneath a thick, brown porridge, and Perche's adapted lungs found that the air was rather breathable, at least more than on other days.

The intense anger he had felt upon returning so quickly to his island ebbed away quickly. He had trained himself to do that. As always, he felt ravenously hungry after the completion of a jump.

Slowly, he got up: caricature of the caricature he had been before. His body now possessed a slaty brown color, and his hairline had receded to the top of his skull. His ribs painted white knobs on his skin and his hipbones protruded dramatically. It was as if his toes had grown, because they seemed terribly long. They had to be that way, because moving in the slush that had replaced the soil was difficult.

But he was still alive, and he had adapted to the loss of his mother. Even more: he now possessed a power no man before had ever dreamed of. It was now eight months since his mother's death, and in spite of his despair, he had survived. He had even found this tremendous power in himself.

It had started the third day after his mother's death. Totally at a loss, he had gone to sleep when a sharp pain in the region of his heart woke him. He glanced around and noticed that he was sitting on his knees between the rotting palm trees. Frightened he was looking at the suffering contours of his mother's body. Bubbles of air foamed around her mouth, and her belly was puffed up like a balloon. She tried to say something but, powerlessly, her head fell aside. With horror, he touched her body and felt her spongy flesh—warm, much too warm, underneath his hand.

Without any transition, he was lying on the beach again. First, he had thought it had just been a nightmare. But the following two days, the same scene repeated itself... and this time in clear day.

Then, he started to suspect something. He was not dumb. He had inherited the brains of his mother but not her character. He understood that he had jumped back in time. For days, he had been living with a deep longing for his mother in his heart, and that had triggered it. After a while, he faced the one and only conclusion: by pure mindpower, he had jumped back in time.

During the following days, a plan ripened in his head. He exercised, concentrated, ascertained precisely what happened in his mind and body when he felt the tug of power in his bowels.

After a few weeks, he had a certain control over the process. It had taken much exercise, but then he had nothing else to do. There was food aplenty, because insect life was abundant and he was not too squeamish in his eating habits.

He drank the blood of the immense but harmless toads.

Again, he began traveling backwards in time. He could jump one year into the past, then two, then three, four, five... more and more his powers reached further backwards into time, but the duration of his stays was much too limited.

He could not stay long enough in the past, and he did not possess the power to choose beforehand the place of arrival. But his solitude kept him busy, and he exercised intensely. To complete his plan, he had to be able to stay for a quarter of an hour, preferably half an hour, in a certain time.

He thought a lot about the possibilities of his plan, and then his dull eyes, encrusted with pus, shone brightly when he thought what he would be able to do if he succeeded.

One day, he felt he was ready. Two days before, he had been able to hold on for about a quarter of an hour. But the place of arrival had been unfit for his plans. Suddenly, he had stood in a big, deserted wood. Like a madman, he had run to and fro. His lungs had hurt viciously because of the overload of oxygen they suddenly received. He had been very surprised by his own endurance, because he had been able to run for about a hundred yards before he got exhausted. Then, he had trotted around in vain: the forest was deserted. But he estimated that he had been there for about ten minutes. That would have been sufficient, if the wood had not been deserted...

Now he had been concentrating for three days to store as much energy as possible, in order to jump backwards strongly. He hoped that this time he would arrive in a ''good'' place, because this time it had to succeed. He could no longer stand this loneliness. Only because of the fact that he had trained so intensely had he kept insanity more or less at bay. But now, he felt he was nearing the end of his endurance.

On the fourth day, he decided to go for it. He shut his eyes and felt the contraction of the now familiar power in his bowels. Then, there was the pain in the region of his heart that told him the jump had been made. He opened his eyes. The first sensation was that of an enormous wailing and howling around him.

He opened his eyes and saw that he was standing on the inner court of an enormous, primitively erected building. People, clad in hauberks, were running out of the court, or stood there transfixed staring at him, emitting raw sounds. Some of them were attempting to draw their swords and roared war cries. Perche concluded he had jumped back somewhere into the Middle Ages. Before the drawbridge of the castle, a retinue of noblewomen was ready to depart. Richly clad women were sitting astride their horses. Beside the horses, squires were standing, falcons upon their leather-clad left hands.

Perche did not lose any time. Deftly, he ducked underneath the blow of a sword that one of the more stout-hearted knights had dealt him, and ran towards the retinue. The squires were frozen with fright. Some stood there, some ran away, making the sign of the cross in the air. The noblewomen were looking with big, round eyes underneath their pointed hats at the skinny, filthy demon that attacked them. They screamed like birds in danger. Perche did not lose a second. With a mighty shove of his sinewy, skinny arms, he snatched one of the screeching women out of the saddle. In his arms, she fainted immediately, probably more as a result of the terrible stench he carried than anything else.

Hopping like an overweight frog, he ran over the drawbridge. His back muscles contracted fearfully when an arrow swished past his head. He had his prey now; why then –; *por Diós*!... could he not go back to his own time?

But the energy he had saved so consciously had begun to spend itself. There was no way out. Panting like a hare, he began to zigzag. He felt his bodily powers diminish. The pursuing roaring behind him gradually increased in strength. He heard horses neighing.

Infernar! A second arrow planted itself beside him, humming into the ground. He could not go on anymore: the air in his lungs seemed to boil, and all that oxygen made him dizzy.

Suddenly, he stumbled with the woman in his arms. He fell, but he clung to her desperately.

The war cries of the pursuing knights became a terrible frenzy...

And then... he was lying in the mud of his island, with his arms around the waist of the woman. She was still unconscious. Perche laughed hoarsely and then began to curse softly: he had done it.

He regained his senses when the woman started moaning and moving her limbs. He did not waste time. He had waited so long, had longed for it, had dreamed of it and had cried for it.

221

With his muddy hands, full of fervor, he began pulling at her clothes. The pointed hat got loose from her head and planted itself as a thick, silvery arrow in the slush.

Her gown was made from a thick velvet, and Perche had a difficult time discarding it. The dizziness, as a result of an overdose of oxygen, became even more intense.

The woman began to cough. Her eyelashes fluttered. She breathed laboriously and her chest moved heavily. Her cheeks became a burning red. She coughed and cleared her throat. Perche understood that she had breathing problems, but she would adapt after a few hard days. These women out of the Middle Ages were used to hardship: she would survive.

With great difficulty, he undressed her. Underneath her upper gown she wore a short dress made of linen. With renewed courage, Perche tore the cloth away from her body...

Three days later, he was sitting with his back to a palm tree. With dull eyes, he was looking at the dirty sky. One of his hands was still bleeding, and with the other, he peeled with abrupt, intense movements some rotting bark of the dying tree beside him. His face was a conglomerate of empty lines, totally empty.

His power to go back to the past had died out. Maybe his last effort had emptied the psychic reservoir. Maybe the frustration he had undergone had been too much for the finely tuned mechanism that had been hidden somewhere in his mind.

As a lunatic, for the past three days he had tried to go back again but to no avail.

He felt that something in him had broken. He was now for eternity a prisoner in his own time.

And beside him, the naked woman was sitting. She still had difficulties with her breathing. She was crying all the while.

Some specks of blood were visible on her belly and haunches, and the steel chastity-belt with the big lock made her look half robot, half woman...

About the translators

WANDA BOEKE was born in Concord, Massachusetts in 1954. She attended the University of Iowa, where she got her MFA. in English.

ADRIENNE DIXON was born in the Netherlands in 1932, moved to England in 1957 and married an Englishman a year later. Her numerous high quality translations of Dutch and Flemish fiction won her the Martinus Nijhoff Prize for Translations in 1974. At present she teaches English and French at a secondary school in Colchester, England.

GRETA KILBURN was born in 1935. For the past ten years she has been translating Dutch literature into English. After spending years in Australia, Canada and England she came to the Netherlands where she now lives.

RIA LEIGH-LOOHUIZEN was born in 1944 in Haarlem and lives in San Francisco. Together with her husband, American novelist James Leigh she started the *Twin Peaks Press*. She returned to the Netherlands in 1980.

SCOTT ROLLINS was born in Oceanside, New York in 1952. He grew up in Connecticut attending high school there before going off to study at Syracuse University. In 1972 he moved to Amsterdam where he studied at the University of Amsterdam for three years. He works at the Foundation for the Promotion of the Translation of Dutch Literary Works in Amsterdam. His own poetry has been published in various little magazines in Europe.

JOHN RUDGE was born in 1945 in Birmingham, England. He attended Cambridge University where he studied in English. Rudge came to the Netherlands in 1971 and earns his living as a free-lance translator.